HALF LIFE

HALF LIFE

HAL CLEMENT

TOR®

A TOM DOHERTY ASSOCIATES BOOK
NEW YORK

HALF LIFE

Significant portions of this book appeared in a different form as a series of stories published in *Absolute Magnitude*.

This book is printed on acid-free paper.

Edited by David G. Hartwell

A Tor Book
Published by Tom Doherty Associates, LLC
175 Fifth Avenue
New York, NY 10010

www.tor.com

Tor® is a registered trademark of Tom Doherty Associates, LLC.

Design by Lisa Pifher

Library of Congress Cataloging-in-Publication Data
Clement, Hal, date
    Half life / Hal Clement.—1st ed.
        p.   cm.
    "A Tom Doherty Associates book."
    ISBN 0–312–86920–7 (alk. paper)
    I. Title.
PS3505.L646H35   1999
813'.54—dc21   99–22199

First Edition: September 1999

Printed in the United States of America

0 9 8 7 6 5 4 3 2 1

To Robert E. Stearns, Jr., in memory of a lengthy discussion a few years ago as we sat on a bench in the exhibit room at the ConAdian World Science Fiction Convention.

Its precise effects on my thinking are far too labyrinthine for me to detail, or even remember completely. Its connection with the events in this book would never have been believed by the late Immanuel Velikovsky, who seems to have been convinced that any such relationship should be direct and obvious.

The connections are there. Maybe you can spot some.

Thanks, Robert.

ACKNOWLEDGMENTS

IDENTIFYING THE SHAPES, colors, and assembly dates of the segments in a million-piece but not quite completed jigsaw puzzle is probably impossible. Doing the same with the factors comprising a human being who has been around and active for over three-quarters of a century is much harder.

Chronologically, I suppose one starts with the parents who taught me and my sister the three Rs well before we started school in 1928, and were understandably miffed when our English usage deteriorated after that date. There were numerous grammar and high school teachers who contributed pieces, even ones I didn't like, such as "Business" in high school, which are still in the picture.

There were college professors I remember well, such as Bart J. Bok, Donald H. Menzel, Fred L. Whipple, Cecilia Payne-Gaposchkin, and John Arrend Timm. There were many I don't remember in much detail, but who certainly also contributed.

There were the taxpayers who provided my education degree under the G. I. Bill, and other taxpayers who supplied my chemistry M.S. via a National Science Foundation grant during the post-Sputnik panic.

There were science fiction writers and editors like John Campbell, Fred Pohl, Jack Williamson, and Neil R. Jones, and legions of fans who liked my work or criticized it usefully or both.

And latest—not last, I hope—there is Adam Goldberger, who, possibly with assistants and co-workers whose names didn't show on the work sheets, confronted me during the preparation of this book with the most complete, challenging, detailed, and professional piece of copyediting I have faced in fifty-seven years of writing. I know I have a good scientific background, and held my end up fairly well there; but I also thought I was a good speller. It's just as well I reached for the dictionary when we disagreed. And grammar . . .

Well, I've been sure for a long time that languages evolve, even in literate societies.

I'm grateful to them all, and apologize for the mistakes I still make; but of course a science fiction writer has to provide some sort of evidence that he may be human.

GENERAL ORDER SIX (GO6)
Northern Research Force

1. In view of the common human tendency, when seeking to explain observations, to favor the first speculation which comes to mind, the following procedures will be observed by all ranks:
   (a) No speculation by any member of the services will be reported to higher-ranking personnel unless accompanied by (i) a comparably plausible alternative speculation, or (ii) a detailed procedure for testing the one proffered.
   (b) If the said speculation occurs during a general discussion, either formal or informal, then (i) or (ii) may be delayed until after the end of the said discussion. Alternative ideas contributed by participants other than the originator of the speculation will be regarded as satisfying 1(a) (i) above.
2. This rule is not intended to discourage speculation, which is recognized as a necessary first step in developing any body of knowledge, but to help preserve objectivity as far as possible in both private reasoning and public debate.
3. The commander of any research unit, whether of observer or theoretician grade, is authorized and advised to use discretion in the detailed enforcement of this regulation.
4. No punishment more serious than reprimand is to be inflicted for violation of this rule.

Rule X

This is not a formal regulation, and cannot be stated with real precision; but reference to "Rule X" in conversation or inferred thought of any person is pejorative. It may be used by anyone to anyone else regardless of any rank involved. The "rule" is to the effect that "I told you so" is unacceptable language. It presumably evolved in the hope of keeping scientific debate as free as possible from, or to delay as long as possible, the use of personalities.

ANTE

THE CREW, OR STAFF, whichever it should be called, of one of the oddest spacecraft ever to lift from Earth was as strange as the vessel itself. Not one of them had previous space experience. They were neither draftees nor volunteers; the best name might have been "persuadees."

And none of them expected, or even very much hoped, to get back. Most of them knew they were dying, and had simply chosen to die usefully away from their home world.

The ship itself was a two-hundred-meter-diameter, slightly prolate sphere, with twenty remountable fusion thrusters distributed uniformly over its surface. It lifted very wastefully from Earth under its own thrust, docked with a supply station in medium orbit, and took on board every possible additional kilogram of water. It was then inserted into a minimum-energy Saturn trajectory.

There were fifty people aboard. All but three were dying and knew it, a far higher percentage of terminal cases than in Earth's now drastically shrunken population. The crew number had been chosen by highly mathematical guesswork, with none of the mathematicians involved agreeing on appropriate assumptions or algorithms.

And few if any had taken their calculations seriously.

For almost two centuries, Earth's population, human and

otherwise, had been decreasing at a rate almost perfectly described by a 69.2-year half-life. Then, twenty-two years before, births had rather suddenly caught up with deaths, and the curve had become a nearly horizontal line.

Hard-line optimists promptly decided that the danger was over, and even praised the mysterious phenomenon which had delayed the climax of the earlier overpopulation crisis. Most of these quickly decided the Saturn mission would now require only a small crew. Even these, however, admitted the importance of finding the cause of the epidemics.

Others pointed out, however, that whatever the general population change, the fact that those who were going were nearly all terminally ill meant that a much smaller half-life should be used in figuring the crew number needed. Neither group ever mentioned publicly that no number of people which could be carried in any practical spacecraft, even with construction and energy costs nearly negligible, could be large enough for half-life calculations to mean anything at all.

This was demonstrated before the orbit of Mars had been passed. Erroneous planning of some of the equipment seeds had been recognized, including those for aircraft to explore Titan's heavy atmosphere, and made it necessary to keep more of the staff active and at work during the five-and-a-quarter-year trip than had been planned. Eleven people instead of the "calculated" one or two were dead, their personalities remembered as friends and colleagues and their bodies preserved as data, before the rings could be seen clearly by the unaided eyes of the survivors. The orbit had been a minimum-energy Hohmann semi-ellipse; there was a vast amount of water on board, but most of it was intended for uses other than reaction mass.

Eighteen more—much closer to the guessed-at figure—were lost during the work inside Saturn's radiation belt, while fragments of ice were being assembled and welded by careful squirts of water into a rough sphere with the original ship in the center. This went on until the ship and its personnel were shielded from particle radiation by half a kilometer of ice that was fairly solid, but not perfectly so;

the fragments had not been melted before assembly and did not fit each other very well.

Two of the eleven, including one of the three not known to be terminal, could only be memorialized; their remains could not be salvaged or even found. The outside work, spotting and capturing construction material and repeatedly relocating thrusters so they remained on the outside of the growing ice ball, all the while exposed to particle radiation which no suit could keep out completely, had come closest to matching the half-life for this part of the task predicted before liftoff.

When the resulting station had been worked into orbit around Titan and the six unprotected and uninhabitable relay stations which allowed observation of any part of the big moon were in place, there were twenty-one survivors.

Not only were they not spacemen, they were not even scientists in the full sense of the word. At least, they were not *specialists*. They were well educated, well supplied with common knowledge, and familiar enough with the cause-and-effect reasoning needed for research to be able to plan scientific work. None, therefore, was seriously inclined toward supernaturalism, and they had a vast information store in the Station on which to base their thinking.

Figuring the seventeen-plus-year half-life which corresponded to the loss on the way out, the nine-month one for the construction deaths, and the nine-year combination which covered the whole Earth-to-station period was mere mental arithmetic to any of them, unless one of the many new Alzheimer's syndrome varieties made someone forget ln2—and that number could always be supplied by Status, their information bank. They, too, attached no weight to the figures; if the calculations had not been trivial, no one would have attempted them. They were like calculating the weight of Earth's atmosphere to settle a minor bet.

Their ailments were under the best available control. They could—probably counting out any Alzheimer's victims—take care of the general run of foreseeable emergencies. If advice—not physical help—was required they could probably afford the roughly three hours needed to send a question to Earth and get an answer.

Or rather, roughly three hours plus the time needed for a repeatedly decimated and largely panicked humanity to find an answer. When this totaled too long, or the problem occurred during
the period every twelve and a half months when the Sun cut off
communication for a few days, ingenuity and imagination would
have to serve.

Contact was to be carefully maintained with home, since the
staff would almost certainly never get back themselves. Whatever
they learned, however, *must* reach the rest of humanity. Even if they
didn't learn what they had been sent for, any possibilities they might
eliminate could be critical for future planning.

Their mission was easily stated: Fill the information gaps between the mineral and biological worlds. This seemed logical, if not
exactly hopeful. After all, if flying machines suddenly develop a fifty-
percent-per-flight crash rate and flight is still necessary, one studies
the *basic physics* of aeronautical engineering as well as the wreckage.
When life itself is failing, the need for basics, probably chemical this
time, is even more critical. *Something* was wrong with life processes
in general; the decay curve, with only modest differences in half-
life, applied to most nonhuman species as well.

When the station finally began operation, its staff consisted of

> Corporal Cheru Akagawa
> Corporal Ludmilla Anden
> Sergeant Gene Belvew
> Corporal Marilyn Calca
> Major Maria Collos
> 2nd Lieutenant Olivia D'Arnot
> 1st Lieutenant Emil diSabato
> Dr. Lieutenant Colonel Samuel Donabed (presumed healthy)
> Sergeant John Paul Finn
> Colonel Arthur Goodall
> Sergeant Barn Inger
> 1st Lieutenant Carla lePing

Corporal Peter Martucci (presumed healthy)
Major Louis Mastro
Corporal Marahla Nemaya
1st Lieutenant James Skokie
Recorder Status, bank of factual and fictional information
Corporal Jenny Vannell
Corporal Xiawen Wei
Major Jennifer Xalco
Captain Seichi Yakama
Corporal Phyllis Zonde

Their ranks stemmed from a century-old attempt to organize along military lines the research obviously needed to salvage humanity. Noncommissioned ranks were "observers"; officers were "theoreticians." The distinction, and much else of the military flavor of science, had blurred badly during the twenty-two-year flattening of the population decay curve. The resumption of the drop on Earth, with a noticeably shorter half-life, during the trip to Saturn failed to clear the blur in the least, though many people suddenly began complaining that the ship and crew as planned had been far too small. Humanity might be dying, but otherwise wasn't changing much.

General Order Six was still in full force because it was good science. Most of the other GOs were remembered only when convenient. Rule X was merely background.

PART ONE

STRATEGY

1

SPOT

IT WAS BAD TIMING, not too surprisingly for a random event. His Mollweide screen was offering one of its occasional, brief, irregularly presented views of Sergeant Gene Belvew's real surroundings. These consisted of his personal quarantined suite in the Station seven hundred kilometers above Titan's surface, and showed nothing surprising at all. It cut him off for little more than a second from the scenes provided by *Oceanus*'s cameras deep in the atmosphere below, but in that second the pipe stall occurred.

It would, a less conscious level of his mind reflected. He didn't believe in a literal, unqualified Murphy's Law, which was strictly for near-civilians like Ludmilla Anden. She was actually a corporal, one of the few people still alive in the Saturn system who didn't outrank him, and for reasons he didn't know himself he tended quite unjustly to regard her as not properly military.

A scientist of any rank should understand the Law of Selective Observation, which tradition, flexible as ever in its details, now attributed to one Murphy. If his engines had chosen any other time to flame out he would have seen it coming, forestalled it easily without conscious thought, and forgotten it promptly as unimportant. As it was, his first warning was the waldo suit's nonvisual input, which kept him in touch with his aircraft even when he could see nothing but the walls, furniture, and equipment actually around him.

Being in two places at once was no longer a logical impossibility but a familiar nuisance.

The suit administered a sharp twinge almost simultaneously to both his elbows. A moment later, when he could see Titan again, thrust was gone and accelerometers showed that *Oceanus* was slowing sharply in the dense atmosphere. His reflexes had already operated, of course, only slightly later than they would have from a visual stimulus; but the trifle made a frightening difference.

Belvew was an excellent pilot except for his tendency to take occasional chances. The aircraft had practically no reaction mass in its tanks, mainly because of the pilot's eagerness to get the seismic lines dropped without wasting time tanking up, so shifting to rocket mode would be futile. It had been obvious to everyone that trying to finish the current line with no thrust backup was silly, but Belvew wasn't the only person impatient for data. The thunderhead over Lake Carver had, however, practically forced itself on his attention, convincing him that he could pick up juice with very little delay after all, and he had been just implementing his decision to refill after all when it happened.

The big satellite's gravity, which his body in orbit couldn't feel any more than it could the ramjet's deceleration, was feeble; if the craft had slowed too much, even the vertical dive he had promptly entered wouldn't get him back to ram speed from his present altitude. Diving into the surface would not injure him physically—the waldo's feedback didn't go *that* far—but would still be a bad tactical mistake. Ramjets, while they were grown products, pseudolife like practically every other piece of modern equipment, could not be picked from trees.

Not that there were trees this far from the Sun. The aircraft were not even single pseudoorganisms, but assemblages of more than a thousand separately grown modules. Replacement would not be impossible, but would be lengthy and difficult and would complicate planning. Carla—Lieutenant lePing—did have two more nearly assembled, and plenty of modules were growing, but like most of the crew she was not always able to work.

For increasingly worrisome moments the tension and airspeed mounted as Gene's elbows stayed sore. Then ram flow resumed simultaneously in both pipes and the speed of his dive abruptly increased with the restored thrust. Still reflexively he pulled out of the dive, very carefully to avoid a secondary stall.

In level flight at last, with fully a hundred meters of air still below him, he put his nose—his own, not the ramjet's—more deeply into the face cup of his suit and moved his head slightly. This ran the screen through its preset half dozen most-likely-useful vision frequencies. He was already pretty sure what had caused the stall, but pilot's common sense agreed with basic scientific-military procedure in demanding that he check.

Yes, he was still in the updraft; the screen displayed the appropriate false colors all around him, and the waldo, which was also an environment suit, and therefore had been designed not to interfere with his own breathing system by using olfactory codes, was reporting the excess methane and consequent lowered air density as a set of musical tones. As usual, there had been no one but himself to blame.

He'd been driving just a little too slowly, trying to get a good look below while filling the mass tanks, and a perfectly ordinary but random and mathematically unpredictable drop in the density of the rising air had raised the impact pressure needed by the jets. He could have *seen* it coming, but if the waldo hadn't been backing up the interrupted visual sensors he'd have learned too late and with probably much less than a hundred meters leeway.

No point thinking about that.

"What happened, Sarge? Or shouldn't I ask?" Barn Inger, Belvew's coranker and usual flying partner, didn't bother to identify himself; only twenty-one people were left of the original crew, and there were no strange voices. As Belvew's copilot, a task fitted in among many other demands on his attention, one of Inger's regular duties was to check with Gene vocally or in any other way appropriate whenever something unexpected occurred in flight; the "shouldn't I ask" was merely a standard courtesy. Few people enjoyed admitting mistakes, however important they might be as data. The terminally ill people who formed a much larger fraction of the Titan crew than of Earth's rapidly shrinking population were often quite touchy about such things.

"I rode too close to stall. It's all right now," Belvew answered.

"Use anything from the tanks?" The question also was pure courtesy; like everyone else, Inger had repeaters for *Oceanus*'s instrument output in his own quarters. Nearly anyone could have taken over control of the jet within seconds of realizing the need. Inger was trying to make the slip look like an everyday incident, to be passed over casually.

"Nothing to use. There was enough room to dive-start." Belvew did not mention just how little spare altitude he had had, and Inger didn't really need to ask. Because of the constant possibility of having to start flying with no notice, everyone kept as conscious as other duties allowed of current aerial activities.

"You're still over Carver. You *could* have put down and tanked up from the lake." This was quite true, but neither speaker mentioned why that option had been passed without conscious thought. Both knew perfectly well; Inger's stress on the "could" had been as close to being specific about it as either cared to go. He changed to a neutral subject.

"You seem to have the fourth leg about done."

Belvew made no answer for a moment; he was spiraling upward to start another pass through the droplet-rich updraft, at a safer altitude this time. Mass was needed in his tanks as soon as possible, and he was now prepared to accept the lower concentration to be found higher up, and to budget the time to get there and make the extra run or two that would be needed. Haste hadn't paid, and had almost presented a very large bill. No one argued, most were relieved at the decision, and Gene was the pilot anyway.

"Not quite," he finally answered absently.

In visible light frequencies his target looked exactly like an earthly thunderhead. There was even lightning, in spite of the nonpolar composition of the droplets, and Belvew faced the piloting task of making collection runs through it at a speed high enough to prevent another ram stall but low enough to avoid turbulence damage to his airframe.

"Not quite," he repeated at last. "But I still have enough cans to finish Four and most of Five. I hope all the ones I've dropped so far work. It'd be a pity to have to go back just to make replacements. There's too much else to do." He fell silent again as the waldo began pressing his body at various points, indicating that *Oceanus* was entering turbulence. His fingers, shoulders, knees, elbows, tongue, and toes exerted delicate pressure, now this way, now that, on parts of the suit's lining, answering the thumps he could feel and forestalling the ones the vision screen let him anticipate. For nearly two minutes the aircraft jounced its way through the vertical currents, and as the turbulence eased off and the air around his viewers cleared, the pilot gave a happy grunt. He would have nodded his head in satisfaction, but that would have operated too many inappropriate controls.

"A respectable bite. Nine or ten more runs at this height should give us takeoff or orbit mass."

"Or a hundred or so stall recoveries," his official buddy couldn't help adding.

Belvew let the remark lie, and two or three minutes passed before anyone else spoke. All not otherwise too absorbed were reading for themselves the rise of tank levels as *Oceanus*'s collectors gulped Titanian air, spun the hydrocarbon fog drops out of it, stored the liquid, and vented the remaining nearly pure nitrogen to the atmosphere. Even Status watched, but used only current-log memory, which would be routinely edited and wiped of nonessentials each Titan orbit.

"There's another odd surface patch a little east of Carver," Maria Collos's voice came at length, as the main tanks neared the seventenths mark. "It wouldn't take us very far off plan to look at it before we start Leg Five." She, too, would have been glad of seismic data—

her growing maps showed a lot of topography in need of explanation—but was willing to pause for other information if the time cost
was small enough.

"Like the earlier ones, or something really new?" asked Belvew.

"Can't tell for sure in long waves. It could be just another bit of
melted tar, if that's what they're made of. It's the biggest so far, but
even if that's all, we're getting enough of the things to need explanation."

"*One* would need explanation!" snapped Arthur Goodall, the
highest-ranking and—excusably because of the ceaseless pain of synapse amplification syndrome—usually least patient of the group. "I
can see and so can you how polymer tars formed up in sunlight
would settle out of the air as dust at this temperature. I can see dust
getting piled into dunes even in the three-kilo breezes that pass for
gales here. I can see it looking like obsidian if it gets melted and
frozen again. What I don't see is what on this ninety-K iceball could
ever melt it."

"I've suggested methane rain, dissolving rather than melting the
surface of a dune as it soaks in and forming a crust as it evaporates,"
came the much milder, thinner, and rather snappish voice of leukemia VII case Ginger Xalco.

"And *I've* suggested landing and finding out firsthand whether
those nice, smooth, glassy patches and hillocks are thin shells of
evaporite over dunes and dirt, as you're implying, or the tops of
magma lenses," snapped Goodall. "When do we do *that*? You've
plenty of juice now, Gene. Why not take a *good* look at this one—
whether it turns out to be just another item for Maria's maps or
something really different? And don't tell me it's against the advance
plans; we're here to find things out, and you know it. To quote the
poetic characters who wrote our mission plan, 'There's no telling in
advance which piece of a jigsaw puzzle will prove to be the key to
the big picture.' "

Goodall, in legal charge of the project, could have given all this
as a set of orders, but the many decades' intrusion of military discipline into basic research was not yet that deep.

"It's not a matter of set policy," Belvew replied as mildly as he could—he had his own troubles, even if they didn't include SAS; but Goodall was his commander, in a rather shaky way. "Dodging risk to the jets before the seismic and weather gear are all deployed is common sense, not just policy, and *you* know it. Once they're in action, long-term studies can go on even if we lose transport for a while. We've made one landing already to deploy a factory, and a couple of others to restock from it, after all."

"I know. Sorry." Goodall didn't sound very sorry, actually, but courtesy also had higher priority than mere discipline. Without it, discipline would quickly evaporate even among adults, as most of surviving humanity had eventually learned the hard way. "It'd be nice to be around when some of the results crystallize, though. And you can't count the later landings because they were in the same place and we knew what to expect."

"Not exactly. The original shelf was gone."

"The area was plain Titanian dirt, mixed tar-dust and ice we guess, with no cliff to fall down this time. Even I could probably have set down safely." No one contradicted this blatant exaggeration. "The old saw about dead heroes—"

"Doesn't apply, Arthur." Maria Collos, somehow, was the only one of the group who could manage to interrupt people without sounding rude. Perhaps it was because her own ailments, a pancreatic cancer and consequent diabetes, were being handled by Status and gave her little pain or inconvenience; she merely knew she was dying. "We're already dead heroes. We've been told so." There might or might not have been sarcasm in her tone. No one else, even Goodall, spoke for a moment. Then Belvew referred back to the landing question.

"I'll be glad to do a ground check after finishing the Four line, if Maria's radar and my own eyes can find me landing and takeoff surface. We can start getting seismic info without Line Five. Actually, we're all as curious as Art about the smooth stuff, and it's good tactics to eliminate possibilities as early as opportunity lets us. Let me top off these tanks just to play safe, and then you can put me back where I left the Four leg, Maria. After that's done we'll scout your new patch for landing risk, if you're not doing that already."

No one commented, much less objected, and Gene made his remaining passes through the thunderhead with no stalls. *Oceanus* was struck more than once by lightning, but this risk had been foreseen. Strips of conducting polyacetylene—no one had expected to find a convenient source of copper or silver near any of the ice bodies orbiting Saturn—extended from wingtip to wingtip and from nose to tail, preventing any large potential difference in the basic structure. The discovery after the factory had matured of silicate dust containing a reasonable amount of aluminum had been a pleasant surprise, and gave hope for more jets eventually than had been planned.

There were no remarks about Belvew's near stall, either; nearly all had flown the ramjets at one time or another. The exceptions were Goodall, whose own senses were drowned in pain too much of the time to let him use a body waldo safely; Pete Martucci, whose reflexes, though he was one of the very few of the staff not known to be dying of something, had never been good enough to trust during landings; and the doctor, Lieutenant Colonel Sam Donabed, who had actually never learned how to fly. Even these knew the ordinary problems of piloting and could take over controls if necessary.

"Standard turn left four five point five," Maria said without waiting for Belvew to report that his tanks were full.

"Left four five point five," he acknowledged, banking promptly to seventy-four degrees. The group had agreed on a half-Earth gravity as a "standard" coordinated turn on Titan. The ramjet's wings, stubby as they were, could still give that much lift at ram speed below thirty kilometers or so altitude. He snapped out of the turn in just over sixteen seconds, since mission speed was an equally standard one hundred meters per second when nothing higher was needed.

"Your heading is good. You'll reach the break in Leg Four in two hundred fifteen seconds from—*now!* Nose down so as to reach three hundred meters at that time. We've allowed for the speed increase at your present power setting, so don't change it. On my time call, level off and do a standard right turn of one seventy-seven point three. Start dropping cans at standard intervals ten seconds after you finish the turn. The leg ends at the twenty-second can." It was still Maria's voice, though Status must have provided the figures.

"Got it." Belvew remembered again, with the aid of the blunt needle mounted in the suit under his chin, not to nod. There were no more words until the time call, and no more after it until the last of the pencil-like "cans"—containers for seismometers, thermometers, ultramagnetomers, and other data collectors—needed for the fourth leg of the planned seismic network had been ejected. There had been only one more of the randomly timed reality breaks which reminded pilots that they were not in fact on board the jets they were driving, and it had failed to interrupt anything important.

"Okay, Maria, take my hand." Gene nosed the jet upward and increased thrust as he spoke. All the others were listening and watching as their particular instruments and duties allowed, except Goodall. He was meticulously testing the output of each of the recently dropped instrument sets. Nothing interrupted the terse directions which followed the pilot's request, and *Oceanus* swung back toward Lake Carver and hurtled northward along the eastern shore eight hundred meters above its surface, with Gene's earplugs still silent. He knew that others, probably more than usual in view of the proposed landing, were examining lake and shore as minutely as they could on their duplicates of his own Mollweide, while Maria was using her station-based instruments, each employing its own combination of active and passive radiation. He could expect to have his attention called to anything he seemed to be missing, so he concentrated on the screen area a third of the way from center to lower margin, which displayed the region he would pass over in the next few seconds. This section was only slightly distorted by the projection that let a single screen squeeze the full sphere into an ordinary human field of vision. This mattered little, actually; everyone had learned long ago to correct in their own minds even for the extreme shape error at the edges. No part of the aircraft itself showed; many of the two dozen cameras mounted in various parts of its skin did have bits of wing, body, or tail in their fields, but Status in blending their images on the single full-sphere display routinely deleted these.

Unfortunately.

The surface of the lake was currently glass-smooth ahead and left of the jet, though even Titanian winds could often raise waves; gravity was weak and liquid density and viscosity low. The highest winds seemed to occur over liquid where evaporation lowered the air density far more than likely temperature changes could. Belvew gave the lake only an occasional glance, keeping his main attention on the land ahead where the feature to be examined should be.

"Three minutes," came Maria's quiet voice. The others remained silent. "Two. You may be able to see it now." The pilot scanned through his vision frequencies again, dodging the wavelengths which were most strongly absorbed by methane.

"I can, I think. Forget timing. I'm slowing to ten meters above ram stall—no, make that twenty for the first run—and going down to a hundred meters. And cut out the reality reminder, Status. If I ever lose track of where I really am we can cut my shift short later. I'll recover. The air looks steady, but I don't want another stall at this height."

No one objected aloud, though there must have been mental reservations. Belvew was the pilot for now; it was up to him to weigh relative risks to the aircraft. Negative comments would have been distracting, and therefore dangerous as well as discourteous.

The smooth patch grew clearer as the seconds passed. It was much larger than most of the many seen so far, about half a kilometer across, roughly circular in shape but with four or five extensions reaching out another hundred or hundred and fifty meters at irregular points around its circumference. It might have been an oversized amoeba as far as outline went. The color seemed to be basically black, though it reflected the pale reddish orange-tan of the Titanian high smog as though from glass.

No small details could be made out from the present altitude and speed. Gene banked, to much less than standard turn rate at this speed, swung in a wide, slow half circle north of the patch, and made a second pass in the opposite direction. This time the reflection of the brighter section of southern sky where the Sun was hiding could be made out; the surface looked more than ever like glass, as Maria had said for the others she had mapped, but there were still no informative details.

He made two more runs, this time at thirty meters above the highest point of the patch and only two meters per second above ram stall, tensely ready to shift to rocket mode—to cap the air intakes and feed liquid and extra heat into the pipes at the slightest drop in thrust. He was not worried about the wings stalling; even those stubby structures had plenty of lift area in this atmosphere and gravity, and the jet had been designed so that they would go out at higher airspeed than any control surface.

Nevertheless, his attention was enough on his aircraft and far enough from the ground so that it was Barn who spotted the irregularity.

2

SETDOWN

THE THING HUMPS UP pretty far at the middle; it's more of a hill than a patch of something," the copilot reported. "There's a hollow about ten meters across halfway from the high point to the base of that northeast arm. It did funny things to our reflection as we passed this time, but I can't see it now. The whole surface is reflecting sky, and that's pretty uniform. I couldn't decide exactly how deep the hole is, but it's just a dent, not a real crater."

"Did anyone else spot it?" asked Belvew. Most of them had, but none could give any better description. Even Maria had not been Dopplering the site. He made another low pass, this time devoting a rather dangerous amount of his own attention to the surface below. He saw hill and hole for himself, but could make out no more details than any of the others.

"You know we're going to have to land sometime," Goodall remarked in what was meant to be a thoughtful tone.

"I know." Belvew was thinking, too. There was half a minute's pause before the commander, who would be operating the remote-controlled labs and wanted to get at it, tried again.

"What time is better than now?"

Gene could answer that one.

"When we know more about the strength of that surface. If it's just a crust, as the rain hypothesis suggests, *Oceanus* could break

through and smother the jet scoops in dust, or mud, or dirt, or whatever form the stuff under it happens to have."

"But we'd land in rocket mode. The scoops would have to be
closed."

"And if the tailpipes were covered too? We haven't even risked
a lake landing yet."

This was quite true, but Goodall was not yet out of ammunition,
and riposted instantly. "You have plenty of cans. See what happens
when one of them hits. Hold the chute; let it hit as hard as Titan can
make it."

"Good idea." The pilot, with much relief, cautiously raised his
speed to standard—too sudden a boost to the heaters could make a
pipe front-fire—and climbed to a full kilometer. There was still no
real wind, but the patch was a harder target than he had expected.
Without its parachute the slender container took much longer to lose
the jet's speed, as all had expected but none could estimate quantitatively. Status's attention had not been called to the problem.

The first drop overshot badly. Belvew couldn't see it, or rather
didn't dare watch it closely, but Inger and Collos followed it with
other instruments until it buried itself beyond detection in ordinary,
firm Titanian "dirt" a hundred and fifty meters beyond the edge of
the glassy patch.

The second try, with Barn calling the release moment, went
much better, and was quite informative in its way. The can's own
instruments stopped radiating at the instant of impact, ending passive measurements, but Maria's shortest viewing waves showed that
the little machine, solid as it was, had shattered on contact without
penetrating. The surface seemed pretty solid.

Belvew was less happy than he might have been. If the can had
broken through undamaged it would have implied a crust probably
too weak to take the jet's weight, much less the impact of a poor
landing. That would have provided a good excuse for not putting
down just here and now, and spared him an increasingly worrisome
decision.

As it was, the next move appeared to be up to him. Even had

the time for shift change been closer than it was, he was mature enough to be embarrassed at the thought of passing a responsibility to anyone else. He thought furiously. Would anything *except* an actual landing tell them what they needed to know?

The jet lacked landing gear in any ordinary sense; there were no wheels, floats, or real skids. Its belly was a pair of solid flat-bottomed keels meant to give stability during a liquid landing and broad support on dubiously solid surfaces, though once stopped the fuselage would sink to something like half its vertical diameter and part of its inner wingspan in the best-guess mixture of Titan's lakes. It would float a little deeper in pure methane. This was why no one wanted to make the first lake landing; it had not occurred to the designers of *Oceanus* and her sisters until much too late to calculate, much less test, the results of attempting a rocket-mode start with the pipes, whose pods were below the wings, totally immersed in liquid. The log of the Earth-to-Saturn orbit had several annoyed entries about such oversights in equipment design. The outbound trip had consequently been much less boring than anyone had expected, and decidedly busier. Many staff members had spent much less time in deep-sleep than had been planned, and so there had been more disease fatalities than expected. This had helped settle the trivial argument about whether the half-life of the crew should be measured from Earth departure or Saturn arrival—trivial because everyone knew as well as the planners back on Earth that the number of units was too small to justify that sort of statistic.

Fortunately, the budget for contingency personnel in the original planning had been based on pessimism.

So far the keels had seemed to be adequate landing skids on a reasonably solid surface. Belview thought carefully. One *could* make a pass at just above wing-stalling speed, grazing the apparently smooth hump. If he did it right, he might really resolve the question of whether the patch was solid or crust—if it broke under him. If it did not, of course, there would be no certainty about its ultimate strength until a real landing was made, the jet had come to a stop, and the wings lost *all* their lift. Might as well do that the first time.

The convexity of the patch complicated the problem slightly. If he landed too hard—easy to do on the upslope side and, now that he thought of it, even easier on the other—the question of whether the crust was stronger than the jet's belly and keels would also become relevant. Here too there was a designed but so far untested safety factor. A whole, especially an extrapolated whole, is never equal to the sum of its parts—Euclid had not been an engineer, or at least had apparently never considered synergy.

The initial landing, a Titan day before, had been on a smooth shelf of ice near the foot of the upthrust side of what looked like a tilted block mountain; Titan seemed to be still active tectonically. There had been no trouble anticipated in detail, though of course the pilot—Inger, that time—had kept alert for the unforeseen. This was fortunate, since the rocket exhausts had started a thermal-shock crack in the ice which chased the jet for most of its landing slide. The pilot had just managed to avoid riding to the foot of the hill on several million tons of detached shelf by a final, quick shot of thrust. The three hours it had taken Goodall to steer the factory seed pod through its climb to the bottom, walk it to a safe distance from the cliff face and the new pile of ice rubble, put down its roots, and start it growing had been spent in a high state of tension—mostly by Inger, who was in no more physical danger than anyone else, but who *was* the current pilot. If he hadn't been able to get *Oceanus* off again, little but remote mapping could be done until Carla lePing and her colleagues had the next aircraft ready.

When it seemed certain that no replacement factory would have to be sent out, the fact that only a short length of ice shelf remained for takeoff had had to be faced. Inger had used maximum thrust, in rocket mode of course, and maximum-lift wing camber. While he concentrated his attention straight ahead, the rest of the group watched another crack chase him along the shelf, and more ice rubble fall, bounce, and roll toward the new factory. There was no longer any ice platform to land on when he did get airborne and reached ram speed.

The two later descents to pick up cans, once the factory had matured and started production, had been on "ordinary" ground and proved uneventful. The drag on the skids, which all had feared might stress the aircraft too highly—this was why the ice shelf had been chosen for the first touchdown, though the ice was merely smooth rather than slippery on Titan—had been strong but not dangerous, and the subsequent takeoffs had presented no problems except a rather larger demand for reaction mass than had been hoped.

Belvew remembered the ice landing vividly as he planned his present one. Some dangers were now more foreseeable, but concentrating on these might lessen his readiness to respond to the unforeseen as promptly as his friend had done. He could, it occurred to him, land on the ordinary-looking ground beside the smooth patch; the labs were mobile and could eventually get the information he was after.

Except the strength of the stuff. That would have to be known sooner or later, and sooner seemed better. His determination to land *on* the patch crystallized firmly.

Well, *Theia* and *Crius* were still available at the orbiting station, or should be in a few days, and the chance had to be taken sometime. No one would would blame him for losing *Oceanus*.

At least not out loud. The aircraft was statistically almost certain to be lost sometime, and *someone* would presumably be flying it. But please, General, someone *else*.

He called for a wind check—even a meter or two a second could make a difference—and held a constant heading for ten kilometers while Inger adjusted a superimposed grid on his own screen's image. Eventually the moving ground features followed one of the lines and let him time their apparent motion.

"Only zero point seven, from eighty-seven," was the verdict. Belvew swept out over the lake without asking Maria for a heading, lined up with the patch from a dozen kilometers to the west, and eased back on his power.

For just a moment. Then, reflexively and almost suicidally quickly, he shifted to rocket mode and nosed steeply upward, with a dozen or so alarmed voices in his ears.

It was not a reality pause which suddenly blocked his view of Titan, but reality itself. He should have seen the slight dimness drifting down the center of his screen against the almost-as-dim sky, but he had allowed his attention to center too deeply on the proposed landing site. Most of his colleagues, even Inger, who should never have allowed any such thing to happen, had done the same.

Rain does not pour, or even fall, on Titan; it drifts, not always down. The gaseous nitrogen is dense, liquid methane is not, and gravity is weak. Terminal velocity for a raindrop is very low, so drops do not get torn into small fragments as they do on Earth; and they don't even start to descend at all rapidly until they are marble- or even eyeball-sized.

A camera lens which encounters such a drop doesn't break but does cease briefly to form an image, and the portion of Belvew's Mollweide covering the space ahead of *Oceanus* went effectively blank though not dark.

He could still see aft, but that was not the way he was traveling. He climbed sharply, watching airspeed carefully. At least there was no other traffic to worry about.

He was out of the rain in a minute or a little more, and flying visually again as the lenses dried. The Titanian landscape ahead was less fascinating than the well-developed thunderhead behind, which everyone was now examining with great interest.

No one said a word of blame. All who had been using the Mollweide image had missed the rain. They had all, including Inger, been watching the intended landing site too closely.

Belvew drove deliberately back into the rain to restock his tanks—he had not used much mass, but had completely lost the urge to save time at the expense of low reserves—and circled while the cloud and its precipitate drifted slowly out of his landing approach path. He felt a slight temptation to pass up the landing and go back to sowing cans, but knew he would lose the resulting debate. Goodall would not be the only one against him. A pilot's authority was not absolute unless he or she was actually aboard the aircraft.

Fifteen minutes later, *Oceanus* was just where she had been when she had flown into the rain, and Gene was once more in the middle of landing procedure, easing back on thrust. His attention again was straight ahead.

Most others', especially Inger's, was more diffused.

He nosed up enough to split the result of decreased thrust between descent rate and speed loss, and reached the shore fifty meters above the liquid and a scant two meters a second above ram stall. Chewing his lower lip, which fortunately affected no waldo controls, he closed the ram intakes and fed liquid to the plasma arcs. There was a grunt of admiration which might have come from Goodall; the shift to rocket mode was almost perfectly smooth. The longitudinal accelerometer shifted slowly from zero to a negative reading, and stayed there as Belvew nosed down and turned his fires even lower. He was approaching wing stall now, and began increasing the camber of his lifting surfaces toward the barrel-section shape which had been used so few times before, and never by him. He suddenly realized he should have done a few practice stalls two or three kilometers higher. He convinced himself quickly that breaking off the approach and going up to do this now was not necessary, but he didn't ask for anyone else's opinion.

The rippled surface of the satellite was forty meters down. Thirty-five. Thirty—

The glassy convexity loomed ahead, rising to meet his keels. He nosed up even more, very gently, killing descent briefly while airspeed continued to drop. The bulge kept rising toward him. Without orders, Inger began calling airspeed aloud. The wings *should* maintain lift down to sixteen meters per second at his present weight, Belvew knew, and the stall then *should* be smooth. Some levels of theory were solidly established.

"Twenty-two zero—twenty-one nine—twenty-one eight—"

The keels were two meters from the bulge, and he nosed up still farther to keep them so as the airspeed continued to fall. That wouldn't work much farther; past the top of the dome he'd have to drop the nose to make contact before stall, and that would speed him up unless he eased back on thrust with a precision which only practice could have given. Not very much speedup could be produced by Titan's gravity, but any at all would complicate the landing.

The side edges of his screen darkened suddenly, but he kept his attention ahead. If there was anything important aft, someone would tell him this time, though he hoped they wouldn't before he was stopped. For an instant he wished he were actually riding the jet, so that he could *feel* when touchdown occurred.

But he knew anyway. The accelerometer and three human voices told him simultaneously. He stopped mass flow and quenched the plasma fires almost completely, but kept ready to use fractional rocket power on one side or the other if a swerve developed. A severe yaw too close to touchdown speed could roll the *Oceanus* onto her back even with the keels three meters apart, and it seemed most unlikely that whichever wing was underneath could take such treatment.

"You're down!" came Ginger's rather snappish voice, this time separate from the others'. Belvew snorted faintly, and spared enough of his attention to utter a bit of doggerel which had survived in various forms from the time of fabric-covered aircraft.

"A basic rule of flying, and one you'll always need: An aircraft's never landed until it's lost its speed."

But deceleration was now rapid as the keel friction made itself felt, and a few seconds later the landing was complete. Belvew knew he wouldn't feel it, but his stomach tightened up anyway for several more seconds as he watched screen and vertical-motion meters for evidence that the ship was breaking through a surface.

Apparently it wasn't, and at last he felt free to let his attention focus on the view aft.

The screen darkening was from a slowly spreading cloud of black smoke, its nearest edge well over two hundred meters astern. It could not, the pilot judged at once, have been produced by friction between his keels and the surface; his landing slide hadn't started that far back, and skin thermometers showed that the keels were at about a hundred and fifty kelvins. This was considerably but not worrisomely above ambient. They were cooling rapidly, but not so quickly as to suggest they had been hot enough in the last few seconds to boil Titanian tar.

Not that anyone really knew what temperature *that* would take, Gene reflected fleetingly.

More to the point, a fairly deep trough in the surface, starting just below the near side of the smoke cloud and extending as far back along his approach path as he could see, confirmed that whatever had happened to the surface had come before touchdown. The most obvious cause was hot exhaust. He was too busy at the moment to devise the GO6-demanded alternative hypothesis, so he refrained from uttering this one aloud.

The smoke was being borne very slowly away from him by the negligible wind. The trough, half a meter deep and ten or twelve wide, remained uniform as the receding cloud revealed more and more of it, extending down the slope of the convexity. The jet had come to rest almost exactly at the top of the bulge, it seemed; both pitch and roll indicators read within a degree or so of horizontal. Luck occasionally assisted virtue, Belvew reflected.

"If it's a crust, it's pretty solid," Goodall remarked.

"Unless the jets melted their way down and just produced more of it," rejoined Ginger.

"Could be, but they didn't touch the spot where we are now," the commander pointed out. Like the rest, he knew that at least one alternative hypothesis, however unlikely or unappetizing, should always be proposed as soon as possible after a first public speculation; Ginger had behaved properly. Still, it was so much better if the alternative was reasonable . . .

It had also been quite proper for the commander to point out possible flaws. Objectivity was, after all, important. "Let's get samples."

Belvew had powered down the flight controls, except for those which might be needed for emergency takeoff, and could safely nod his head, not that the others could see him from their own quarantine compartments.

"All right, in a few minutes. Nondestructive examination first. I assume everything in sight's been recorded; now let's *look.*"

"Right." Goodall's voice was a fraction of a syllable ahead of the others'. Belvew activated the short-focus viewers on the lower part of *Oceanus*'s fuselage and allowed their images to take over the Mollweide screen as his friends above chose—no, not above, he reminded himself; *he* was *above* with them; another real-surroundings reminder must be about due. No one, however, said anything for several minutes; the surface still resembled obsidian or tar at every magnification available and at every point the viewers could reach. The depression seen from the air was now hidden by the curve of the hill ahead, even though they were looking from the top of the bulge, and the nearest point of the track left by the landing approach was too distant for a really good look.

"I guess we dig," Pete said at last. Belvew nodded again, as uselessly as before, but operated more of his controls.

The object which dropped from between the keels might almost have been an egg-shaped piece of the surface itself, as far as texture went, though its color was much lighter. It measured about fifty centimeters in its longest dimension. Until it reached the ground, which took an annoyingly long two seconds in Titan's gravity, it appeared totally featureless. When it did strike, it flattened on the bottom to keep from rolling, uncovered a variety of optical sensors on the top and sides, and deployed handling, liquid-sampling, and digging apparatuses, coring tools, and locomotion equipment.

Structurally and functionally, it straddled the accepted arbitrary borderline between nanotech equipment and pseudolife; it had been grown like the cans and the jets, not manufactured, and much of its internal machinery was on a molecular scale. It was about as capable of self-repair as a healthy human being, both ranking far below a starfish.

"Take it, Art. Where to?"

"Aft, I'd say. I'll sample at each meter until we reach the exhaust trail, if that's what it is, and then really dig. The smellers report ready."

The "smellers" were of course the analytical equipment, and

everyone began to tense up again as the egg crawled to its first sampling point and its iridium-coated scraper went to work.

"How hard?" queried several voices at once.

"Only about three. If it's a crust, it must be pretty thick to take
Oceanus's weight."

"Composition?" This answer was slower in coming, naturally,
but overall percentages were ready in less than a minute.

"Carbon fifteen point seven one; nitrogen eighteen point eight
eight; hydrogen four point one one two; oxygen twenty-eight point
two five; phosphorus—"

"Phosphorus?" Again several voices merged. The first three elements had all been observed in samples of the atmospheric smog,
and there was nothing surprising about the oxygen in view of all the
water ice; but this was the first third-period element other than aluminum and silicon to be identified on Titan.

Study of presumably prebiotic substances had the main mission
priority, of course. Whatever was decimating humanity was probably biological and therefore chemical in nature; new diseases, new
varieties of older diseases, even newer combinations of both were
appearing and spreading faster than causes could be identified and
treatments devised. It had seemed at least possible that Titan might
be in a prebiotic stage, and might provide origin-of-life data which
could fill the still broad gaps in existing theory—broad in spite of
the advanced development of pseudolife equipment. Of course even
such data might not be meaningful for terrestrial biology, but with
energy and construction expenses almost zero, this expedition or
almost anything else seemed worth trying. Human beings were des-
perate and individually expendable; one might as well die *usefully*.

And of course this was another excuse for a few people to get
away from Earth, which might or might not be a good idea.

No one had been sure, of course, that there would be anything
even prebiological to study on Titan. Even the now obvious tectonic
activity might not go deep enough to bring all the elements presumably needed for life from very deep in the satellite. That would depend on the still unknown causes of the seisms.

Regardless of the fact that only two-thirds of the sample mass had been accounted for, Ginger Xalco snapped out emphatically, "Structure, for goodness' sake."

No one suggested that the elemental analysis be finished first, certainly not Goodall, who might have pulled rank if he had chosen. He shared her feelings. He set the appropriate internal machinery to work while the lab crawled on to its next sample site, and its next, and its next.

"It's a gel, really," he said at last. "The solvent—pardon me, dispersing agent—is methanol. Simple methyl alcohol. Most of the rest of the material seems to be polymers of one sort or another. Some of it's carbohydrate, a lot has nitrogen, but it's going to take a while to find whether we're dealing with what we'd consider proteins—polypeptides made of the same amino acids we are."

"Left or right?" asked Collos and Martucci together.

"You'll have to wait even longer for that—"

"Wait a minute!" Inger cut in. "Even at this temperature and gravity a gel has no business holding up a jet for very long. And it's just been rained on! Gene, outside coverage! *Quick!*"

3

STATUS

Belvew didn't bother to ask what his partner had noticed, but instantly but flicked his own screen back to the full-sphere coverage. For a moment he felt relief, since the standard view excluded the aircraft; but a moment's manipulation let him see his keels. Without word, warning, or delay he fed the plasma arcs and tensely watched the longitudinal accelerometer, wishing once again that he could feel the jet's response directly.

For a moment the meter trembled around zero. The surface seemed to be clinging to the keels, which all could now see had sunk into it for several centimeters, and Belvew slowly increased thrust. Another black cloud appeared at the sides of the screen, supporting the idea that surface material was being boiled off by the exhaust. No one commented, yet.

The glassy surface underneath was nearly featureless and for a second or two he was unsure whether or not it was letting *Oceanus* move at all. Then the accelerometer swung, the whole landscape suddenly jerked backward as the jet snapped free, and a moment later he—no, *it* was airborne.

Goodall gave an indignant exclamation as his lab unit, in the path of the exhaust, stopped sending data. The pilot paid no attention for a moment as he concentrated on reaching ram speed as quickly as possible using a minimum of mass. It was Inger who expressed sympathy.

"Sorry, Art. We can grow new labs much quicker than new planes. What else came in before we blew your machine into the lake?"

"Some more numerical stuff. Nothing structural, and we don't have the samples anymore, either."

Inger pondered for a moment, then suggested, "Maybe we can find it. The lab should be all right, at least. The exhaust cools pretty quickly, and the data were coming by beam to the plane. That would have been thrown off line when the lab was pushed. Tell the lab to broadcast, and Gene can make some low passes back along the track; maybe we can get its signals."

"What if it reached the lake? It must have been blown that way, and it's mostly downhill."

"So much the better. We could use a reading on the composition of that juice. Maybe we could find out something about its depth, too. If anything's certain, the liquid's not exactly like what we get from the clouds. Look at the bright side, Chief."

The answer was a grunt which might have meant anything up to "*You* look at it." Barn's instruments, however, showed that Goodall had indeed sent the broadcast command to the lab; whether he was waiting more eagerly for resumption of data flow or for a chance to go on complaining was anyone's guess. He would have denied the latter, of course, probably pointing out that griping was much less effective than useful work at keeping pain out of his mind. Everyone knew this already.

Gene had been listening, even with most of his attention on piloting. In spite of his sympathy for the colonel's feelings, he went up to a little over a kilometer, steered out over the lake to the rainstorm, and replaced the reaction mass he had just used. Then he increased thrust and nosed down—he was actually as impatient as any of the others for the lab data and more optimistic about the unit's survival than most of them—and headed back toward shore and the landing site.

He was down to fifty meters by the time the glassy patch showed ahead. He eased back thrust, allowing the jet to slow to ram stall plus twenty, and made four passes over the area at that speed, first following and then paralleling the line of the landing and takeoff.

Nothing from the lab registered. With a grim expression which no one could see, and some muttered remarks which he took care no one could hear, he reset the wing camber, closed the ramjet intakes, and went back to rocket mode; but two more passes at a bare fifteen meters altitude and just above wing stall—neither Goodall nor anyone else was going to say he hadn't tried, whatever they might think of his flying judgment—still produced no signals. Either the lab had been wrecked, though that still seemed to Belvew to be rather unlikely, or it was too deep in the lake for its signals to be picked up. Nobody, curiously, thought of its being deep in anything else; after all, it was far lighter than the ramjet.

The presumably nonpolar liquid shouldn't interfere seriously with radio frequencies, but in broadcast mode any great depth certainly would. Titan was a weird place by human standards, but the inverse square law and rules of optical absorption still applied there.

There was no basis yet even for guesses at the depths of the numerous lakes. That would depend on details of the still hypothetical methane cycle as well as tectonics. There seemed, for example, to be practically no major rivers either to feed lakes or to fill them with sediment, though each liquid body was usually supplied by a number of small brooks.

Such items of information detail had a low priority in the early part of the program, though they would all be faced eventually.

"Sorry, Art," Belvew said at last as he increased thrust, returned to ramjet mode when speed sufficed, and began to climb back toward the thunderhead. "I had hopes too, but I guess we've lost it. Have you any ideas what could produce a gel here?"

"I have enough trouble guessing what could produce methanol."

"Why?" retorted Belvew. "The makings are all there. Ice and methane could do it directly, with release of hydrogen. Maybe some of the prelife catalysts we're hoping to find are actually here, if you think the reaction would go too slowly at ninety K's."

"Naughty, naughty!" cut in Maria's gentle voice. "Catalysts wouldn't help. That reaction's endothermic by over a hundred kJ."

For a moment Gene wanted to kick himself. He knew the woman hadn't had that datum in her head, but he, too, could have checked quietly with Status before making himself sound silly. Then he saw a way out.

"The energy could come from local heat," he said, trying to keep smugness out of his voice.

"At ninety kelvins?"

"Sure. I did mention the other product. Hydrogen would leave the scene, so no back reaction—"

"That would happen only if it *could* leave the scene." Goodall had pounced on the hypothesis and was enjoying himself. "That would be at or very near the surface, not deep underground—"

"Or in or just under a lake," Ginger cut in. "We'll have to look for bubbles."

"And lower than ordinary temperatures, if it's happening fast enough to show bubbles from the air," Belvew finished. "All right, we'll look. Do some planning, you types with imaginations. I'm just an observer. I'm going to hit Line Five. Give me heading and time, Maria."

The fifth planned seismic array was a quarter of the way around Titan from Lake Carver, ten or eleven hours flight at standard observing speed and over two even at full ram thrust in the thinner air tens of kilometers up. Belvew set everything on automatic, turned *Oceanus* over to Maria's attention, and decided to eat and sleep. He needed the rest. A healthy twenty-year-old might have gone through the last hour casually, but he was neither. Very few human beings now alive were.

Evolution of disease organisms had gotten further and further ahead of medical research; dozens, counting new variations of older and once solved ailments such as the various leukemias, leprosies, and cancers, were now on the list of major health problems along with AIDS TA, VL, and XL. At least four of these involved sterility, three of them in women. The average age was now barely twenty years in spite of, or more likely because of, the species' usual reaction to any major threat. STDs shared the increase.

Belvew and Inger were twenty-eight, quite elderly; Goodall was forty-four, almost unique.

Suggested explanations among the less panicked survivors were legion, and even ones which seemed worth testing were quite numerous. Satisfactory ones were almost nonexistent, except very briefly. Even supernaturalists had had to fall back on Noachian-flood divine wrath aimed at general materialism rather than at specific sins.

The scientists had done better as far as testable ideas were concerned, but not very much; each virus, prion, genetic warp, and other cause of each given ailment had usually been identified beyond reasonable doubt quickly enough, but the information seldom produced an effective treatment before the disease in question had killed or incapacitated a few million more victims. The basic, general, underlying cause of the whole pattern was simply unknown.

There were two favored speculations—they showed little sign of graduating to real hypotheses—among scientists. Either new disease organisms had been tailored by people with motives that were unspecified, but presumably unsane by most standards; or the sudden appearance of so many ailments almost simultaneously was merely a statistical event like a baseball hitting streak. Both speculation sets took synergy for granted, and humanity still had many conspiracy fundamentalists to defend the first.

Those who preferred the second could point out how and why common worldwide travel could bring infective agents to critical concentration, at which hosts could be found and invaded faster than victims died off. They could not, however, explain why drastic restrictions on transportation and actual collapse of many travel systems had failed to show the opposite effect.

Belvew, who liked people, was not a conspiracy believer but was too well informed to feel sure of his own correctness. CPRS—calcium-phosphorus recrystallization syndrome, the ailment which would presumably finish turning his own bones to something like eggshell china in another two or three years—was known to be caused by a virus which would have taken only a little manipulation to produce from a normal human gene.

Or, of course, a very modest natural mutation.

An occasional message from Earth suggested that progress was being made in the search for its cure, but this offered Belvew little comfort. The same claims had been current for most forms of cancer for centuries; occasionally, and much less rationally, someone would even claim a cure for cancer in general. This might be why most of Belvew's generation tended to be skeptics who had no real need for GO6.

If success for CPRS was actually achieved, it was unlikely that the treatment could be duplicated by the Saturn crew's relatively limited synthesis facilities. Factories could be reprogrammed or even replanned, but this shouldn't be done for merely personal reasons.

Gene, sure that Maria was having no trouble with the aircraft, extracted himself from his suit. It could use servicing too. He floated back to his sleeping cell and napped while the waldo's life support devices were recharged, cleaned, and otherwise readied for further use, and Status ran test programs on the control systems. The suits were not full-cycling, indefinitely lasting affairs; they had been designed mainly as waldoes. They did, of course, have fusers and life support capacity designed for Titan's environment, but they could keep the wearer comfortable for only thirty hours or so, and alive for perhaps twenty more, on the surface.

Calcium-phosphorus recrystallization syndrome, while robbing him of energy, also kept Gene from sleeping for very long at a time. He was back with *Oceanus* sometime before it reached the planned site of the next seismic array, and Maria returned her full attention rather thankfully to her general mapping. There was nothing for the pilot to do but watch scenery and, of course, speculate on the causes of its various features. He could see the ground well enough from this height, using frequencies able to pierce the small amount of smog which was below him.

There were block mountains and rift valleys; there were plains and what looked like volcanoes—these would come early on the investigation schedule once the weather and seismic nets were established; prebiotic chemistry, if it was happening at all, would presumably need a large variety of materials and a source of energy, and volcanic action offered the best hope of both.

There were lakes large and small. The background surface, the covering of nearly all the more or less horizontal areas, could be the hypothetical tar and ice dust; the factory had been planted on such a surface, but at that time no analysis had been possible. Neither cans nor labs had yet been grown.

None of the lakes was large enough to be called an ocean, as mapping from orbit had already made clear. However, it now seemed that fully a tenth of the satellite's surface was occupied by liquid bodies, ranging in size from Carver, about the area of Earth's Lake Victoria, down to puddles. The Collos patches were neither as numerous nor as a rule anything like as large as the one where *Oceanus* had just had its mishap, but they were far from rare.

The locations of the lakes were to some extent controlled by topography, of course; water has many unique properties, but other liquids including methane share its tendency to flow downhill. Nobody, however, had yet found any order or sense in the size, location, or arrangement of the Collos patches. Belvew amused himself, as he had done before, by trying to organize patterns out of those he passed over. He reached his target area, however, without coming up with any shapes more meaningful than constellations.

Maria, who had also slept briefly, warned that it was time to decrease thrust. The jet began to slow and settle. A real-surroundings interruption occurred just after the descent started, and Belvew wondered briefly whether he should have Status stop this procedure for a while. He decided against it: his tanks were full, he would be traveling high enough and fast enough to preclude any kind of stall as he sowed the cans, and vertical disturbances could be seen at a safe distance. It was only while inside them, slowed down to juice-collecting speed, that there was any danger.

Any *known* danger, he reminded himself. Any known danger except the ever-to-be-remembered one of identifying too closely with the aircraft, which the reality interruptions were intended to prevent. He brought his attention back to the job as Maria began issuing more specific directions.

He had lined up on course, reached standard speed and delivery altitude, and released the first dozen of the Line Five cans when an interruption came from a voice rarely enough heard to catch everyone's attention.

Its most recent and important all-hands announcement had come when the last of the six relay units which kept the station in potential instant contact with all of Titan's surface was properly adjusted in orbit, thus clearing the crew to get the actual project under way. Few had thought of it since except when receiving personal health guidance; it was as much background as traffic noise had once been.

"There is a change in map detail at the factory site. Someone should evaluate." The speaker was Status, the data processor dedicated to constant recomparison of surface maps, maintaining of orbits, supervising the operation of all closed-cycle life support systems, and monitoring the current medical condition of each of the explorers. Its announcement automatically put Maria, currently responsible for surface mapping, in charge. As usual, the voice with which she responded was calm.

"Gene, you're still on track. You have forty-four cans on board, which will complete about two-thirds of Line Five. When they're gone, your heading back to the factory starts at three eleven. I'll get back to you with more headings for the great circle when you need them, or have Status do it if it seems likely I'll be too busy. Barn, standard; monitor Gene. Art, get any readings you can from the factory itself while I check details Status couldn't sense. The rest of you carry on. I'll keep everyone informed." She fell silent for several minutes while she examined the surface around the factory with every frequency at her command.

"The change," she resumed at last, "seems to be the appearance of another of what you so kindly call Collos patches. Its texture is identical with the others', as far as I can tell. It is almost perfectly circular, just over twenty meters across, is essentially flat, and its center is one hundred forty-four meters from the opening of the factory's delivery port and directly in line with that opening—that is, directly north. Azimuth zero."

"How long did it take to reach that size?" asked Goodall. "Can you or Status tell us when the last check of the site was made? And are there enough observations to tell whether it appeared all at once or grew from a center?"

"Less than four hours, four hours, and no," replied the mapper. "That's the time of the last routine check of the spot, and there was no sign of the patch then. Does the factory itself have any data?"

" 'Fraid not. It's been finishing twenty cans and one lab an hour and paying no attention to aboveground surroundings since it ripened."

Everyone could hear this exchange, of course, and Belvew cut in without allowing his eyes to leave his screen.

"Aboveground? But how about below? Do any of its roots go toward the patch?"

Goodall was silent for some seconds, and finally answered in a rather embarrassed and surprised tone, "I can't tell. Roots went out in all directions, of course, and I can tell what materials have been coming in through each major one, but we never thought of wanting to know which absolute direction any one root was taking."

There must have been a spectrum of reactions to this announcement. However, neither laughter nor anger nor surprise was audible. The jet ejected several more cans before its pilot could think of another useful question.

"The root which went east, toward the cliff, would be picking up more water sooner or—well, sooner. The factory couldn't have started production without oxygen. Does any one of them show a richer water take than the others?"

"Yes, though not impressively greater. Number Twelve."

"Then it's a reasonable guess that that one went toward the mountain, which seems to be a block of ice. Whichever is ninety degrees counterclockwise from Twelve must be pretty close to under the new patch, right?"

"Wrong. Unfortunately—"

"Unfortunately? You mean you don't know the *relative* directions either?"

"No. I don't know whether the numbers go clockwise or otherwise, or even if they are in sequence. I labeled them as they started to pick up raw material. Sorry. Even if we'd wanted to, there was no other way to identify them."

"So there goes any chance of analyzing that patch with the factory instruments."

"I'm afraid so."

"So I go back and plant more labs around the factory."

"You drop the rest of Line Five first," Maria cut in. "It won't make much difference in time. You'll be a couple of hours getting back, and it's where you'd be going anyway for more cans. There's no reason to suppose there's any hurry; we don't know what causes these patches even though you've found out they're a bit gooey—"

"That *one* is a bit gooey," muttered Corporal Pete Martucci, who was more regulation-minded than most.

"—and we can learn more sooner by watching this one grow if it does. There's no need for speed."

"There could be if the factory itself has anything to do with the appearance of this new one," Goodall pointed out. Belvew started to say something, but Maria was first.

"We should worry about that if and when it seems in order, I think. I'll watch how fast, and which way if any special one, this thing grows. If it does. Art—no, you're too busy; you, Ludmilla— keep on top of the factory's behavior; that's the only other thing I can think of which might warn us of any such connection. Any other ideas?"

"Five cans to go," Belvew answered, with no obvious relevance. "What's that return heading again?"

Maria told him, and he finished his run in silence. He then climbed to compromise height—air thin enough for low resistance while still dense enough to feed the ramjets—eased in full thrust, took up the great circle heading back to the factory, set *Oceanus* on automatic control, presumably somewhat safer than letting Status handle it through the communication links, and shifted his screen to the instruments being used by Art, Maria, and the others. There should be no intense verticals at this height, and he refused to worry over unknowns, especially when Barn was also watching.

As far as general crew attitude went, scientific-military procedure was of course an important and sometimes even a life-and-death matter, but freedom to pay attention to a problem was more so. The rank distinction between commissioned theoreticians, mere observers, and essentially civilian technicians—even the doctor attached little weight to his technical rank of lieutenant colonel—meant nothing in that respect. The smooth patches might not be a military or any other kind of risk, but they now involved a basic situation change near the only equipment source currently on Titan—one which would take days at least to replace, if they did have to plant a new factory. The more minds speculating on the problem the better.

Sergeant Barn Inger felt just the same, and allowed the fact to direct his thinking and capture most of his attention. He had only the same data as the rest, since he couldn't see *Oceanus*'s wings either. He *could* have looked at parts of the aircraft, since the software omitting it from the full-sphere screen was controllable merely by asking Status, but no one had ever bothered to do such a thing since the aircraft had first flown. Status could see what was happening but had been given no reason to care.

Barn saw no more reason to worry than did Gene, or anyone else. There was a more obvious and presumably more immediate problem.

4

SETBACK

IT WAS DAYLIGHT AND would be for several more days at the factory site. *Oceanus* was on the night side, though Belvew expected to see the fuzzy reddened blob of the Sun—much of the smog was still above him—in another few minutes. Both factory and flier were on the hemisphere away from Saturn; to see the big disc, pierced by the needle of its edge-on rings, would have required relay from the main orbiting station and possibly one other. Even had it been above the horizon, he'd have had to use very carefully chosen sensor frequencies with *Oceanus*'s cameras or, much better he suddenly realized, shift to cameras in the base above with him. Even this might not work since the station spent over a third of its time in Titan's Saturn-shadow. Usually no one knew any more exactly where they were in orbit than the average person on Earth knows the current phase of its moon. They had no reason to care; that sort of thing was for Status.

Even by Titan day, visible light was no use for examining the factory from above the atmosphere. Much longer waves were needed, and for these to have really high resolution the readings from at least a few kilometers of orbit travel had to be combined statistically, also by Status, into single "pictures." Maria could never quite watch her surface images at high resolution in real time. By now it had occurred to everyone in the group how nice it would have been to provide the factory with a camera, but this was another don't-mention-it. "If onlys" were against military, scientific, and medical discipline as well as common sense, all of which demanded dealing with things as they were. Rule X, in fact.

How things were was slowly becoming more apparent. Before Belvew could see the Sun, Maria announced that the new patch was six centimeters broader on the east-west line and eight on the north-south than it had been when first measured. Half an hour later both amounts had increased by another ten centimeters, and the distance from the centroid of the patch to the factory was smaller by nearly a meter.

"Suggests it's actually moving, not just growing more one way than the other," Barn pointed out.

"Suggests I was wrong about the things' being caused by rain," was Maria's less enthusiastic comment.

"Are you sure? Would the factory report rain?" asked Belvew.

"No, but my viewers would. Status says it hasn't rained there since we planted the rig. There isn't—"

"Not during *any* of the four-hour or whatever it is intervals between his regular checks?" asked Emil diSabato, doing his best to keep any suggestion of a pouncing cat out of his tone.

"No storm we've seen yet has lasted less than seven or eight hours," Maria answered. "There isn't any lake close enough to make it likely, either. And I know rain when I see it; there's been plenty of it here and there on Titan. You ought to know, Gene."

"I do. It's always been from verticals either over the lakes or very close to them. The background circulation is so slow that a thunderstorm usually dies before it gets very far from the lake that spawned it, even if it lasts for ten or fifteen hours; and the factory's over twenty kilometers from the nearest lake."

"They *seem* to die," was Goodall's more pessimistic contribution. "In any case, if all these things are made of gel like the one which tried to swallow *Oceanus*, we still have to explain how liquid methane turns into methyl alcohol."

"There *was* a suggestion about that, and the factory is close to an ice source," Ginger pointed out.

"But not to a lake," Maria admitted, still rather sadly.

"So Gene drops another lab the second he gets to the factory."

"Of course, after I land and pick some up," replied the pilot. "That'll still be nearly an hour, though. Aren't there a good many labs already there? Why not get one of those on the job—or two or three, if that'll make things faster?"

There were several seconds of silence.

"Pete, you're the strongest of us by a good deal. If I unseal my room, would you take the chance of a quick visit and kick me? You can hold your breath long enough, or wear a suit."

"No, Art," replied Martucci, "but not because I'm afraid of breaking quarantine, or even regulations. I'd come and take the chance of staying even longer if it would help the lab work, but I don't see how kicking *anyone* would do that."

"Don't be so literal. It might remind me not to let my mouth outrun my brain, but we needn't rub it in, I suppose. I have a lab on the way, Gene." Goodall was obviously embarrassed, as the others would have been for him if all hadn't been equally blind. Neither the commander's morale slip nor the general oversight was mentioned again. Failure to get ideas as soon as they might be useful was a common cause for annoyance but not a reasonable one for guilt. Even replacing the "you" of "if only you'd thought of that" with a "we" would not make such a remark an acceptable, much less a courteous, utterance.

"Better have the lab do samples on the way to the patch, not just after it arrives. We'll need to compare the patch with the ground in its neighborhood," pointed out Ginger. This obvious suggestion made everyone feel better; they could all share the onus of delayed conception, and the point that Goodall needn't consider himself the only offender had been properly raised.

The readings from the alternately scraping and traveling lab held everyone's close attention while the jet neared the site and began its

letdown. Since neither Belvew nor Inger could see the white accumulation starting to grow on the leading edges of its wings, nose,
and empennage shortly after the descent began, this made no real
difference. Status, to whom the complete camera fields were accessible, could see some of them, but had no programmed reason to
pay them any attention. He—even the women seemed to regard the
device as a male personality—just didn't care.

So when the pilot shifted full alertness to his job as final approach and landing neared, neither his eyes, his waldo sensors, nor
his partner told him what was coming, though the frosty ridges leading the wings and stabilizers were now projecting nearly three centimeters. In effect they sharpened the wings and fins, but did not yet
make perceptible difference in lift, drag, or stability. With a few
hundred more flying hours experience at a wide enough variety of
altitudes and speeds, Gene—or anyone—might have learned to recognize and even interpret the tiny discrepancy between thrust and
airspeed. Had he actually been riding in the jet for that much time,
he might even have felt it.

And if the material had remained where it was until after he had
touched down, no one might ever have known about it. There were
instruments to read and report on skin temperature at many points
on the machine, but not at leading edges. Even with nano and pseudolife technology, and their effect of making complex devices almost
costless to build even when rare elements were involved, there were
limits to how much could be installed on a flying machine, fusion-
powered or not.

The heat which leaked from the pipes was at once carried away
by the airstream, of course. Status, while not interested, kept a running log of everything it sensed. This was not "cleaned" to save
memory more often than once a Titan day, sixteen of Earth's in
length, so that events not recognized as important when they occurred could be reviewed in detail afterward. All but a few centimeters of wing adjacent to the ramjet pods themselves stayed at
ambient temperature. Warmth was now, however, beginning to
creep farther out as the speed dropped to and below tens of meters

per second; but no living mind knew it. Status was not, even by those who thought if it as him, a living mind.

The increasing camber applied by Belvew as wing stall approached may have contributed to what finally happened, but no one was ever sure. The operator's tiny pitch and yaw corrections as he maintained a straight and steady descent may have, or may not. Even a trace of turbulence in Titan's own air may have been all that was needed.

Whatever the cause, most of the sharp white rim on the leading edge of the left wing suddenly fell or blew away from the now slightly warmer surface, and the lift on that side, already as dependent on wing area as on shape, dropped.

Slightly. So did the wing tip.

Slightly. Slightly was quite enough, since it also happened suddenly. Probably not even an automatic control, or even Status if it had been on call for such a purpose, could have reacted effectively at such low airspeed.

The wing, short as it was, grazed the ground with its tip, and *Oceanus*'s nose whipped down and to the left. Belvew felt practically simultaneous kicks, nudges, pinches, and stabs from practically all his accelerometers and other rate instruments. At the same instant most of the central area of his Mollweide went blank, and the mosaic of sections which should have shown the view to the rear displayed only Titan's pale peach sky.

There was nothing useful to say for the moment, and Gene again made sure no one heard him saying it.

"There couldn't have been any turbulence there!" sounded too much like an excuse to be uttered by a disciplined civilian, much less a moderately high-ranking observer. Everyone's thoughts reached the same point on that logic route, though not all passed the milestones in the same order.

No ground camera views. No transport until. Seismic nets not finished. Weather tracers not even started. Labs now available only at their source, where they'd have to stay; and something odd was happening there.

Humanity is a visually oriented species, and in seconds Maria and Status were building a new image of the factory site, whose details improved moment by moment as data poured in from different sensors. The factory itself was simply a block with rounded corners, a little over five meters on a side now that it had finished growing, saved from resembling a child's toy by rain-gathering, light-reading, gas-ejecting, and other apparatuses on its roof. No one was looking at that image yet, however.

The jet's nose could gradually, as details were filled in, be seen crumpled back almost to the wings; the "coffin" in which a pilot could ride must be occupying only a fraction of its former volume. The ground the bow had tried to displace had not yielded significantly. The left wing and ram pipe were hidden under the fuselage, whose tail pointed upward at about sixty degrees. The right wing and engine, also pointing upward but less sharply, seemed undamaged, even after image resolution got down to single centimeters.

"So much for *Oceanus*. Is *Theia* ready?" asked Goodall finally.

"Just about," Carla responded quietly.

"I'll check her out," came Ginger's voice. "I think I'm nearest, and I've just slept and done my suit."

"Are you willing to drive again, Gene?"

Belvew hesitated only a moment before answering. The crash was presumably his fault, but there was no reason to suppose that anyone else could have avoided it; and the idea behind the old custom of a pilot's flying, or a horseman's riding, again as soon as possible after an accident was probably still valid even when the pilot wasn't in the aircraft at the time.

"Sure. I'm fresh enough. I'll nap, though, during the preflight. Call me when she's ready, will you, Ginger?"

"Should I hurry?"

"No!" Goodall was emphatic. "*Theia* hasn't been flown at all yet. Cover everything on the checklist, and anything else you can think of. If Maria reports some other ground change we may have to hurry, but not unless or until. It'll be two or three days before we're at a radiation-minimum launch point, and we won't wait that long; but since we're heading toward one, we needn't rush."

"I'll be good," Ginger lied. "Gene needn't worry."

"Who worries?" asked Belvew. He received no answer, and relaxed in his suit. It seemed unlikely that there would be time enough to get out of it for a real nap, or even a video.

This estimate, of course, was based on foreseeables, not on human behavior.

The station was far too massive for anyone to feel the reaction when a person pushed off from or stopped against a wall, but the departure of *Theia* was noticed by everyone. It was also identifiable, since everyone had felt such shoves before.

Reactions differed. Goodall and one or two others wondered momentarily whether they had been asleep and missed the end-of-checkout report. Peter Martucci's movie-idol face made a wry grimace in the privacy of his quarters, as though something he had expected had happened in spite of his hopes. Dr. Lieutenant Colonel Sam Donabed gave a snort of irritation. Lieutenant Carla lePing shook her head disapprovingly.

No one saw any of this, of course. Looking into someone else's quarters was almost worse than entering them. Gene Belvew was, for a fraction of a second, the most surprised, and of course Ginger Xalco was the least.

But Belvew was quick on the uptake.

"Ginger! Why?"

"My suit's fullest, and it'll save time."

"We don't need to save time!"

"Do you really know that? I certainly don't!"

"My suit was serviced almost as recently as yours," Belvew tacitly conceded the other argument. "It has nearly as much life supply."

"And Status says I use less than three-quarters the food and oxygen you do, gorilla. Stop being futile; I've already cut speed."

Everyone by now understood the situation, but no one was ignorant enough to suggest, much less order, that the woman return the jet. There was no point in anyone's making speeches about poor discipline. There was nothing to be done; Ginger was not merely flying *Theia*. She was *riding* the machine, physically on board. That was a point which had to be remembered consciously by everyone until, and if, she got back to the station.

Instruments showed that she had already killed enough station orbital speed to take the craft into atmosphere, and used most of the little reaction water in *Theia*'s tanks to do so. Return was not physically possible until she had refilled on Titan.

Nor was there any question of taking over from the rebel even if this had been useful. Her waldo suit was in the space designed for it on the jet, and any suit on board automatically had control priority unless the wearer deliberately ceded it. "Dead-man" override from outside was not possible; this was another of the unforeseen needs.

However cheap construction and energy might have become, design had not; people charged more heavily than ever for their skilled services. Predictably, most structures and machines were now delivered with performance well short of ideal, and commonly somewhat short of specifications. Even the best usually turned out to lack *something*. The situation was far from new in history, but had been greatly aggravated in recent decades.

Even Goodall said nothing for general hearing. There was nothing useful to say for the moment, and what would be said later would never mention penalties, or violation of rules, or disobedience of orders. Hunger for understanding had replaced much of the desire for personal property, for influence over others' behavior, or for simple glory which had motivated so many of humanity's earlier high-risk activities.

The need-for-knowledge culture, however, had not evolved in quite the same direction as the economic-religious-military one. Social awareness—idealism or patriotism—was fully as great as ever in the vaguely militarized ranks of science, and of course required as much team effort as war; but it did not usually demand the prompt and blind submission to orders which militarism had had to evolve when the opponents were other human beings. A universe with no personal wants, enmities, or survival urges was not an *enemy*.

The new patriotism, if it could be called that, was not nearly so blind as the old, but it still could demand personal risk and sacrifice. Ginger knew exactly what she was doing, and why. So, in spite of their hasty questions, did Gene and the others. Nothing critical was said during the hundred minutes that *Theia* took to touch atmosphere and start to kill her nearly two-kilometers-per-second relative velocity; and even when she was flying rather than orbiting, navigation instructions from Maria and flying advice from the others made up most of the conversation.

The advice was not needed. Ginger had spent as much time in simulators and roughly as much actually flying *Oceanus* as had any of the others, but those still in orbit felt a need to keep meaningful conversation going—to "stay in touch."

Xalco, after carefully purging the remaining water from her mass tanks and filling up above a convenient lake, deliberately landed by the factory at higher speed than Belvew had done. There was no way yet to tell whether this made the difference. *Theia* approached from the north, touched down, and slid to a stop half a kilometer west of the factory. She would have come closer, but there were numerous objects on the surface between cliff and factory, and some even west of the latter, which had been identified by Maria's equipment as boulders of ice from the fallen shelf. One of Goodall's labs had by now confirmed this; three separate specimens were nearly pure water ice, with traces of carbonate dust. A debate on why this was not silicate, led by Louis Mastro and Carla lePing, had taken up much time between the discovery and the jet's landing, but no conclusions had been reached except that the news had better get to Earth promptly. There may be no telling in advance which will prove to be the key piece of a jigsaw puzzle, but anything unexpected screams for upper-level attention. Goodall had sent the report before *Theia* touched down.

The landing approach had not been directly over the new patch, but the exhaust had melted or blown a shallow trough in the regular surface like the earlier ones, and like them raised no cloud of smoke of the sort that Belvew's recent landing by Carver had done. It was still possible that this superficially uniform area—uniform except for ice blocks and the still-growing patch—differed here and there in composition. Goodall had all ripe labs now out and in action, and was sending out others as quickly as the factory completed them. He ignored the small size of the stock of inert metals—gold, platinum, and iridium—which the labs needed for chemical and electrical apparatuses and of which the factory had only a limited supply in the "yolk" of its original egg. This stock could, for a while at least, be replenished from the station; a fairly large reserve had been brought from Earth. It had seemed unlikely that any such materials would be found on or near Titan. Certainly none, not more than a few atoms per cubic millimeter, had been found in the E ring and nearby material which had been collected to protect the station.

Most of the group, including Ginger, were listening to the analyses of the local area which Maria was numbering, tabulating, and locating on a large-scale map which now usurped part of everyone's screen, and trying to make sense out of them. Belvew was the only exception. His attention was aimed more narrowly.

The crumpled form of *Oceanus* showed a few hundred meters from her sister jet and much closer to the strange patch, and he was trying to see why it had fallen. If the cause was actually turbulence there would probably be no evidence, but he still found this hard to believe.

"Art, could you spare a lab to sample right around the wreck?" he asked at length.

"We'll get there pretty soon anyway. Any reason for special haste?"

"Well, Ginger landed hot, but there'll be a couple of seconds after liftoff when she'll be as slow as I was. It might be worth at least a check. Maybe the ground was warmer, or colder, for some reason, and grew verticals."

"How could it be?" The question, from Peter, was ignored by all but Barn.

"We're looking for chemical action," he pointed out, "and there's the methyl alcohol to explain."

"All right," admitted Goodall. "Two labs on the way. Tell me where you want your samples, Gene."

Belvew went back to the view provided by *Theia*'s eyes, and strained his own looking for points of special interest on and about the wreck. It would be a few minutes before the slow-moving labs reached the spot.

Several of *Theia*'s cameras covered the remains, and he ordered Status to process their images with interferometric routines to produce the best possible resolution. He didn't think of asking for a stereo image. For some time he concentrated on the ground plowed up by *Oceanus,* but he could detect nothing special, and finally shifted to the jet itself. The labs had arrived and without anyone's specific instructions were starting to scrape dirt samples with their iridium-coated hoes before he saw the interrupted white ridge along the leading edge of the uptilted right wing. Some of the material, especially toward the tip, had not been shaken off by the crash. He pointed it out to the others.

"That shouldn't be there! How do you get wing ice on Titan?"

5

SORTIE

"How do you know it's ice?" asked Barn reasonably.

"I don't, but it's where you pick up wing ice in Earth's atmosphere, and it had the same effect!"

"You're blaming it for what happened?" came Maria's quiet voice.

"Well, not yet." GO6 was sometimes soft-pedaled, but it was seldom completely ignored. "Can you get a lab up there, Art?"

"I doubt it. They weren't designed to climb a smooth surface."

"That skin's hardly smooth anymore."

"All right. I'll try." The colonel followed up the words with action, and for over fifteen minutes sent one of his devices rolling and clawing its way along various upward-leading wrinkles in the crumpled fuselage. Each, sooner or later, narrowed enough to spoil his grip and let the machine topple back to the ground, undamaged in Titanian gravity but ineffective.

Goodall finally gave up. Belvew, less skilled but more anxious, tried from some time himself, with no better luck.

"It looks as though some of the stuff has fallen off," Inger pointed out at last. "There should be bits of it on the ground."

"If there are, I can't see them," replied Belvew. "I suppose we can just do lots and lots of tests all around the wreck, but how will we be sure that any offbeat result can be blamed on the white stuff?''

"We can be quicker than that," Ginger assured them.

"How?" asked Gene.

"Very simply." Several of the listeners guessed what was coming but kept their mouths shut; there was nothing they could do about it, and objectively Xalco was being smart. She was economizing on her suit time.

Those who failed to read the implication from her words understood a few seconds later as a fluorescent orange environment suit with a black "GX" stenciled front and back entered the field of view of *Theia*'s eyes and started to make its way toward the wreck. Its walk was unsteady; even Titan's less than fourteen percent of Earth gravity was a lot more than most of the group had experienced for many months. The station rotated, but very slowly. Centripetal acceleration just inside the equator of the original ship's skin was much less than a hundredth of a gee.

Few of the crew could now have stood a full Earth gravity. The major made good speed, however, never actually fell, and reached *Oceanus*'s remains very quickly.

"I don't see anything white on the ground," she said. "It either fell off farther back or got buried in the dirt *Oceanus* plowed up. Here, Art." She needed to jump only a short distance to bring one glove against the rime on the wing. It stuck to her suit when she tried to set it down beside the nearest lab, and she had to shake it off, leaving some liquid on her palm. All watchers tried to draw inferences while the lab unit inhaled this juice through its gold-plated liquid sampler and did its work.

"Mostly ethylene, a trace of acetylene," Goodall reported tersely after a moment.

"Melting points?" Gene asked promptly, sure that Maria would have them on her screen at once. He was right.

"About one hundred four and one hundred ninety-two respectively," she reported promptly. "Check your own wings, Ginger; if you picked any up after you cooled down from entry, it would still be there."

"It is. I see it. It's lucky I landed fast, I guess. I'll wipe it off right now."

"Bring the lab and sample yours, too," said Goodall.

"Right." Her suit disappeared intermittently, its image reappearing as odd patches and parts from time to time as she moved into and out of the parts of view fields the computer was using for Mollweide projection.

"Why did we pick that up these two times, and not on any of the earlier landings? And why pick it up at all, for that matter? There isn't much of either of those in the atmosphere." Gene was still puzzled.

"I think I can guess," Barn said slowly. "You don't need much, after all; water vapor usually doesn't compose very much of Earth's air, but it freezes on wings if they're cold enough. These landings are the only ones made so far so soon after the jet had spent a long time up at compromise altitude or in space, and really got its wings chilled. I spent a lot of time on practice stalls before the first landing. We can test that, if there's ever time, by going back up for a while and doing stall exercises, at a safe altitude of course, after we get down again." He did not suggest merely asking Status to make wings visible; this was a scientific problem, not just a matter of safe flying. Avoiding the problem would not have answered questions.

"And we make it a point to land a little hotter than we have been." Gene was relieved. "Good work, Ginger. You'd better come back up; you've used up hours of suit time already."

"I have plenty more. I'm going to take a *close* look at this patch while I'm here."

"I don't mean to be insulting, but I trust you're budgeting time to refill your tanks after takeoff," Goodall interjected.

"I am. But thanks for asking. Don't apologize." Her suited figure dwindled on the screens.

"The labs can do gas analyses, can't they?" she asked suddenly.
"Sure."

"Then hadn't we better look for free hydrogen? Remember the idea about the methanol production."

"We'd need water, too," pointed out Barn. Ginger kicked at one of the boulders, almost overbalancing in the weak gravity.

"These *look* like ice," she assured him.

"They are. I checked them already," growled Goodall. "If you want a repeat—"

"I know. That can wait. I want to see this tar-patch stuff." She moved a few gliding steps farther and squatted down. A lab moved slowly toward the kicked boulder, guided from above, but the oldster said nothing aloud. *Of course* this would be ice, too.

"Give!" came mingled voices. Ginger's suit had no camera.

"It looks and feels through my gloves like black glass; it could still be the melted and refrozen tar someone suggested. I can't scratch it with a glove claw. Labs, please."

"Already there, as you should have noticed," answered the colonel. "Analysis so far matches the other one; it's a methanol gel, basically. I'm still working on the polymers."

He would be, Belvew thought. Arthur, of all the group, was the most optimistic about finding prebiotic material on Titan, though Seichi Yakama was a close second. The colonel had also informed himself most extensively from Status's encyclopedia on autocatalysis and other phenomena presumably involved with the chemical evolution stages supposed to precede actual life. He was the only one whose training had actually included more than the standard educated adult's basic chemistry.

He was also hoping desperately, his companions knew, to find a key piece of the biological jigsaw puzzle while he still lived, even if that piece failed to provide a cure for his particular ailment. He was as close to being a pure idealist as anyone in the group—a scientific Nathan Hale, though none were tactless enough or historically informed enough to make the comparison either aloud or silently.

The screen brought Belvew's attention back from its brief side trip. Ginger had started to rise from her squatting position and was putting on a rather grotesque show.

She had been slightly off balance as she straightened her knees, and reached vertical with her center of gravity a little outside the support area outlined by her feet. There is a normal human response to this situation, usually acquired during the first year or so after birth: one picks up the foot nearest the direction of tilt and moves it farther in that direction to extend the support area, but not so far as to make reaction initiate a fall the other way. The reflex, of course, is normally acquired in Earth gravity, and one or two of the watchers wondered very briefly whether she would overcontrol, but they never found out. The major started to pick up the appropriate foot, the right one, but it refused to pick up. The couple resulting from pull on this one and third-law push on the other tilted her even farther to her right. By the time she reached thirty degrees all eyes were on their screens, and at least three hypotheses were being developed.

"You've melted yourself in!" cried Martucci. Inger, whose idea involved close contact between soles and surface plus Titan's high air pressure, said nothing but thought furiously. Goodall, already wondering how simple the chemistry for a thermotropic reaction could possibly be, called, "See whether it's pulling in around your boots or if you're just sinking!"

Major Xalco was moved to answer this. "*Just* sinking? I'm *stuck,* you old idiot! What do I do?"

"Find out why," the colonel replied calmly from the safety and freedom from immediate responsibility of a seven-hundred-kilometer-high orbit.

"Try to tilt and slide one boot at a time," proffered Inger.

"Can anyone guess how much jet exhaust a suit will take from, say, twenty meters?" asked Belvew. "I assume no one *knows.*"

While the woman tried unsuccessfully to implement Barn's suggestion, and then less enthusiastically to follow Goodall's instruction, Gene, already in his waldo suit, silently preflighted *Theia,* which he could now control. Xalco had filled the tanks conscientiously on the way down, apparently without melting her wing "ice"—that would have to be discussed sometime—and the landing had depleted them only a little; there was much more than enough juice for a takeoff.

Keeping careful watch on the gauges, Gene fired up the plasma arcs and fed liquid to the pipes. Carefully checking the relative whereabouts of woman and factory, but not letting himself worry about a few labs, he raised thrust on the right jet enough to drag *Theia* in a curving trail—the keels wouldn't let it simply pivot—until it was heading almost toward Ginger. He then equalized thrust on both sides and sent the machine dragging forward until it was only fifty meters from the still-anchored suit. Rather than attempt another tight turn, he went on past, leaving the woman on his left and turning only slightly to the right, until the exhaust was streaming past her only a few meters away.

"Better let me take it," she said at this point. "I can tell if it's too close, and the response will be quicker."

Gene made no argument. He relinquished control, but only briefly.

Using the waldo control while standing up in even a weak gravity field was not merely more awkward than Ginger had expected but essentially impossible. Uncontrollable pressures on control areas in the feet shifted the jet to rocket mode and very briefly applied heavy thrust. She would probably have been incinerated had Belvew been even a little slower resuming control.

The blast for a split second swept over part of the patch, behaving just as it had during Gene's landing hours before. The tar, if it was that, was sinking into or possibly vaporizing out of a shallow groove along the track of the warm gas. This time no smoke appeared. Then the thrust was cut.

Ginger's jump was equally reflexive. It was also, to everyone's surprise, effective; she was free of the sticky surface. Her suit went up for more than two meters and away from *Theia*, kicked by the hot gas stream. She landed closer to the center of the patch. She leaped again, this time with deliberate control of her direction, and reached safe ground.

The unspoken question which had briefly crossed everyone's mind, whether enough surface could be removed or persuaded to let go without cooking her in the suit, was answered the risky way.

"I still can't tell whether it vaporized, melted and sunk, or just crawled out of the way,'' she reported, her voice lacking its usual snappishness. "I'll watch more closely this time." She stepped calmly back onto the patch. Two or three voices started to say something, but all stopped before finishing a word. There seemed no other way to get the information.

"Is it crawling over your boots?" asked Goodall. Xalco squatted once more.

"No," she replied after a moment. "I'm more like melting in. The stuff isn't closing in around me. You know, this might work. This is interesting; I wish I could send you pictures."

"Damn!" said Arthur with feeling. Not even Ginger criticized. All watched tensely from *Theia* but learned more from the verbal report.

"It still looks tarry, but acts more like fairly soft wet clay. It squeezes up around my boots even in this gravity, but isn't closing around them as a real liquid would."

"Or something that was trying to swallow you," interjected Goodall. Neither Ginger nor even Belvew could think of an appropriate answer to this, and she continued reporting.

"I can pick up one boot without much resistance. I get pulled that way, I suppose by air pressure on the boot—not suction, Arthur—and the other foot goes down a little—"

"How about sidewise motion?" asked Belvew. The watchers could tell that she was trying this.

"No problem. Still like soft clay. I could ski on it, I think."

"Can you still get *off* it, or will I have to risk cooking you again?" Again the ship cameras provided the answer before Ginger's voice. There was a little backward slipping of one boot as the other moved forward, but forward won out.

"I'm off the patch. Don't waste any juice."

"There are three labs near you. Save me some time. Put one on the patch about where you were standing and the other two at the edge—one on the side toward the factory, the other on the opposite one. Then grab a sample and get it up here."

"But Art—I have hours left in my suit!"

"I'll give you five minutes to think of something you can do down there that would be more useful than bringing some of that glop up where we can really study it. I admit it's probably not alive, but anything squishy at that temperature needs explaining. Think on your feet!"

"You've already grabbed first-landing glory," remarked Inger. "The first person to walk on Titan."

"I wasn't thinking of that!" the woman snapped back, indignantly but perhaps not quite truthfully. "Anyone willing to face the unforeseens which might keep her from getting back could have done that."

"Four minutes."

"I—I didn't have a—all right. I'll bring one of the ice chunks, too. You were wondering about the carbonates, weren't you?"

"Yes, I was going to suggest that. Can you carry both samples? The storage bins in the jets aren't all that large, and I don't suppose you took any specimen bags down with you."

"I didn't, I'm afraid."

"Good."

"Why is that good?"

"It helps me believe you didn't premeditate this trick very long or very carefully. Got your specimens?"

There followed some seconds of silence. The watchers could see the armored figure bent over a glassy boulder, but for some reason it wasn't moving. Belvew's worry was the first to reach speech pressure.

"Something wrong, Ginger? That's a lot too big for any of the bins." Goodall didn't seem to be worried at all.

"I'm afraid it is," Ginger finally said as she straightened up. "But it's interesting. We'll have to carry personal cameras after this. Do we have any small enough to attach to our suits and built to stand local conditions?"

"We'll see," snapped the commander. "Someone can design and grow one, maybe. Tell us what you have there. Maybe you could bring a piece of it up."

"I didn't foresee needing a pick, either. How do I break off a piece?"

"Just tell us what it is!"

"A vug. A geode, if the word can be used on Titan. A cavity in the boulder, about half filled with crystals—well, maybe not crystals; the stuff looks more like mold or absorbent cotton. White and rather fluffy."

"Hit it with another rock. Get a piece off somehow!"

There were plenty of smaller fragments around, presumably relics of the fallen cliff dating from Inger's first landing. One of these, a rough cube half a meter in each dimension, was no problem to lift even for an ailing human being. Ginger carried it over to the larger fragment, raised it above her helmet, and slammed it down as hard as she could, lifting herself well off the ground in the process but landing on her feet.

Titan's gravity was little help, but the ice was brittle. The piece she was using as a tool shattered into dozens of fragments, but her target split only in two, with the vug in the larger part.

"Lucky you knocked that cliff down, Barn," she remarked as she sought another hammer.

"Any time."

The third blow produced a fragment bearing some of the "mold" on one of its surfaces and, Ginger judged, small enough to go into sample bin.

All watched her approach the aircraft, the screens losing bits of her image in the odd patterns the watchers had seen before. No one had thought to have Status save the human figure rather than exclude the plane.

The ice fragment did indeed fit in a bin. The other specimen would have also, but another problem came up. She couldn't let go; it was too sticky to detach from her glove.

"What do I do now?" she asked after several minutes of effort that merely distributed the stuff over both hands.

"Just bring it back, of course. All the controls are *in* your suit. Stuff outside won't interfere with flying." Goodall's impatience was getting the better of his courtesy; the "of course" had been unnecessary. Even Ginger could sympathize, however.

"Better take off to the west," cut in Belvew. "Make as tight a turn to the right as the skids will let you, and—"

"Don't hit the factory on takeoff!" Arthur added; then, "Sorry."

Ginger made no answer. Seconds later *Theia* slid into the air, and moments after that had reached ram speed with nearly a thousand kilograms of mass still in her tanks.

"There's a thunderhead at forty kilometers, two hundred degrees," Maria informed her.

"Right. Thanks. Is there anything I should do while I'm here after I juice up? Or have I already earned a mission credit? I did pick up data."

Belvew wondered whether his own contribution should be mentioned, but he was far too polite to suggest this explicitly. Besides, someone might have suggested including the loss of *Oceanus* in the balance.

"All yours," he answered innocently. The pilot was too busy to answer.

Goodall had been technically right; nothing outside a suit should have been able to interfere with use of the Waldo controls. However, the inside of the aircraft, especially the coffinlike compartment where the pilot rode, was a great deal warmer than Titan. The specimen lockers had temperature controls, since the planners had foreseen a possible need to keep samples in their normal environment, but the "cockpit" was another matter. People might have to open their suits there. When Ginger entered and sealed herself in, the temperature began automatically to climb from ninety kelvins to two hundred ninety, and the "tar" began to melt.

This still caused no piloting problems, but there was no way to tell where the liquid might be going—or even if it was remaining liquid. Nothing *should*, of course, be able to escape into the rest of the aircraft's structure, but several people began wondering about possible corrosion effects. None of them said a word; the pilot was busy.

Ginger tanked up, climbed to optimum speed altitude, followed instructions to the right point on Titan's equator, and began to climb once more. Neither Belvew nor his partner gave any advice. The former nodded approvingly—his suit was now disconnected as far as Waldo activity was concerned—as she made a smooth transition from jet to rocket mode and from airborne flight to orbit.

Enough time had passed before she docked to ease some of the worries about possible effects of melted or vaporized tar, and at least her gloves were now free to move; only traces of the stuff now coated them, and this, while still black, was no longer really flexible.

"Stay put for a few minutes after you unseal." Goodall's words had the force of an order in spite of the casual tone he used. "We'd better check the dock spectroscopically before you come inside. You can hold out, can't you?"

"Sure. Hours yet." Ginger was in fact thinking longingly of her comfortable quarters, food, sleeping facilities, a show, and especially a bath, but she had no intention of arguing with obvious common sense. "I expect the methanol will have vaporized pretty well; you ought to find it easily enough."

The answer was indirect. "Get a bit of that frost or whatever it is from the other specimen, quickly so the whole thing doesn't warm up, and see how decent temperature affects it."

"All right." There was a pause. "Got it, and the locker's sealed again."

"Don't leave it on your gloves. Spread it—"

"I can't. It vanished almost at once. It can't be water."

Another pause, during which everyone visualized the colonel's manipulating instrument controls, taking readings, and generally keeping his attention away from his own suffering.

"Your frost seems to be ammonia. And I can't find a trace of methanol in the dock."

"Yes, you can have the mission credit, Ginger," repeated Belvew. "Or does raising more questions than you answer count as a minus?"

PART TWO

SACRIFICE

6

SURFACE

IN HIS QUARANTINED QUARTERS at the level just inside the outer skin of the original ship, protected by the architecture from the ailments of his colleagues and from Saturn's radiation belt by half a kilometer of ice, Barn Inger clipped a sensor to his earlobe and waited. The entity responsible for keeping track of the station personnel's physical conditions as well as of the information they were accumulating presently reported aloud.

"Phase zero point two two; sixteen percent above accepted normal, presumably trending downward. Subjective?"

"I feel fine. I *need* something active."

"You should be all right for about twenty hours allowing standard safety factors, twenty-five to thirty without them, possibly fifty considering your personal variability. No confidence at all in the last."

"Fine. Someone has to go down to the factory to map those roots. Arthur's labs can scrape and suck but not really dig. Any of the rest of you feel you're better set than I am to do it now?" The other twenty staff had of course heard the whole exchange; no one ever *saw* into someone else's quarters, but all could hear. Privacy in the station ranked high, but took a poor second behind the need to know whether and when someone needed medical help. Sometimes a patient could call a verbal warning or a plea for help before even Status detected symptoms.

The only answer came from Gene Belvew. "I'm flying *Theia* right now, on polar air circulation. If you'd rather not go down physically, you could take over this run and I could land in *Crius*. She's ready at last, apparently. Any preference?"

"Maybe I'd do better if the drill kicks," Inger pointed out, stroking his luxuriant blond mustache, which none of his colleagues had ever seen. He did not, of course, mention Belvew's bone problems, and not merely because these were common knowledge. Courtesy was not quite the same thing as privacy, but they were related.

"Good point. *Crius* is yours if no one else has anything to raise." Ginger Xalco's clipped voice came with a question.

"What route will you take to the dock?"

"Standard. Straight to the axis, then along it to the pole. Unless—"

"That's all right. Just be sure of your suit before you leave your own place, please."

"Sure. Don't worry; I'm a careful type."

Niether speaker, and none of the listeners, had to be more specific. Actually, Ginger's query had been superfluous, though no one blamed her for speaking. She had the usual reason for concern; her own blood was slowly being wrecked by a very ordinary but remarkably unresponsive leukemia variant, and no one had any idea what adding Inger's ailment to that might do to either of them. His "Cepheid sickness," misnamed by a medical worker who knew very little astronomy, caused him to cycle between extreme polycythemia and severe anemia. Unlike that of a Cepheid star, its period was unpredictably variable, ranging from one hundred fifteen days to one hundred eighty and, rarely, more. The almost unique quality of the ailment was that no one had yet established its cause, far less any treatment, in nearly forty years. It had killed over seventy-five million people in that time.

Most of the diseases currently decimating the human species

followed a standard course: they appeared suddenly, killed a few thousand or a few million people, had their causes identified, and then yielded, except for an unfortunate minority of the victims, to quickly developed treatment. Science was trying to catch up with evolution—from far behind, now.

The minority tended to join the shock troops in the all-out research war which blended all the disciplines into a service dedicated to the hope of finding *in detail* how life could start and how it really worked.

In detail. Repeat aloud.

Nothing less sweeping seemed likely to account for the surge of emerging new ailments. Even the advance of genetic engineering seemed inadequate—there just weren't, most people hoped and believed, enough mad scientists or even mischievous genetic hackers in existence to account for even a fraction of the new mutations.

This did not prevent some people from firmly believing in conspiracy, which *did* have enough supporting evidence to rank as a theory. It seemed better, at least, than the vague suggestion that all mutation rates in viruses and prions had suddenly risen far enough to override the damping effect of transmission delay.

Barn inspected his environment suit carefully, made sure it was fully charged, donned it, disinfected its exterior with chemicals and radiation, and issued the routine warning to the others that he was leaving his quarters. He unsealed and passed through the prion-tight door and made his way along the passage "upward" toward the center of the rotating station—whose two-hundred-twenty-minute rotation period did not really produce an effective gravity. Here, his weight now really zero, he drifted along the axis to *Crius*'s dock, and in a few minutes he reached the craft.

He devoted over three hours to the preflight check, only partly because he would actually be aboard this time instead of waldoing the jet from the station. With only two remaining ramjets—no one had any real hope of salvaging *Oceanus*, though the possibility had been discussed—no avoidable risks with the craft themselves would be taken. Also, while Saturn's particle radiation was feeble at Titan's orbit, it was safest to make transfer flights while the satellite was nearly between Sun and planet.

Emergency sometimes justified a greater risk, of course. Danger was taken for granted, and none of the group really expected ever to get back to Earth, but it was still hoped that enough of them might survive to finish the project. After *that* few gave much thought, though an occasional "What'll we do then?" crossed one mind or another.

Inger had weighed privately, without consulting Status again, the importance of this job against the likelihood of his becoming helplessly anemic before it was done, and had decided that a modest delay in the descent was all right.

Satisfied at last, he drifted into the pilot's "coffin" and spent another twenty minutes testing his suit controls. Finally, using the spring launcher, which saved reaction mass, he kicked the vessel free and allowed it to drift slowly away from the roughly spherical structure of welded ice fragments.

He could see both Saturn and Sun, at screen coordinates which meant that they were in nearly opposite directions. The lumpy assemblage of ring chunks from which he had come blocked out nearly half the sky and much of Titan, while the satellite in turn occulted a large fraction of the remaining starry blackness. Their almost spherical shapes were distorted grotesquely by the equal-area projection, but this bothered neither Inger nor the others sharing his view. He allowed *Crius* to drift until the station filled less than a tenth of the screen's area, spun her on a lateral axis until the pipes pointed "forward" along the station's orbit, made sure she was in rocket mode, and vaporized a small amount of reaction mass.

This craft had not yet made any descents, and her tanks contained only a small amount of water remaining from the original journey and construction work. Even the little he now used up committed *Crius* to atmosphere after two minutes of falling away from the station, but the man wasted no time or thought on the fact that he, too, must descend.

Rather more than an hour later and a third of the way around Titan he felt the touch of drag. He had used a little more water than absolutely necessary. Orbital velocity, less than two kilometers a second, was too small to cause a serious heating problem, and before making a full half circle from the point where he had left the mass of ice—which was still in view: it had not fallen very much behind him during the descent—he was using wings and aerodynamic controls, and had uncapped the pipes into ramjet mode.

The rest of the flight was uneventful; it was a new adventure for the aircraft, but not for Barn. Finding an adequate cloud, and using it to fill the tanks with liquid hydrocarbon, had long been routine. Clearing the tanks first of the traces of unused water was not, but he well knew, as he had known on his first landing and Major Xalco had known on hers, what ice crystals at liquid methane temperature could do to *Crius*'s pumps. He took care of the matter early enough so that even Belvew, letting his attention wander slightly from the jet he himself was operating a quarter of the way around the satellite, felt no temptation toward outside-the-coffin driving.

Finding the factory and landing beside it were also routine; Inger had been the first to take one of the ramjets to the surface. The fact that he had not been physically aboard that time was unimportant; the waldo suits worked either in direct-connection or remote modes, the latter suffering only signal-travel delay of a few milliseconds.

Crius slid to a stop a couple of hundred meters from the factory. Inger had not checked for wing "ice," but he landed hot as a precaution. He completed the power-down check of the aircraft and the Titan environment check of his suit, and emerged. There should be no need to report the fact even to his partner; everyone was presumably watching carefully.

Even Belvew, who was having a minor problem of his own.

Theia was high enough in the smog layer for Saturn and its nearly edge-on rings to show dimly on her screen, though they were rising and setting too fast for comfort. Gene ignored the sight as best he could. Circling Titan's south pole at one hundred meters per second and increasing the radius of the circle by half a kilometer each time around took no attention, of course; that sort of thing could be set up in advance. The satellite's rotation axis's being a couple of degrees from perpendicular to its orbit plane was merely background information, though it was responsible for Saturn's present peekaboo behavior. The bothersome item which did demand attention was a steady altitude loss by his aircraft.

It was not frightening. The ground was tens of kilometers down and the descent mere centimeters per minute, but it was puzzling. It was also annoying; correcting the altitude manually every minute was a nuisance, while setting the automatic controls to do it might hide important data in unrecorded corrections. Not even Status's log covered everything.

There was also the matter of self-respect; the sergeant wanted to explain the phenomenon himself before Status, whom he preferred at times to think of as Nursemaid, made him feel foolish again. His rank might imply a mere observer rather than a theorist, but he considered himself perfectly qualified to think.

Thrust and attack angle were correct, and corresponded to the airspeed. Energy consumption matched the mass of atmosphere being piped, the thrust indicated by the ramjet mounting sensors, and the weight of the aircraft. There were no lake thermals at this height and latitude. There must be some obvious factor he hadn't—

There was. The calm voice of Status, committed to reporting changes of background whenever they reached a certain level without regard to their probability of danger, made itself heard.

"There is a slow general descent of the polar air mass covered so far on this air circulation run. Symmetry suggests it to be quite precisely centered on the pole itself. There must be poleward flow above *Theia*'s present altitude, and equatorward below. Repetition of the present flight pattern at a larger number of levels than originally planned appears in order. When the entire volume has been vector-sampled I suggest comparison with the total upward flow over the lakes."

Belvew could think of only one response which might restore his morale.

"How does the air density match norm for this height? It should be greater if there's such a huge downdraft."

"It is. Qualitatively this could explain the effect."

"And quantitatively?"

"Unanswerable until the vector analysis is more nearly complete. More data will be needed for that."

Another thought restored Belvew's self-esteem even further, and he voiced it before the analyzer beat him again.

"Is there enough more smog in the air to account for the higher density?"

A human voice cut in. Even now it sounded slightly amused, though no one knew why.

"Wouldn't more polymer drop the density? It's made from the surrounding gases, and would use them up as it's produced."

"It would drop volume, Maria. The mass would still be there and contributing to pressure, I'd say; and that would start inflow, which would carry solid and liquid particles from a distance—" The debate was interrupted.

"The inflow wouldn't be in. It would be around. There's Coriolis force even with a sixteen-day rotation and small planet size, and no surface friction fifty kilos up." The new voice was Arthur Goodall's, and no one added anything for a moment; the old fellow had an annoying habit of being right, aside from being officially their commander. Belvew was about to take a chance on mentioning the minuteness of the Coriolis effect, but was saved by Status's voice.

Goodall himself, in his sealed quarters two hundred meters from Belvew's and closest of all to the station's spin axis, paid no attention to what the computer said. He had known as the words left his mouth that his reasoning was sloppy. It was getting constantly harder for him to think coherently, and more and more of his time was being wasted wondering how long he could be useful at all to the project. The pain kept getting worse, and distraction from it more difficult.

Of course he couldn't work all the time, or even all the time he was awake. Rest and relaxation were essential, but relaxation which would hold the attention firmly was, he had found, almost a contradiction in terms. Reading was better than watching shows, he knew. He suspected that this was because it was a less passive activity, but he had never raised the question publicly and had therefore never been obliged to produce a challenging hypothesis. He had been told long ago that the discomfort of SAS—synapse amplification syndrome—was less severe than that of shingles, but he had never learned how his informant knew. If anyone had ever suffered from both it must have been at different times for the effects to be distinguishable, and whichever had been experienced later would have been remembered as being worse. Arthur Goodall had the normal, reasonable mistrust of data dependent solely on human memory, and a chain of human memories was far worse. Besides, he knew of no reliable technique for actually measuring pain, though he had heard of units intended for the purpose.

He knew all he wanted to about SAS. Unlike shingles, it affected every square centimeter of his skin at one time or another, but caused no external markings. Like shingles and chicken pox, it was produced by a virus, one which had been identified and mapped within weeks of the first recognition of the syndrome. It differed from the shingles/chicken pox agent in only four amino acids at specific points plus one bundle, perhaps originally an independent organism, which rendered it unresponsive to both natural and engineered human immune systems. The four acids were few enough to be explained by natural mutation, but numerous enough to make human tampering a reasonable suspicion; the bundle was natural, but might have joined the virus either with or without human assistance. It made no difference to Goodall whether he should be blaming nature's indifference or human malice; the molecular engineers who now made up most of the medical profession had not yet worked out either a nonlethal contravirus or a straight chemical treatment. Sam Donabed, the only remaining medical specialist of the expedition, occasionally discussed the matter with colleagues on Earth when his other duties permitted, but neither they nor he had come up with any helpful procedure.

Sam was officially only a lieutenant colonel and Goodall could reasonably have lost patience and told the doctor to leave him alone; but neither the commander nor any of the others thought of him as a military type, scientist or otherwise. His rank was irrelevant; he was a doctor, and rational people still tended to follow doctors' recommendations even with the full knowledge that they amounted to experiments with no two identical subjects. Human beings vary in more than hair color.

Besides, losing patience would have been ungentlemanly, immature, and rude, and at Goodall's age he didn't want to risk his reputation for maturity.

Doctors had, of course, a lot of work to do on other ailments, and there were only a few hundred cases of SAS at a time to worry about, so there was no use in Goodall's complaining about being at the short end of a triage situation. Most people now alive shared that distinction.

With the pain growing ever worse, what he really wanted now was not a cure—not exactly. He wanted an opportunity. He had even worked out in some detail just what sort of opportunity. It should, he felt, occur *somewhere* on Titan. The plan needed only one of Maria Collos's gel pools, not too far from a lake, and isolated in some way from the rest of the big moon's surface.

There were a few impact scars on the ever-growing map he was developing on his own without consulting Maria. Crater walls might provide the isolation, though all mapped so far appeared badly weathered or nearly buried. This might seem surprising, since there appeared to be no high winds in Titan's heavy atmosphere, and methane rain should be a far weaker erosive agent than water, but on the other hand both had presumably had several billion years to do their work.

At least two of the craters on Maria Collos's less specialized maps did contain small lakes. This was hopeful, and the maps were still being revised and extended, partly in the standard course of planned operations and partly in Goodall's personal, private files. He wondered more and more frequently how long he could keep that up. It was this sort of solid, detailed work that could best turn his attention from pain, sometimes for hours at a time, but the distraction by his body was getting harder and harder to fight.

The chances of finding an ideal site for his slowly developing personal project were decreasing, though he was not admitting this yet to himself. Titan's equatorial regions had now been well mapped, and his personal travel problems made the rest of the satellite much less suitable. He still had hopes, however. He might be short on time, but not yet on patience.

He turned his attention back to the display of Belvew's—more correctly *Theia*'s—Mollweide screen, and resumed looking for ground images which might bear detailed study. Even polar areas *might* be usable, although much less accessible.

But watching quickly became boring, and boredom gave the pain access to his attention. He wrenched his mind back to the Station, the best place to find the immediate, serious work which he needed. No immediate work? What should he read?

Belvew was in no trouble, and the new atmospheric data seemed trivial, however interesting. There was one bit of chemistry to be rechecked, but it would be a while yet before any more data could come from Maria's tar pools, gel pools, prebiotic sites, or whatever they were.

To Goodall, the mistake about methanol's being part of the gel had been interesting and somewhat embarrassing. He had of course corrected it with Status, but without calling the attention of his living colleagues. He did not intend to tell them until someone asked him why there had been no methanol found in the dock to which Ginger Xalco had brought *Theia* days before. Not having to explain the matter had been pure luck; Louis Mastro, bless his rapidly deteriorating heart, had been loudly and emphatically interested in what seemed to have been ammonia crystals in the ice specimen Ginger had also collected. The dear fellow kept hoping aloud that another piece of the "geode" specimen might be brought up to orbit.

One could see why, of course; ammonia crystals growing in an ice cavity could be very informative about details of Titan's history, as calcite and quartz geodes were about Earth's . . .

Good. Even that thought, though not important to the work as far as anyone could tell, could hold Goodall's attention. For a little while.

And there were the brittle black chips which were all that remained available of Ginger's originally sticky tar sample. Goodall really should get on to that stuff. Let's see; it was still in the collection locker removed from *Theia* . . .

He hoped passionately this stuff would contain proteins, or at least amino acids. His plan could be justified by any such discovery.

He was decades past conclusion-jumping or even hasty action, however. At least, he hoped that he was.

The plan itself, though still very tentative, was also able to hold his attention, sometimes for a full hour. He did not cut off his connection with *Theia*'s screen—there was always a chance of something's happening—but turned to another display. The argument about atmospheric currents and polymerization had ended, and Goodall neither knew nor greatly cared how it had turned out; he was a theorist, greatly outranking Belvew, and would consider that matter when and if it seemed important.

The screen he now faced showed most of the scenery around the wrecked *Oceanus,* minus a few gaps which her remaining cameras could not cover even though Goodall had unobtrusively repointed them. While he himself did not fly because the pain smothered his needed senses too often, everyone had waldo suits and could control the aircraft.

The factory was there. The ice mountain also showed. The mysterious gel area which had caused Ginger's misadventure and had now expanded or moved to include the wreck was only partially on the screen. He couldn't tell whether the tar, or whatever it was, was crawling or growing or even with any certainty whether *Oceanus* was sinking in it.

And he didn't want merely to wait around until the jet completely disappeared. That would certainly take much too long, and there was no way to tell how much longer he'd stay competent.

7

SLIP

BELVEW'S EARLIER EXPERIENCE with another land-
ing suggested to everyone that the wreck might indeed be sinking,
but offered no basis for guessing how far down it might go. The
depth of a typical pool, or rather the one which now claimed his
interest, was also something Goodall wanted to know; but it was
more important to get the research program properly set up while
enough of the group were left to handle routine. Also, he could see
no way of even being sure that any given pool was typical. He didn't
want to modify any of the existing plans without very, very good
reasons—reasons which would convince, or at least suggest to,
everyone else that change was in order. It could be awkward if anyone were to suspect his real plans, especially since Ginger Xalco's
recent escapade. General drat the woman.

The colonel was, in fact, feeling the irritation of a would-be bur-
glar who has discovered, during the casing stage, that his planned
victim is under observation for drug activity. That was just the mental part.

He also wanted to remove his gloves, which just now seemed
lined with needle points. It was like his only flight test, as though
the pain were being deliberately directed; each and every control
contact he had tried to make had been swamped with agony. He had
not at that time conceived his current plan, but even then he had

resolved to remain as independent as possible of routine, which seemed invariably to lead to boredom and pain. He'd have to keep wearing a suit all the time, and *practice.*

At least no one could possibly expect now . . .

But they could, of course. Especially now, curses on the presumably red head of Major Xalco. He'd have to be really careful.

His project was not merely private but illegal and by some standards immoral, and would be quite unacceptable to the rest. It would involve breaking the agreement everyone had accepted after the unauthorized Xalco landing. It would also be a major violation of regulations, though that would mean less to this group. Science was a military discipline out of necessity, granting the necessity of continuing the human species; but scientists, especially the commissioned ones, were still individualists.

He might, of course, get his answer about the depth and other qualities of the tar pool, if that was what it was, by simple luck. The instruments showed that the third ramjet, *Crius,* was now in descent orbit with Inger aboard—Goodall suddenly wondered how long his mind had been wandering; he did not remember the launch—and her cameras after landing might supply some of the information he wanted. Maybe all of it. At the moment they didn't, of course. From space he could do better with Maria's observation gear. It would be hours yet to *Crius's* landing, hours while he had to occupy himself with *something.*

A red-hot whip suddenly fell across his shoulder blades, and almost at the same moment his waldo boots seemed to shrink several sizes.

Something . . .

He found *something,* real brain-stretching work after careful thought and data checking, and decided hours later that the job had been good for him. It had held his attention.

Barn Inger had by now landed and emerged, and was examining the ground. The embarrassing gap in the factory data due as usual to poor planning had to be closed. A suit camera had been improvised, so there would be less need for the person on the ground to divert his attention to verbal reporting. Goodall brought the image from this instrument to his main screen, magnified as far as possible.

This was not, he thought ruefully, as good as eyes on the spot; Inger himself might already have observed, without considering it important enough to mention, what the colonel wanted to know but was afraid to ask. Maybe Inger would need to shift his ramjet, so the old man kept *Crius*'s Mollweide image on one of his own screens and checked it frequently.

It would have been so nice for a native Titanian to walk, or crawl, or fly into view. That would . . .

The commander took a firm grip on himself. If his mind was going—well, he thought wryly, that would at least justify the plan. In his own mind. Circular argument . . .

But it might also prevent him from carrying it out.

Barn had known like the rest that the wreck was now in the pool rather than beside it, but motion of the tar had long ago been left for Status to keep track of. He did remember how Ginger had stuck when she had stood on the glossy surface and how Belvew, on his first landing on another one in *Oceanus*, had started to sink; but he had too much else occupying his attention to think of these right now. The wreck had been powered down and allowed to cool to the local ninety kelvins. Anything about it which anyone might want to check later would presumably still be there when and if the time came.

Inger's work on the root hunt called for holes in the ground. The dirt was largely water ice, heavily laced with silicate particles—not the carbonates found in the fragments from the cliff—and microscopic grains of polymer which had presumably settled from the atmosphere during the ages. Physically it was rock rather than dirt. Inger was not trying to resolve fundamental questions like how the silicate had found its way up from Titan's core or why the tars had mixed with the water instead of forming a layer on top of it. This was for the theorists, later.

He needed to find which of the numerous roots that the growing factory had extended in various directions corresponded to which analytical reader in the orbiting station; the roots themselves were numbered to match instruments, but no one had thought to provide any way of telling which way a given root was growing. This, to put it mildly, was hampering the surface analysis part of the project.

Low-pressure ice—Ice I—at ninety-plus kelvins is not slippery, at least not under the Titanian weight of a suited human being. Neither is it fragile. It is simply rock, perfectly usable for construction when pure and presumably, though no one had had a chance to try yet, tougher but less workable when full of the mess of hydrocarbon precipitates which chemists still called "tar." Getting a drill into it was going to be a problem, all could guess. Barn Inger massed, in space gear, just under a hundred kilograms; on Titan's surface he weighed almost exactly thirteen, less than he would have on Earth's moon. Even with the ice not slippery he lacked both weight to make the drill bite and traction to avoid being turned by it. The tool itself was powered, but at the first high-speed try it simply skittered around on the surface. At the lowest rpm available the wielder found himself pushed sideways whenever it started to bite. Newton's third law was still valid, even here.

There were ice boulders from the cliff scattered around the area which might have provided backing, but none was in just the right spot. The proposed hole was not started at random; Inger had located a root by microseismometry before attempting any drilling. If the seismometer had been able to identify it as well as locate it, there would have been no trouble; but it would be necessary to drill to a point near the conduit and feed in some chemical identifiable by the factory monitors when the root picked it up.

"Can any of those ice chunks be moved?" Maria Collos asked at length. "You could build yourself some sort of backing to lean against, or even to brace the drill against." The amusement which sometimes bothered Goodall even when he didn't think he had inspired it was in her voice.

"Worth trying," Inger admitted. He set the tool down and walked in the awkward fashion dictated by Titan's gravity to a lump of ice whose volume he guessed at nearly a cubic meter. It was clear, apparently one of the fragments fallen from the nearby cliff when the factory had first been planted. He got a grip on one of the rough sides and tried to lift, without success; even on Titan it must weigh seventy kilograms or so, he suddenly realized. At the present phase of his illness, it was too much for him in armor.

Rolling, while still awkward, was more successful, and in a few minutes the boulder was over the root. He settled it on one of its narrower sides to provide more height to lean against, picked up the drill, and made another try.

Heavy as it was, the ice slab fell over as the tool made a brief, tentative bite.

"Right direction," he said thoughtfully to the watchers as he picked himself up. "A pile of smaller stuff against the far side should take care of that." The smaller stuff was plentiful and much easier to transport, and in a quarter of an hour a slope of what had to be thought of as rather low-density rock and gravel was bracing the back of the largest fragment.

The direction might be right, but the distance was still short. Another burst of power on the drill sent the man *along* the wall.

It was more than an hour before the structure had grown to an acute-angled V with solid bracing on the outside, an inward lean on the inside to give him backing for a downward push, and a pair of small but reasonably heavy blocks which he hoped would keep his feet from slipping toward the opening of the V.

They didn't, and by this time Maria was not the only one feeling amused, though all knew it wasn't really funny. It was a concatenation of unforseen events in a deadly environment. Tension was mounting far above; Inger said nothing about his own feelings, but they could be guessed by all but Status.

He got back on his feet, breathing heavily—not entirely from fatigue, though even the best-designed armor still makes manual work difficult. His glove clicked against his faceplate as he unthinkingly started to stroke his mustache.

"All right. Friction just isn't enough to count, even if ice isn't slippery here. Ginger, or someone, turn *Crius* so her pipes point this way."

"Better get behind your wall," the woman promptly snapped. "A push that'll turn the plane may be too much for your armor. I suppose you want to weld the stuff down, which will take more than the dose I got, and even if you don't fry, getting blown away could be risky."

"That was the idea. I won't get behind the pile, I'll get away from it; then neither of us will have to worry. In fact, I might as well get on board and do it myself."

"I'm already tied in," Ginger responded, "and you can tell better from outside when I'm lined up right, and which pipe to use when I stop swiveling. They're far enough apart so it will make a difference. How much reaction mass should we budget for this?" She had become just a little less impulsive since her escapade, though her voice remained clipped and snappish.

"It shouldn't take much, and the tanks are practically full. I didn't use much on the landing. Once you're lined up I can get right next to the wall and tell you when melting starts; you can cut off right away when I call. We *could* use a quarter of the juice and still have plenty for a takeoff and even return orbit. There's nothing to worry about." Barn moved away from his rock pile toward the left side of the jet, so that the exhaust—the pilot would have to use rocket mode, of course—would reach the wall before touching him. Only a little more than a sixty-degree swivel to the aircraft's right would be needed for proper aim, and not too much thrust; the ice was smooth, even if not actually slippery.

Goodall was now watching the *Crius*'s main screen with his fists clenched near his knees—*on* them would have hurt, and even the clenching was painful—and unblinking eyes. The aircraft's position shouldn't change much, but the direction of the tail-fin camera, which had the highest viewpoint available, surely would.

Ginger checked the pipe caps and fed power and reaction mass into the left one's chamber, gently at first. She, too, was watching the screen, but not for the same reason as Goodall. She stopped the thrust increase as the runners began to scrape and the scenery to move, and began feeding brief jolts to send the craft in a rather jerky turn to its right. It slid forward slightly each time; there was no way to stop that, though it increased by a few meters the distance from Inger's wall. No designer had foreseen a need for reverse thrust, either.

She cut power at the same instant the man on the ground called out.

"Right pipe is just in line—you overshot a bit. It'll be easier to use that one for melting."

"Obviously. I'd have to light it anyway to turn back. I certainly don't want to waste mass swiveling all the way around, and I'm sure you don't either. All *I'd* be risking is the ship. *You're* down there."

Barn made no answer to this point. Neither did Goodall, though he did not fully agree. A full turn would have provided a fine variety of viewpoints both high and low. Enough, he felt, to let a little image processing give him a fully detailed three-dimensional model of the pool. At least, of its surface.

"Shouldn't you get a little farther to the side?" asked the woman. "I'd hate to either blow you away or cook your armor."

"I'll be all right. The exhaust doesn't spread much in the first few meters."

"Wrong," Belvew cut in. Not quite all of his attention was on flying. "Believe me. That's dense air."

Ginger, from personal experience, agreed emphatically, and Inger moved a few meters farther away rather than argue the matter.

"You're lined up fine," were his last words. "Light it." The woman fed liquid and energy to the engine, and all watched the loose pile of ice rocks with interest. The last hour or more had been typical of the group's problems from the beginning: unexpected factors had time and again caused what should have been foreseeable procedure and equipment use to go awry. Imagination had not been built into any data processor yet, so Status's fellow processors on Earth hadn't helped; they had no imaginations either. Well-known facts had either not been considered at all, or dismissed as irrelevant.

One of them was *not* irrelevant . . .

The watchers expected the surfaces of the ice chunks which Inger had used for his wall to liquefy quickly and start to drip, or possibly blow away in the stream of hot gas, but it didn't work out that way.

Within a second of the exhaust's enveloping the wall everyone heard a series of sharp snapping sounds, not quite explosions. Not everyone saw the flying pieces of thermally shattered ice. At least, not in time. One of them, half the size of his helmet, struck Inger in the face. The others heard the impact; no one ever knew whether Inger himself did. He toppled backward with fascinating deliberation in Titan's gravity, and settled to the ground with his feet more than a meter behind the point where he had been standing.

He neither spoke nor moved.

"Left one forty-seven standard." Maria's mild voice was the first to be heard. For once, the amusement was gone. There was no question whom she was addressing, and Belvew banked *Theia* sharply to the left. A real-surroundings view chose that moment to appear on his screen, but he didn't heed it. He knew he was in the station, flying with his waldo suit; he knew he would have to bring *Crius* back up, board it physically, and get back to the surface before he or anyone could help his partner. Briefly he wondered whether it would be quicker to climb to orbit from where he was instead of getting to the equator first, but mental arithmetic disposed of that notion. A nearly polar orbit would take less time to get him near the station from where he was than a trip to the equator, but would not leave enough exhaust mass to match velocities. He had a quarter of Titan's circumference, south pole to equator, to traverse before leaving atmosphere, and there would be hours after that before he or anyone else could get back down.

All three jets were now in atmosphere or on the ground. No one expected him to be in time. No one seriously believed there was any time even now, but no one even privately denied the need to try. People were people, especially friends. Even dead friends.

Not even Goodall escaped the emotional blow. He was jolted enough to forget for several minutes to record for his private map the new surface features Belvew's cameras must be covering. Even when he did, he was clumsier than usual in setting up the equipment, and when the adjustments were complete he realized that little would probably come of it. *Theia* was traveling as fast as ramjet mode would permit, which meant that she was in thin air well above much of the heaviest smog. Her cameras did range into the near infrared, which gave some surface detail even from this height, but the jet had no radar and there was little chance of catching the sort of feature he wanted, at least with the detail he needed.

Nevertheless, he watched. The southern hemisphere was not yet mapped in anything like the detail available for the latitudes between the factory and Lake Carver. Terabytes of data had indeed been recorded by Maria's instruments, but were not yet combined and translated into readable map form even in Goodall's quarters.

He watched tensely and silently as images flowed across his screens. Sometimes they were quite clear, sometimes entirely meaningless; Titanian smog was far from uniform. Annoyingly, the regions around lakes tended to be worst, since the bodies of methane mixture created vertical air currents capped by clouds; methane vapor, at any given temperature and pressure, is little more than half as dense as nitrogen. This had long since ceased to be a surprise, but it could still be a nuisance.

Twice Goodall thought he glimpsed a lake with hills around it. The first time he reacted too slowly, and recorded only an approximate position. The second time he was more alert, got precise satellite surface coordinates, and then had time to realize how the concentration had spared him whole minutes of pain. He thought briefly of Barn Inger, then for a moment of calling up records immediately to build a detailed map of the area; then he decided simply to watch and note positions until *Theia* reached the equator, banked east, and started her climb to orbit.

By the time this happened he had four more possible sites in his notes. He decided to work on them in reverse order, since the last

were closest to the equator and potentially most suitable for his purpose. The presumably rock-hard human body by the factory was
almost as far from his mind now as his own pain.

The first site, after details had been added from Maria Collos's
files, indeed turned out to be an irregular lake covering about two
square kilometers, near the southern edge of what almost had to be
a badly eroded impact crater some fifteen kilometers across. Unfortunately, nothing Goodall could do quickly with the images revealed
the slightest sign of any of the smooth areas of glassy/tarry material—the "Collos patches"—which were central to his needs.

The second, over three hundred kilometers from the equator,
seemed ideal almost from the first glance. The lake was much
smaller, but two of the tar patches lay inside the crater; and the
surrounding ringwall, only seven kilometers in diameter, appeared
to be much more recent than the first. Its minimum height was over
fifty meters, and it rose in some places to nearly three times that.
The commander drew a deep breath of satisfaction, ignoring the agony as his expanding chest rubbed the soft material of his suit liner—
his waldo was off now, of course—and began to think furiously
about many things, both positive and negative.

Sometimes even including Inger's misfortune.

STRATEGY

THE COLONEL WAS still thinking when *Theia* reached the station, docked, and departed again with Belvew now physically aboard. He did not worry as the craft left; there was nothing he could possibly have done toward executing the plan just yet, even if he had had all the tactical details worked out. Also it crossed his mind briefly that what had happened to Inger might make the whole idea harder to justify.

To the project, that was. Goodall was getting more and more certain that he himself would not be able to get on without trying it for much longer.

Not *too* much longer. But there was still a chemical problem to solve before he could dispense with analytical equipment, heavy thought, and—most troublesome—physical contacts.

He had reported the material of the tar pool on which Belvew had landed earlier to be a gel, with methanol as the dispersing agent. No one had pointed out, politely or otherwise, that methanol's melting point was something like a hundred kelvins above the local temperature. Frozen jelly doesn't flow even under Titanian atmospheric pressure. Presumably none of the living minds had noticed—they might not even have the fact in their memories. Status *knew,* since both the current data and much of the chemical information known to humanity were in its memory, but would never *notice* without guidance. Goodall himself had not thought of the point for some hours after his original report, and when he did he was more dismayed at having had his word accepted uncritically than by the fact that he or his apparatus must have made some sort of mistake. Even the observing ranks should have known better.

He made all reasonable tests of the apparatus he could, strongly annoyed that the original sample and sampler had been lost, and found nothing wrong. There had been three or four carbon-hydrogen bonds, one carbon-oxygen, and one hydrogen-oxygen per molecule in the principal material present. There was no crystal structure to provide a background, either helpful or otherwise; the stuff *was* essentially liquid in spite of the temperature. There were many other compounds there, of course, to help confuse the readings; but this was plainly the general background. Testing for individual, unbonded atoms seemed pointless, though the labs could do this; they had pore sensors adjustable to virtually anything. They could even isolate and accumulate such things; atoms like gold, platinum, and iridium were potentially so useful in the manufacture of equipment that the ability had been designed into them in spite of what seemed negligible chances of finding such stuff on Titan.

Goodall had not thought to look for other bonds once the carbon, hydrogen, and nitrogen ones had been read out; it was not at once obvious what others could be fitted into the pattern then being sought. Four for carbon, three or five for phosphorus, two for oxygen, one for each hydrogen—

He had allowed the hope of finding amino acids to steer his imagination, of course. The inspiration that he might have overlooked carbon-carbon *double* bonds had come embarrassingly late. He hadn't mentioned it to anyone yet because he had no way of checking it. The original analyzer was gone with the sample, while the ones around the factory were busy on the planned routine now and in any case couldn't be moved up to the Belvew site until another ship went down. Also, the appropriate reference material was too vast to digest quickly.

And not even Status knew the melting point of the vinyl alcohol monomer. At terrestrial temperatures it existed too fleetingly for such properties to be measured. On Titan—who knew? It *could* be lower than that of methanol: the molecule was larger, its one hydrogen bond presumably less effective—or maybe not; what did the charge distribution of a carbon-carbon double bond do to the polarity of other bonds on the same atoms? Embarrassingly, Goodall didn't know. Status might, but the colonel didn't want to ask it now. The question might tell the others too much.

There were analytical labs from the factory around the place where Ginger had had her misadventure. Should he reprogram one of them to do a more complete basic analysis? *Could* he without being noticed? The mere question of whether the wrecked jet was being engulfed was not excuse enough; that had already been considered and the program planned to include it.

However, a possible major error in the data which had been supplied to Status was something else. Goodall *must* make as sure as possible about this point before doing anything irrevocable, however tempting his planned final experiment was becoming. Status should be given the right answer to file. Merely knowing that the present one was wrong was not enough. *Why* it was wrong should also be known. Personal vanity was irrelevant.

Belvew entered atmosphere, did a routine refill, and sent his aircraft plunging toward the factory site, following the great circle vectors transmitted by the still deadly serious Maria. Neither he nor anyone else expected to reach the place in time to do Inger any good, but the effort had to be made. Humanity was still, in spots, more moral than logical and more emotional than pragmatic. The word "inhuman" was still a pejorative, though it was seldom now directed at science and scientists. Inger would have to be brought up for the data mausoleum, and properly memorialized.

And he was—had been, since there was no real possibility that he was still alive—a good friend.

Theia flashed across the factory site half a kilometer up, banked sharply, and was worked into a landing pattern. For just a moment her pilot allowed himself to picture all three of the jets on the ground

at the same place and time, and to think what would happen to the
whole project if even one more of them should fail to get off again;
were there enough reserve heavy elements in the station to grow
another aircraft? Then he focused his attention on his landing.

He chose to come in from the west rather than the north, as the
other setdowns had been made; he knew that if he overshot he
would have the ice cliff ahead of him, but the cliff itself made a
landing near the factory in the opposite direction impossible, and he
didn't want the complications which might ensue from involving the
tar in his landing slide. He had gotten away with that once, and felt
he knew how much luck had been involved. He was going to land
hot, to make allowance for the wing ice which might have wrecked
Oceanus, and he could not even guess what higher friction would
do to the gel which he planned to miss.

The need to stop as close as possible to his partner left only the
eastward landing feasible.

He was out and running the three-hundred-meter distance, if
high-speed human locomotion on Titan could be called running, the
moment he had completed his landing checklist. Neither he nor any
of the others was surprised to see the shattered faceplate, nor at
Inger's failure to show any sign of life.

The suits, like the station, contained pure oxygen at one-fifth of
a standard atmosphere, an eighth of the Titanian surface pressure.
A flood of ninety-kelvin nitrogen must have washed into the victim's
face; it was unlikely that he had felt much, if anything. Certainly he
had made no sound.

There was no basis actually for sight judgment; the space behind
the smashed plate and some of the region outside it were solid with
frost. Inger's mustache was still invisible; no one would ever remember it.

The rest of the body was not yet frozen; the environment armor
was effective where it was intact. Most of the group could see how
this accounted for the frost in the helmet, but nothing was said about
the details.

No one, not even Belvew, displayed feelings, unless the lack of conversation counted. Like the soldiers they had become in name and almost in fact, they were hardened to sudden death and to the knowledge that any of them might be next. The large fraction of the original group which had gone merely in the setup of the station and its relay units had been expected and accepted by the survivors and, apparently, by the victims; but there would always be sorrow and memory.

Belvew did note that his sight was slightly blurred as he gathered up the kilograms of mass which had been for many months now his best friend, but he refused to admit to himself what might be causing this. There was still a job to do; the body had to be gotten off Titan quickly. There was little likelihood in this chill that it would cause chemical—still less, biological—contamination and invalidate the entire project's labors, but this was research; the chance had to be eliminated as completely as possible.

To his relief and very slightly to his guilt, Belvew found his main conscious emotion one of thankfulness that the body was still flexible enough to be fitted into the ramjet's coffin—he was bothered, fleetingly, by the appropriateness of the name—and that since Ginger's escapade an override system had been installed in both surviving craft to allow them to be controlled from outside even when the coffin was occupied.

What Goodall was thinking at this point the others of course did not know, but he was still thinking. Inger's condition might affect part of his plan; should he suggest that the body be placed at the site he had almost decided on for himself? Or would that give some of the others a clue—too early a clue—to what he had in mind? Someone, probably more than one, would wonder what had called the commander's attention to this particular spot on Titan. Explaining why it was nice to have the place isolated by a ringwall would cause someone to wonder whether he had been thinking about deliberate local contamination, which he was. And that, in the main plan, was not supposed to happen until ground laboratories had been built.

Pain made the decision.

Belvew reboarded his own jet and lifted off, after spending some reaction mass to swivel *Theia* far enough to point her nose to one side of the ice cliff; he could not possibly have climbed fast enough to clear the elevation. Ginger took control of *Crius* and did the same without the preliminary, since it already had a safe heading. Maria guided them to different cumulus clouds to tank up. This was the first time two of the jets had been in the same airspace at the same time, and some of the group wondered whether Status would have done anything about traffic control if Maria hadn't. No one but Belvew was moved to ask, and he restrained himself.

Tanks full, *Crius* headed eastward and upward, climbing back toward orbit. *Theia* turned south to resume the air-current study; there was no hurry for Belvew to get back personally to the station, since his suit was well charged, and he could stand missing an occasional real-surroundings interruption for the next few hours. It would be nice to have the sight of his real surroundings continuous and relevant.

The station's mausoleum, a fifty-meter cube of emptiness among the roughly welded ice chunks that was separated from the living space inside the original hull, already held twenty-six occupants. Gooodall offered to remove Inger's remains from the docked jet and convey them through the passages to join the others. Not even Yakama, officially in charge of such station maintenance as could not be handled by Status, objected. Contagion-fear was realism, not paranoia, and no one had the slightest idea that the old man might have any ulterior motive.

Actually, the motive was now a little shaken; the sight of his frozen friend brought forcefully to Goodall the fact that one aspect of his plan was now superfluous.

But there was another facet. He did what he had to do, returned to his quarters, and reported to the others that his quarters were prion-tight once more.

Gene Belvew conducted the memorial. He had been the most closely associated with Inger, and knew more and could say more about him than anyone else.

He couldn't remember afterward just what he had said, but he knew he had meant it.

The job left unfinished by Inger's death still had to be done somehow. Just *how* was a subject of intense discussion, but no one seriously advised that drilling with the present equipment be tried again, or that anyone should be present physically no matter what was attempted. Common sense overrode heroism.

Thermite was suggested, with the admission that this might be risky for the root being checked. The risk was, after some argument, accepted; then it was realized that while oxygen was plentiful and aluminum at least available in the silicate dust of Titanian soil, there was probably not enough iron, oxidized or otherwise, accessible on any square kilometer of Titan's surface to make a child's horseshoe magnet. There might be lots of heavy elements in the satellite's core, and tectonics plainly did occur; but how much core material had ever been brought to the surface was still an open question. One which had low priority on the basic plan, and which the present situation wouldn't change.

Goodall surprised himself, though not the others, by coming up with a workable suggestion inspired by this general line of thought. The gel of the patch could be analyzed for trace elements and the input from the various roots could be monitored thereafter for a statistical match. This should eventually identify the north root. He did not mention that this might also furnish a chance to check for carbon-carbon double bonds in this batch of tar.

He was delighted at the opportunity, but deeply worried by the immediate and uncritical acceptance of his suggestion by the others. They shouldn't be that dependent on *him*.

And if they were, should he carry out his plan?

Of course. What else would cure them?

Yes, this provided another justification for what he was going to do—soon now, he had to admit. No research group could ever function effectively staffed exclusively or even largely by Arthur Goodall fundamentalists, and this one had to function. He had no living children, but he did want the human species to go on. It might still accomplish something if it got itself past this crisis, and in any case it could certainly enjoy itself. He had been able to do that himself, once.

Arthur Goodall would have to keep his mind on his own problems for just a little while longer, but at least there were no more policy decisions to make. Just tactical details.

Those could keep his mind off his pain, but for how long?

Status would—

He would have to think about Status.

First, though, a careful job of data processing had to be finished; he needed a very detailed chart, in three dimensions, of his crater and its lake, its tar patches, and all its other features—detailed enough to satisfy his own conscience in the matter of isolating the planned contamination. The information was available in Maria's surface studies, of course. It just had to be compiled.

Five-centimeter radar got through the smog easily but did not resolve one-centimeter details. Images from points—many points— many meters apart along the station's orbit had to be combined using interferometric algorithms which were straightforward but tedious without Status's public assistance. Analyzing some forty square kilometers of surface to one-*milli*meter accuracy took even the station equipment many hours. Status took no "conscious" part; this was theoretical work which might come to nothing. Only when results seemed valid and relevant would they become part of the basic record, and it was up to Goodall to decide when and if they were. So far, therefore, there was no worry that he could see of anyone's noticing his activities.

With the detailed map's completion came the need for personal judgment, which meant careful examination of the model. This took even longer.

The twenty-two kilometers of the nearly circular ring had to be examined for possible cracks which would let a methane stream flow outward. There were rivers, or at least brooks, on Titan; most of the lakes were fed largely by small, winding methane-courses, fed in turn principally by rain from their own cumulus clouds. Very little rain had been seen to fall elsewhere than on or very close to the lakes themselves. There was nothing like the vast drainage basins so characteristic of Earth's topography. This was why no one felt confident that all the lakes would turn out to have the same detailed composition. Each gathered its solutes from its own neighborhood.

The lake which was currently keeping Goodall's attention from his own troubles was small, about six hundred meters east to west and little more than half that north and south, about a hundred and fifty thousand square meters of, presumably, impure methane. It had the usual smooth shoreline except at the dozen or so points where rivulets entered it. The number of these was unusually large for the size of the lake; presumably the crater funneled an even higher percentage of the precipitation than usual back to its source.

GO6-inspired conscience deflected the colonel's train of thought for a moment here; he should, of course, try to produce an alternative hypothesis for the cause of the extra brooks. None presented itself for several seconds, however, and this was no time to publish a request for one.

Besides, he wouldn't be reporting to higher authority.

And the problem didn't seem serious.

The depth and detailed composition of the liquid would of course have to be determined. There was more than one way to do this; Goodall had not yet decided which to use.

One of the tar patches was less than a hundred meters from the shore, of typically amoeboid shape, and little more than twenty-five meters in average diameter. The other had nearly ten times the area and was located, to Goodall's surprise, within half a kilometer of the northeast rim of the crater. He noted the sizes, shapes, and locations of these as precisely as he could, and filed the information in his private speculation record, to be released to Status on his personal order. This file was getting quite large.

There was no evidence here of tectonic activity—no ridges, ice boulders, nothing like the tilted block near the first factory. He wondered briefly whether he'd better search for still another site, but convinced himself that the small number of variables was really an advantage.

Besides, the general smoothness had another good point, he suddenly realized. He was certainly not a good pilot. An obstructed landing area might make the whole project impossible.

The major remaining decision was *when*. One problem presented by Status still had to be solved. He had had one idea about this, but the inspiration had not come until after he had left the mausoleum, and it was then too late.

Distracting the robot was pointless as well as impractical, since the device could do nothing in any case but inform the rest of the staff; it controlled little physical except its communication links, pressure safety valves and doors, and some dedicated medical equipment. It was the people who had to have their attentions distracted.

If Goodall left his quarters without announcing his intent, Status would certainly warn everyone about the quarantine violation and keep them informed of his moment-by-moment location. There had to be a good reason for leaving again, one which would either satisfy Status that no warning was needed or satisfy his colleagues that the action was line-of-duty.

Naturally this reason should involve no danger to any of his friends.

Well, *preferably* no *real* danger. But each time the pain came back this restriction seemed less essential, and Goodall was getting worried about this in his more objective moments.

What problem—not too major a problem—would call for his roaming the corridors again?

Certainly nothing involving life support, even if that was an acceptable risk from his own viewpoint. He'd be the last to be chosen to do station maintenance; the nature of his illness was known, as was its effect on his manual skills.

Observing equipment? More promising, but he'd have to go out first to cause the trouble—and causing real trouble there would do more to harm the main project than his current plan possibly could to help it. So would *real* damage of any other sort.

How about unreal damage? He had the normal scientific abhorrence of intentionally falsifying data, a repugnance which for thinking people both long preceded and vastly exceeded the military offense of violating regulations, but if he could straighten out such an offense before any ripples spread . . .

Yes, he could indeed. Slowly a smile spread over Goodall's lined face. It hurt, but he did it anyway.

9

SETTLEMENT

Sergeant Belvew, are you awake?"

"Of course, Colonel. I'm flying—I mean, I'm actually down here."

"Sorry. I lost track of time, I'm afraid. I knew you had stayed down after picking up Barn, but I thought your suit would have needed recharging by now."

"Another few hours. I thought I might as well be here on the spot for as long as possible, since I had to come down anyway. If there's something you've thought of for me to do I should have stocked up on suit power and sleep earlier; I can't stay down too much longer now."

"It was just a question. When you retrieved Barn, did you shut off his suit heaters? His body was flexible when I took it from the ship."

"No, I didn't. Silly of me, but I couldn't bring myself—and if he'd frozen while Ginger was bringing him up, you might have had trouble getting him out."

"He wouldn't have *frozen;* the coffin is heated. But he might have—well, the fact is that I didn't think about that, and I didn't power his suit down either. I'll have to go back to take care of it. I know it's not exactly critical, but the sooner the better."

"I can do it myself when I come back. I could start now, and meet the station in—how long, Maria?"

"Just a moment." The woman was busy, of course, but nothing ever seemed to disconcert her. "Since you're just about at a pole—one hundred twelve minutes to the equator, half a minute to turn, seven and a quarter to orbit speed and clearance of atmosphere, one hundred ten to intercept and two more to match—"

"Forget it," Goodall interrupted firmly. "It should have been done long ago, and I can do it in a few minutes. You must be flying a planned pattern, Gene. Finish it out and come back whenever you intended. I'm leaving quarters, everyone, as soon as I've checked my suit."

There may have been doubts, though no one claimed later to have had any. There was no objection; almost certainly there was no suspicion. Goodall was a theoretician, with rank to do as he saw fit. He was, in fact, the boss, as far as such a group could have a boss. The others were qualified, and commonly quite willing, to raise what they considered reasonable objections to his decisions, but none was likely to do it on such a trivial issue. Five minutes later he was climbing the short distance to the station axis.

He actually visited the mausoleum. He had indeed failed to shut down Inger's heaters—that memory was what had inspired his present plan. A direct and total falsehood would probably never have occurred to him. He was now, however, facing a need to lie—really lie—probably in a very few minutes. Of course he didn't want to until he absolutely had to, since something might always happen to make it unnecessary. Never lie until it becomes unimportant whether anyone ever believes you again or not; this was pragmatism, not morality, he told himself.

The body had stiffened by now, though not from cold. This bothered Goodall slightly; it was general policy to forestall as much as possible the irreversible chemistry which followed death and added additional variables to any study involving a body. One never knew when more information might be needed. However, there were other possible subjects—other former friends whose memorials and personalities he could remember, he thought briefly and grimly—and as long as the error was on file with Status it shouldn't matter much.

The frost that had filled Barn's faceplate area was gone, but Goodall didn't see the mustache either. He was too careful not to look closely as he opened the heater switch.

He filed the report without caring whether any others were paying attention. He left the mausoleum and headed not back to his own laboratory/hospital cell/quarters but toward the pole of the station and *Crius*'s dock. Status would pay no attention without specific instruction, since he was legitimately outside his quarters, and the more imaginative staff wouldn't know in time.

The remotely controlled override which would allow the jets to be handled from the station even if a waldo suit was aboard was a recent improvisation, of course. It was considered less effective and less important than the unanimous agreement that no one would do anything of the sort again—the agreement whose breach was about to make Arthur Goodall a liar. It had been installed anyway because someone had now thought of illness taking over a pilot at an awkward time.

Goodall had been mainly responsible for its design, and knew what to do. Disabling it was a matter of disconnecting a single jack, easily done floating above the coffin even while wearing a suit.

He did not remember whether this would be noted by Status, but this no longer mattered. He was aboard within seconds, with the outer canopy closed. Everyone would know what was happening in a few minutes, but no one, including Status, would be able to do anything about it.

He closed the coffin hatch and started the prelaunch check. This was entirely passive at first, a matter of reading instruments, and would call no attention from outside the ship. All seemed ready. The tanks were not full, of course—most of their mass had been used to get up to the station—but there was much more than enough to break orbit and get back to atmosphere. The fusers were solid-state devices which went wrong only catastrophically when they failed at all, and they must certainly be all right now, since the jet and surrounding areas were intact. Chemical batteries were at reasonable charge. So was Goodall's own environment suit; he had made sure of that before leaving his quarters. He could see that the launching springs were compressed, as they had been when Ginger docked. There was no status indicator for the remote controller which would release them from inside the jet, but there was no reason to worry about it; the device was too simple to be tricky. At least, nothing had gone wrong with it so far.

He energized the small tank heater which would make sure some of the reaction mass was vapor and would reach the feed pipes, waited for the required three seconds in tense anticipation of Status's voice asking what was going on, realized at last that the jets were not part of the robot's responsibility except through direct orders, and sprang the launcher.

That brought the questions, a confusion of voices from everyone in the station. Goodall ignored them. He had never actually flown one of the craft before except for a brief try in upper atmosphere, but in spite of the pain he had followed through with his suit many times while others were doing so; and like the others, he had received plenty of training before they left Earth.

He had more than one reason for concentrating on flying now, of course. He had no intention of being talked out of this, and if he allowed himself any distraction he'd be noticing his pain again. Right now handling the craft took *all* his attention, blissfully.

Crius drifted away from the station and achieved regulation distance for minimal rocket use, and her pilot swung and applied the thrust. It was only a tiny fraction of a gravity, and nearly five minutes passed before the departure was irrevocable—before distance and accumulated orbital change would make return impossible with the available mass—and until that happened, and he had applied the brief but more solid thrust which would bring him down to atmosphere, he paid no attention to what anyone said. Then he uttered only one word.

"Sorry."

Argument had already stopped; everyone but Belvew, who had not had access to the instruments in his quarters and had only a confused idea of what was happening from the equally confused tangle of voices, knew that argument was pointless. There was no way for *Crius* to return to the station until she had replenished her tanks in Titan's atmosphere. Most of the staff had inferred even more than this, using the broken agreement as a basic datum. Ginger Xalco, whose own malfeasance had been responsible for the agreement in the first place, asked the obvious question.

"Why, Arthur?"

"I know I'm being a bit early," he replied with no tremor or other sign of worry in his voice. "I'm starting Stage Three—settlement. I've found a place to start the control run, a place where there are Collos patches, a lake, and good isolation from the rest of the surface. We can now test the patches without too much contamination risk for what we hope they are—prebiotic areas, made of what may become life someday if Titan has time for it before the Sun's a planetary nebula. Anyone can run the analyses. You know what we want to find out: mainly, whether chemical evolution is really taking place, and how fast. I think the chances are good; there is *something* making those tar pools far more mobile than they should be at Titan's temperature, and *something* seems to be making them responsive even to simple stimuli. Also, the responses aren't all the same. Ginger found that out; so did you, Gene. Different prebiotic molecules? We'll have to find out. And why didn't any of you notice that my methanol report had to be wrong? That methanol doesn't melt until it's a hundred kelvins hotter than that stuff can—pardon me, *should*—be? I'm only guessing what it is, but I think it's a good guess. I'll run an analysis when I get down, and supply a batch of enzymes afterward; you'll have to keep track what they do, if anything, and watch for evidence that my crater system isn't as isolated as I hope. We mustn't contaminate all Titan; that would spoil the whole project. But we do have to see what contamination by non-native enzymes can do, so we have a chance of recognizing it if it

happens accidentally, and the contamination needs to be in an isolated spot. You know that as well as I do. We were going to do it,
eventually; I'm afraid I just lost patience."

"But why? Why?" it was Maria Collos's almost frantic voice.
She was upset at last; she, at least, had now guessed his full intent,
Goodall felt sure. "It could have waited until the planned time. It
should have."

"It couldn't, and you know why." Goodall's voice was gentle.

"Where are you getting the enzymes, and what ones will you
use?" Belvew, perhaps because he had less information, was less
quick than usual on the uptake.

"I don't have a complete list, but there are a good many
thousands. You and Pete, or Seichi, or whoever takes it on, should
have fun reading chemistry. Don't worry about details; Status's
memory is there. I'm priming it with a background based on what
I've done so far, and there's a lifetime's worth in it already." It was
not until the end of this sentence that Belvew caught on. He practically screamed his next words. He wanted to do something, but was
completely helpless except for talk.

"You old idiot! You could drop a steak from the food plant into
the pool and get the same result! Get back up and be useful!"

"The steak will be more useful to you than I will. Shut up and
think." The colonel regretted his own lapse of courtesy, but was
pretty sure that nothing less would make Belvew listen. "I haven't
really driven this thing before, and will have to plan the flying part
of this mission. I wish I had enough mass for a few practice maneuvers, but I'd better not risk that. It's less than an hour to atmosphere,
after all." Belvew actually did shut up. He could see why the theoretician needed planning time.

Goodall had never flown the jets not because he was incompe-
tent, but because the pain which resulted when anything touched
his skin drowned out the sensations supplied by the waldo suits—
sensations which provided the feedback necessary for real reflex-type
flying control. Without the service of his sense of touch, he could fly
only by visual inspection of his instruments. A living pilot in an

ordinary airplane a few centuries before would have had no problem
with this, having been trained to ignore everything *except* the visual
input—the seat-of-the-pants sensations had killed far too many early
fliers for anyone to trust them.

Neither Goodall nor anyone else in the group had had such training; the waldos provided more tactile input than any other kind, and
they all had learned to trust this. The colonel was going to have to
reinvent airplane-type instrument flying, and his principal visual information would come not from gyro-referenced attitude sensors or
radar displays but from a full-sphere screen distorting its picture into
a Mollweide equal-area projection.

Like the others, Goodall was used to allowing for the screen
distortion, but that seemed to Belvew the only bright aspect of the
whole situation. He was pretty sure that no sort of argument would
now swerve the chief from his plan, though the sergeant intended
to keep trying. He could—thankfully—only guess at the sensations
the old fellow had had to endure for the last few years. He knew
that he himself might have done the same thing long ago, in Goodall's place. That knowledge might weaken the emotional intensity of
his arguments, but he was still going to argue.

But not until *after* the jet's tanks were full, or at least after *Crius*
had completed atmosphere entry, and everyone had had a chance to
see what sort of piloting Goodall could actually do.

Entry was not too difficult. *Crius* was after all an aircraft, designed for stable aerodynamic flight, and she lined up easily and
without pilot assistance along the proper axis once drag became perceptible and airfoils effective a couple of hours after leaving the station. Initial entry speed was only about one and a half kilometers
per second, which offered no thermal problems and quickly decreased. Goodall lit the ramjets in the appropriate speed range and
spent some minutes practicing turns, climbs, dives, and even pipe
and lift stalls. No one even offered advice. No one realized that his
microphone was off most of the time so that no sounds of pain would
reach the station. Handling the waldoes still hurt, but was at least
possible for the commander. Reading their tactile input was not.

The watchers did grow a little tense as Goodall started a long, gentle descent to deep atmosphere and began to hunt for a thunderhead. There was less room for error recovery with only a kilometer or two of air underneath, and as others besides Belvew knew from experience, the low airspeeds needed for mass collection offered perils of their own. When a cloud did loom in the center of *Crius*'s Mollweide and Goodall slowed still further, even the imperturbable Maria Collos had to remove her hands from her mapping controls. Belvew, for the first time, offered advice.

"Watch airspeed and pitch, Art, with thrust the controlling variable. Don't let anything else distract you." He spoke with a little tremor.

"Right. Thanks." Goodall's voice showed no emotion, though his actual feeling was one of pleasure. He hadn't noticed much pain since entering atmosphere; he had been far too busy even to think of anything but *Crius*'s behavior.

He had stabilized now at what the others had found to be the most effective collection speed, about five meters a second above pipe stall, and he plowed into the cloud with his eyes on the instruments Gene had recommended.

He could feel the bumpiness of the air as his craft met upward and downward currents. It hurt, of course, but by keeping pitch and thrust constant as directed he held his airspeed close to optimal. It was pitch which gave the most trouble; entering an updraft tended of course to lift the jet's nose. This would slow her down if it was allowed to happen, and the colonel's reflexes were unpracticed. He tended to overcontrol, like any novice.

The first pass through the cloud had to be written off as practice; he had forgotten to set up collecting mode, and none of the others had noticed either. The practice, however, did help, and on the second try he not only took a respectable amount of liquid into his tanks but held his airspeed within three meters a second of the planned value—with the errors all on the high side. He was being *very* careful. He knew, in his head, the recovery procedure from a pipe stall, but thinking it through was one thing, reflex quite another.

Belvew noted all this without taking too much attention from his own flying procedure—after all, he did have the proper reflexes—and gave a rather obvious sigh of relief when *Crius*'s tanks indicated full. Goodall must have heard it, but he made no comment about it. He probably felt much the same.

"So much for that," was his only remark. "All right, Maria. My spot is at seven point one degrees south, one twenty-five point five east of the factory. Give me a heading, please."

Maria hesitated for just a moment, and everyone including Goodall knew why. If she refused guidance, he'd have to come back—

No, he wouldn't. He'd order Status to guide him, or if that was blocked in some way he could do a rough mental calculation. He must have kept *some* track of his entry point and subsequent flight path. Any lack of precision in his figures would simply waste suit time and fuel, and interfere with whatever he hoped to get done.

"Heading zero nine six. Climb to eighty kilometers for best speed. At thirty-seven minutes, start descent at ten k per minute. You'll see it when you're down to two k, about five ahead."

"Thanks. The rest of you: this can be considered the planned settlement. We'll have to plant another factory and plan possible manned ground structures. If you can do that soon enough I may be able to do something about checking the orientation of the factory's roots, this time—no, you can't manage that. It should concentrate on making structure blocks, and someone will have to come down from time to time to do the actual building until habitable quarters are ready. I know this is sooner than we planned, and someone will still have to finish the rest of the seismic lines and atmosphere checks, but I've decided the chemistry needs to get started right now. There'll have to be a few, but only a few, analyzers at first—maybe a dozen or so. I have four, the dials say. The new factory can turn out any more we need, and then get at the bricks. Maria, you can slow down on mapping and take general command."

"But I'm only—"

"You're a light colonel as of right now. Sam Donabed has date of rank on you, but he won't raise a fuss—will you, Sam?"

"Good General, no, sir. Who wants to spend time running things?"

"Well, Maria doesn't either, so don't let her argue you into it. Maria, you're the best for it. I know. I knew long ago. That's an order, and Status has it on record, for what that may be worth to anyone. Use your Athenian organizing powers. Set up as many more surface analysis sites as seems good to you and that the factories can supply, and concentrate first on comparing the Collos patch compositions at random locations with the ones by the settlement. You'll know which one to watch most closely for change—I'll use the one closer to the lake here, partly because it is closer to where I hope to land and partly because it's smaller; what I add will have higher concentration and be easier to measure. Don't ask any questions until I'm down; just think over what I may have missed. There's bound to be something."

The reference to the ancestry suggested by her name almost revived Maria's chronic amusement. Long ago she had said something which had inspired the misunderstanding—a silly one, in view of the thorough mixing of ancestry and variation of naming customs which now characterized humanity—and she had been looking forward, someday, to letting him see her face, which was emphatically not Greek. Now—

"One question," Belvew cut in. "I'm starting up now, and will have to concentrate on making orbit for a few minutes. How sure are you that you can make your landing—yourself?"

10

STAND-DOWN

THE COLONEL GAVE NO sign of being insulted.

"I'll make some practice runs when the place is in sight, and decide. I promise I'll let you know if I need help."

No one pointed out that he had broken one promise already, and for long minutes the two craft went their respective ways. Little was accomplished at the station.

Belvew was still in orbit when *Crius* came in sight of the crater and lake, and Ginger was standing by to help talk the colonel down. However little anyone approved of what was happening, and however much arguing might yet be done with their nominal commander, it was still critically important to save the jet. Everyone but Belvew, who had only his own screen and had to use it for his own flying, watched tensely as *Crius* passed slowly—too slowly, some felt—over the ring.

Still two kilometers up, Goodall shifted briefly to rocket mode, slowed down, and felt for wing-stalling speed. It seemed to be just where it should be with the tanks full and wings at landing camber. He repeated the trial several times, making recoveries with various combinations of added thrust and lowered nose, and eventually satisfied himself and almost satisfied his watchers.

"You might make it at that, Arthur," Ginger admitted after the fourth try, "but it will be a lot safer if you let me set you down. It may not make much difference to you"—she had pretty well re-signed herself to Goodall's completion of his plan—"but keeping the machine in one piece is still pretty important to the rest of us."

"And to me," the commander assured her. "I want the job finished as much as you do. You know that. My judgment may be off orbit now, of course. I'd be the last to know about that. But what I'm doing is based on my considered opinion of what's best for the job, including the fact that I won't be able to do useful thinking much longer."

"Moon wind!" snapped Peter Martucci. "If your judgment is off, you have no business pulling this trick!"

"I have no business doing anything else. I have other reasons for working it this way. One of them I'm sure you know or can guess, some I'm just as sure you don't and couldn't, but I don't have time to argue them all. I have work to do and not much time after I'm down."

"Then let me land you, Arthur," Ginger said quietly.

"Well—there's a problem with that—"

"You promised! We know you broke the one about not making unauthorized flights, but surely that's the only one—you wouldn't break another—"

"I didn't mean to; but there's a problem I didn't consider."

"What?"

"I unplugged the override before I floated into this thing, in case someone caught on too soon and wanted to bring me back before the ship was committed. I'm still in the control niche, and no one else can fly it while my suit is here."

"Reconnect the override, then."

"That's what I didn't think of. I can't reach the jack. No one could who is any larger than lePing, and I'm not sure about her. I can't move around enough to reach it. I'll have to take her down myself. Ride as close as you can, and say anything you think may be useful, Major Xalco, but I'll have to do the real flying."

There was silence for half a minute as Goodall swung away from the crater to set up a landing path. Ginger Xalco briefly wondered if she could persuade him to wait until Belvew was back at the station and could do the talking, but this was only for a moment; then she realized that the old fellow wouldn't—couldn't—waste that much time. There were the others, of course; everyone but Martucci and the doctor was an experienced pilot. But after Belvew she was the best and knew it. Responsibility can sometimes be disconnected from authority, but never from competence.

"Don't land across the lake," she said carefully. "It has the usual cumulus cloud above it, and you'll hit turbulence just before touching down. I suppose you want to stop near the patch."

"Right."

"Then come in on—oh, seventy-five. Drop to five hundred meters, shift to rocket, and slow down to wing stall plus twenty by the time you're five kilometers out."

"Why five?"

"Don't ask questions either. I'm allowing for corrections when you overcontrol, if you must know. If you even think you're starting to stall, feed full thrust, wait a second, and nose up two degrees; that will pull you out of trouble, and we can always make another pass. Or a fuel run."

Goodall remained silent this time. If he wondered how many landing passes he really had time and mass for, no one knew it. Mass was less critical, of course; he *could* tank up again, as Ginger had said, if he wasted too much.

But time was different.

A minute later he was on line and altitude, and settling down to speed.

And feeling every signal of his waldo suit as agony.

There was no way to turn the impulses off; such a need had never been imagined. He did have ointments for dulling his skin sensitivity, but their last application had been well before his leaving the station, the stuff itself was back there, and even if it had been on the jet there was no way to apply anything through the suit. He should have been able to concentrate so thoroughly on the landing that the pain couldn't get his attention, but it wasn't working out that way. If he wrecked the jet—if he killed himself or hurt himself too badly to let him do what still had to be done—

"Airspeed and pitch, you idiot!" They were his own mental commands, not an actual message. The ones Belvew had provided earlier.

"Nose down just a hair." That was Ginger. He tried to obey, but the hair would have been thick enough to hold a kite, at least in Earth's atmosphere. The woman's tone didn't change; she wasn't snapping now. "Up a little. That's better. A little high now, but take it out in power drop—down to five sixty." Thrust lessened, speed decreased. He didn't want to look at the indicator, but had to.

Two meters per second above wing stall. There'd better be no turbulence.

"Good. Hold that. Rocket mode—good. Altitude fifty. Fifty seconds to touch. Don't change a thing. Forty meters, forty seconds. The ground is level. No complications. Twenty meters. Ten. Five to go—hold your attitude—don't touch anything—stand by on thrust— *cut!*"

The pilot felt the keels touch, surprisingly gently.

"Let it slide!"

For the first time he felt free to look at the outside screen, and immediately forgot his pain again.

The lake was behind him and to his left, the chosen patch almost at his left wing as *Crius* came to a halt. The crater rim was over three kilometers ahead; there would be plenty of space for whoever would do the takeoff. There was nothing left to do but the job.

He dropped two lab units between the keels, thought a moment, then dropped the remaining two. There were some seismic cans on board, according to the indicators, and he released two of these. He didn't know where he was with respect to any of the seismic lines, but someone could check that later.

"If someone can get a factory pod down here pronto, I might last long enough to check its first root or two," he called. "Just don't drop it in the lake. I don't know its bottom contours, and don't want to take a chance wading. I'm getting out now and taking one of the lab units over to the patch. Don't take off, Ginger or whoever will be doing it, until I get the instruments out from underneath. I won't waste any time."

He opened the canopies, which groaned slightly with the effort until their seals cracked and the outer air rushed in, and slid out. He was able to move easily enough in the thirteen-plus-percent gravity, though not with the ease that Belvew and Inger and Xalco had shown. He was, he reminded himself, a good deal older than any of them; allowances had to be made.

There was plenty of room for his suited form between the keels, and he quickly retrieved the equipment and carried it to the patch fifty meters away.

"I'd get a bit farther," Ginger said soberly as he stopped. "I don't know the surface friction—you stopped pretty quickly—and I want to use full thrust."

Goodall didn't argue, but moved another hundred meters past the tar patch, carrying the instruments.

"All right," he said. "This should be plenty."

"If you can risk it, I can."

"Risk it. The plane's what's important now."

He watched and listened as the exhaust thundered in the heavy air. *Crius* trembled, then slid forward. She reached lift speed in about three hundred meters. Her keels cleared the ground by millimeters, then by a meter, and Ginger nosed her abruptly upward. The exhaust roar died out in the distance as the wings flattened.

Goodall got to work, wondering vaguely why he didn't feel more lonely. His feet and joints hurt, of course; that was where there was most pressure from his armor. But that was just physical. He had expected that these last few hours would be somehow more emotional, but he found himself approaching the work as calmly as—as—he couldn't think of an analogy. As calmly as he had ever approached anything.

He set the apparatus down for a moment, walked over to the tar patch, and inspected it closely. The view was better than he had had of the others on his screens in the station, but he could see no significant difference: the surface was smooth, glossy black, reflecting the orange sky where the Sun's location could just be guessed at. Saturn was of course invisible; Goodall had no idea whether or not it was above the horizon—yes, he did; he knew his longitude, he suddenly recalled. It wasn't.

He touched the glossy surface gently with his armored hand. Prelife? He'd never really know. It wasn't sticky, in spite of Ginger's experience. He pressed as hard as his weight would allow, and it seemed in no hurry to yield, either—well, it had taken a while even for a pair of jet keels to sink in significantly where Gene had landed. The major had stuck much more quickly, he now recalled. The patches couldn't all be the same. That was *good*. Not just good to know.

Human senses gave too little information. He fetched the analyzer and set it on the black surface.

Reading the results would be something of a nuisance, since the device transmitted to his own receiving/computing center in the station and took its orders from the same place. Goodall spoke aloud.

"Pete, you know my system. Get it running, and have this unit scrape up a sample and look for carbon-carbon double bonds, will you? I had Status switch my general board to you while I was coming down."

"Sure. Some special reason?"

"Yes. I told you I messed up with my original analysis. I found three or four C-H bonds. I supposed the uncertainty came from bond direction—a C-O and an O-H—and assumed methanol. Now I doubt it. There could be two carbons there, and if there are—"

"If there are, you have an impossible structure." Status's words came flatly.

"I'm not sure, at this temperature. The point is I'll have a really high energy molecule with a really low activation energy either for reacting with others or simply breaking up. That would be the best situation for pre-bio that anyone's found yet. If it turns out to be true, you check other Collos patches here and there and find out whether it's general, and then watch what happens to this one when my enzymes get distributed. If anything does, *keep it confined* and watch it come alive—if anyone can decide where the fence between pre-bio and alive is. I think we really have something here—or will if you find that double bond.''

As he spoke, the lab unit had extended its iridium-coated scraper and managed to free a sample, with no more obvious trouble than had been experienced earlier near Lake Carver, and ingested it. Goodall could visualize the miniature NMR, neutron, and gamma diffraction devices going to work; he wondered briefly how many labs they could afford to lose before running out of beryllium for the neutron sources. They hadn't brought much, and recycling might not be practical. He could visualize the patterns they were providing for the computer far above—but he shouldn't do that. He should wait for the data. Predicting them at this stage was highly improper.

He wanted to hold his breath, but things already hurt enough. It was more than three minutes before the answer came down.

"The bonds are there." The pain disappeared.

"Then it's—well, unless you can think of something else, it's—"

"Yeah. Vinyl alcohol, not methanol. Do you want me to figure energies for its breakdown to water and acetylene, or can you think of other likely reactions, or don't you care if your enzymes boil the patch off the planet?"

"Think of any you want. I won't care, and it's time for the rest of you to start the thinking anyway. That's all I really wanted to know; my job's done. You needn't really hurry with the factory." Goodall looked thoughtfully and silently at the glistening surface for a moment. His friends were equally silent. Then he spoke again. "Well, not quite done."

Maria gave a choked, "No—"

"I have hours yet on my suit. I'll take a lab unit to the other pool, over by the rim, and we'll test that too; it won't be much of a walk, and I haven't walked for a long, long time. It might be fun."

Ginger spoke firmly. "I'll have full tanks in a few more minutes. I'm going to bring the plane down, and you're getting back aboard. You've been right again, and we need you to go on being right. This is really a boost; maybe we can get some really critical knowledge back to Earth while we're—"

"While *you*'re still alive. I've been right too often for your health, and I'm looking forward to not hurting anymore. Subjective and selfish, but that's the way it is. Start a systematic analysis of the patch, Peter, Seichi, anyone with the interest and ideas. We need to know everything that's *in* the gel. It's a pity Gene had to blow the earlier unit away; we might have finished this part of it by now. I'm taking one of these for a walk."

A trifle over three kilometers is not much of a walk under Titanian gravity, even for a disease-wasted and age- and pain-racked human body. Two or three times, as his skin seemed to catch fire in another spot, Goodall considered turning back and initiating his final experiment, but each time curiosity maintained its grip and drove him on.

Even when *Crius* roared overhead once more and settled back to the surface near the lake he merely pursed his lips in annoyance and continued his hike, with no words of irritation or anything else. If they chose to leave the jet on the ground until he was finished, there was nothing he could do about it. Arguing was almost always a waste of time, except of course about points of reasoning. He was not planning anything reasonable, and the arguments of the others would be irrelevant.

Since the craft was under remote control, with no one else down even back at the factory, there was nothing they could do about *him*, either.

He reached the larger tar patch and had the unit put through its paces. While he waited for answers, the pain came back, but was somehow not as bad. He could wonder—was there a range of odd materials in the patches scattered over the big satellite? Or were they all the same? If they were the same, was it because highly probable reactions—nearly inevitable, it would have to be—had built them? Or was there transfer of material over Titan's surface in ways no one had yet figured out? Could any of this stuff *evaporate?* Surely not in significant amounts at this temperature. He thought all this aloud;

Status would store the words, and speculations were always starting points.

And he would't have time to fall in love with these.

Was subsurface transport of solutions possible? More would have to be done to keep proper track of factory roots when the new ones were planted.

Those few minutes while he waited for the next set of results raised thoughts that came closer than had any of his friends' arguments to making Goodall change his plans and persuading him to climb back aboard *Crius*. There was so much still to do!

But the places where he was pressed, however lightly, by his suit made their own counterarguments. Yes, there was a lot to do, but he simply wouldn't be able to do it.

He heard the report that here, too, the liquid part of the gel was probably vinyl alcohol—*probably;* don't jump to conclusions, you old idiot; once is more than enough—took it as a fitting summary of what he'd done so far, and started back toward the lake.

Crius was still there, of course; he would have heard the departure if anyone had decided to take her off. For just an instant he panicked; had he plugged the takeover jack back in? Then he remembered that with no one in the coffin there was no need, and it had already flown without him.

He looked the jet over carefully—there was no hurry about the final experiment—and noted that there was no frozen hydrocarbon on the wings. He should have checked that earlier; it would have been more likely on his own landing. Had he been merely lucky, or had Ginger's talk-down been designed to keep a little extra speed? No, he had been frighteningly close to wing stall those last few seconds, he recalled.

Your mind is wandering, old fellow. You're doing the right thing. Do it *now.*

He took the seismic cans and drove them firmly into the surface, one midway between lake and tar patch and the other a quarter of the way around the lake to the north. He wished he had thought to bring at least one of them over to the crater wall, and briefly wondered about doing so now—did he have enough time in the suit for such a trip? Probably, but he couldn't spend it for that. He was burning up.

One lab unit he set down a meter from the edge of the lake, another just in the liquid, positioning both carefully. He watched for a minute or two to make sure that the latter wouldn't roll—there was no way of telling the slope of the lake bottom, since the liquid was not very clear. He pointed the latter fact out to Peter. The remaining lab units he set down on areas which had been scorched, or seared, or melted, by the rocket exhausts of the two landings and one takeoff. This didn't matter much, since the devices were mobile anyway, but it would be nice to see—for them to see—what chemical effects there might be from brief warmings of the ninety-K surface. Maybe the earlier landings had already caused contamination, especially *Oceanus*'s. No, don't think of that.

And now there was only one thing left to do. No, two. He repeated the order releasing the detailed crater information to Status's regular files. Then he took one more look around the crater, clearly enough visible in the faint sunlight filtering through the smog. He looked at the lake, the parked aircraft, noted happily that he felt neither pain nor temptation for the moment, and walked out on the patch.

"Arthur—," came a faint, distressed female voice.

"Be sure you don't miss any readings from here for Status," he answered. "Here's where I'm betting the changes will be."

He turned off his suit heaters—I remembered this time, he approved himself—and waited a few minutes. The suit insulation is really good, he reflected.

Then the cold did begin to creep in. It was not at all painful. He should have tried this before; he couldn't feel much of anything, for the first time in years.

But he couldn't enjoy it for long. His personal enzymes would need access to the tar, or vice versa, and if he waited too long he wouldn't be able to move. His hand went to his faceplate release as he knelt down and leaned forward.

But nothing happened to the plate. The outside pressure was far higher, and the plate wouldn't open. It was held against its gasket by Titanian air. He gasped in surprise, and for a few seconds actually worried. Was this all wasted? Would he just lie here, accomplishing nothing, while the tar surrounded him without being able to get at him? Should he turn the heaters back on? *Could* he? Maybe the tar could get through anyway—

He was nearly prone now. The pain was coming back, where gravity pressed him against the front of his suit. Was even the release of the cold being lost?

"Arthur. Emergency oxygen. You need pressure." Maria's voice was still unsteady, and she was clearly neither arguing nor amused.

"Thanks," he muttered. He groped for, found, and opened the manual cock of the topping tank, and fell silent again while the oxygen hissed from the container to his suit, raising the inside pressure. Luckily, high oxygen concentration took a while to get one drunk. Or maybe it would be good if he did—

Everyone in the station heard the faceplate pop open.

PART THREE

SEISMICS

11

SHAKE

Maria Collos was feeling philosophical. Personal danger usually makes one brush even the most basic personal strategy aside in favor of immediate tactics, but Commander Collos, who disliked both the title and what went with it, had a strong sense of responsibility.

She knew all about the ninety-kelvin ambient temperature and the twenty-five-hour remaining charge in her life suit. She knew the minimum time needed to get back to the station. She recognized the small but far from infinitesimal chance of an aircraft problem which would keep her from getting back at all. Increasingly frequent trembling of the ice underfoot hinted at still other perils; but her mind still kept wandering to matters of policy. Physical exhaustion forced her to pause often in her work, and when she stopped she simply couldn't keep from thinking.

She was a sensible person, though her present whereabouts and occupation might have suggested otherwise. Her philosophy was basically of the take-care-of-what-you-can-and-don't-worry-about-the-rest sort; but a colony of what's-the-use germs had somehow invaded it. She had come to Titan firmly convinced of the prelife project's importance, despite its low chances of success. She even had a fairly optimistic view of those chances, though knew as well as anyone that there were many more wrong pieces than right ones waiting to be added to the barely started jigsaw puzzle of the Human Universe.

It certainly wasn't a complete picture yet, and not even the as-sembled part could be counted on as fully accurate. Shifting an old piece to a new place or tossing it back in the box was everyday science.

She still felt sure that adding to humanity's store of knowledge—finding more pieces of the puzzle which the physical-realists were so desperately trying to fit together—offered the only hope other than pure luck for survival of her species. She realized that the concate-nation of diseases decimating humanity might turn out to be mere statistical bad luck, as did nearly everyone else but the conspiracy fundamentalists; but knowledge seemed to promise more hope than resignation did.

Looking at it one way, the assignment of the Titan group was to establish at the world-is-round level, rather than just a reasonable scientific presumption, that life could and sometimes did originate from purely natural causes, and, if at all possible from only two examples, to try to estimate the chances of its doing so.

This had been strongly implied for many decades by the partly assembled pieces of the puzzle found so far, but to the non- and antiscientists who used the word "theory" as a synonym for "guess" it was "only" a theory.

Finding something on Titan which seemed halfway to life might not be a very promising goal, but it offered hope as a lead to the solution of medical problems in general, and Titan was the only accessible body in the solar system other than Earth to make the offer. Jupiter and Europa might be more probable places, but they could not yet, if ever, be regarded as accessible ones where biogen-esis seemed likely to occur. Europa was far too deep in Jupiter's radiation field to allow a long-term human project, and Jupiter had no surface, though there had been talk of balloons.

Humanity was, after all, clutching at straws. It was much too late to see what had actually transpired when Earth conceived life. While most thinkers had taken the "natural origin" concept for granted for many decades, there were detail gaps in the assumed process; filling them *might* help what was left of humanity to save itself.

But was this really worth doing?

Collos, now head of the project, was herself human and wanted very much to live—to live longer than she probably would. Presumably most other people felt the same way, though Arthur Goodall's example a few weeks before might justify some doubt. As long as *anyone* did, then probably one should try.

Even when tired. Maria hadn't used to get this tired. Her cancer seemed to be in remission, and nanotech devices were handling the sugar control it had long ago destroyed, but she could detect her own deterioration just the same. She knew all about her own ailment, of course, and the knowledge widened the mental crack which was letting the what's-the-use feelings leak in; but she had caulking for that leak.

The sealant was a perfectly rational thought: If we quit, we *won't* find out. Ever. If saving humanity is indeed worth any trouble, then quitting is certainly a mistake; if it isn't and the fact finally becomes clear, one can always quit later. After the futility is solidly demonstrated, of course.

In the meantime, finding things out was *fun*.

She was certainly being useful right now, though not finding out very much. She was alone on Titan's surface. *Crius,* which had brought her down, was back in service, doing shuttle flights to and from the station and other work of its own rather than waiting for her. There was so much to be done down here, so much which had to be useful, and so much needed to be done everywhere else to support the useful activities.

Much had already been done since Arthur Goodall's final experiment. A hundred meters north from the mouth of the tunnel where Maria stood was a quarry in a cliff face, with a power saw and hundreds of ice fragments lying near it. The work had been done so far by powered hand tools; programming a factory for construction of blocks of ice had been surprisingly difficult.

Many of the pieces were square-cut bars of varying lengths and thicknesses; many more were fragments of such bars. It had taken much effort, and more time than had been hoped, to learn enough about the structural qualities of ice at local temperature to let Status calculate how deeply the surface base would have to be dug or how big a structure could be made of the blocks; but now the excavation had started.

During the testing, as usual, more questions had been raised than answered. The top of the low cliff containing the quarry had shown layering: three clear and obvious sequences of the dark smog-tar which had settled over so much of Titan, alternating with a few centimeters of white material which was probably compacted ice dust but which there had not been time to analyze yet.

Unless, of course, Louis Mastro or Carla lePing had filed a report which Maria had not yet had time to hear. They had, she remembered, been almost as insistent about investigating similar layering at the top of the cliff near Factory One; but that had been inaccessible to anything but cameras.

Crius, since landing her at Settlement Crater, had already restocked its mass tanks and was in orbit back to the station, probably being flown by Gene. *Theia* was in atmosphere dropping seismic cans or checking air circulation or something. Her pilot could have been almost anyone at the moment, and anyone else the next. *Oceanus*—well, that hadn't been her fault. In not too many hours Seichi Yakama, still physically able to fly and work in spite of advanced Hansen's III syndrome, would relieve her on the ground here at Settlement, and *Crius,* after taking her back to the station to rest and restock her suit, would descend once more and resume adding details to Status's image of the satellite. Routine went on, in other words.

It had been Status's decision, actually. The deaths of Goodall and Inger had brought the personnel count down to nineteen, which the data handler apparently considered a critical value in spite of the low relevance of statistics. He—it—now insisted that spending time ferrying people back and forth between station and surface was wasteful of their chief resource, time, as well as dangerous. As long as any surface work by human beings was necessary, it would be better in the long run to construct a base below and transfer everyone down for good. The extra commuting needed while construction lasted should be offset by time and personnel saved later.

When Maria and others had doubted this, Status had shown detailed calculations. These seemed to be correct, but only a bare majority of the surviving researchers had accepted them. They were emotionally negative, like those about the population crisis in the days when human population had still been rising. Showing mathematically how little time it would take to transform the planet into human flesh at whatever growth rate was then current had never had much effect, at least where it was most needed.

The Saturn group of educated nonspecialists was presumably better qualified than most to judge whether a silly conclusion was due to faulty math or to faulty assumptions, but its members still had the normal human difficulty believing anything which would make for personal inconvenience. They also had the normal human skill at finding excuses for the attitude, even under semimilitary discipline.

Status had won the vote, however, and there was no point standing there brooding. After all, resting wouldn't really help Maria's fatigue, which was not caused by work, and delay would only lengthen the time being used—wasted?—on this construction. She moved back toward the tunnel mouth.

In front of her as she faced east was a vertical cliff some fifteen meters high. To the south its top descended gradually, merging with the crater floor about half a kilometer away and about equally far from the impact crater's central lake. South of this point lay the area where the jets had been landing. Northward, past the quarry where the test bars had been cut, the scarp seemed to grow higher, but how far this continued only Status knew so far.

This human ignorance was embarrassing to Maria. She had been responsible for the original mapping from orbit. A fault like this, which presumably postdated the crater itself, should have been *noticed* by herself, not just recorded, if it had been, by a machine. As it was, not even the pilots landing in the crater had seen it. Arthur Goodall had not reported it. Only after the decision to move down, when the ringwall and its floor had been mapped more carefully even than Goodall had done, had it shown, and even then no one had bothered to trace it farther north than the quarry site.

Of course, pilot attention would have been taken up by other matters like landing, but still . . .

No one believed yet that it could have formed in the last few weeks. Possibly no one wanted to believe it. Maria could easily imagine how Arthur, who had searched so long for his ideal experiment site, would have reacted to the idea.

Most of the cliff top showed the light rusty brown edge of the smog deposit that, mixed with varying amounts of ice dust, covered so much of Titan. The ground at its foot, however, was bare ice. It must have taken time for some weathering agent to wash away the dark sediment on the west side of the fault, and something more mysterious to do so without also clearing the high side. A few crusty deposits like candle drippings, perhaps dissolved from the top of the cliff by rain and precipitated again at the foot by evaporation, were all that marred the level surface near tunnel mouth and quarry.

Even these should have taken a respectable time to form. Titan's surface was clearly being reworked by erosion and tectonics, but there seemed no reason yet to suppose that this was happening any faster than on Earth. If anything, the absence of liquid water suggested the contrary.

Maria would have liked to see what the fault had done to the north rim of the crater, but she firmly rejected the temptation to go and iook. There should, after all, be a nicely detailed answer already in the unexamined data above, but this was not the time for talk. Status *might* "know" in a sense; but the processor was neither omniscient nor imaginative. It would come up with correlations it had been told, explicitly or sometimes even implicitly, to seek, but never with theories.

It could only criticize these.

On the other hand, if Maria herself seemed likely to be too far from the landing site when the jet came back, so that she might not reach orbit while her suit supplies lasted, the computer *would* foresee that and firmly recommend return before she got anywhere near the rim. Suits could not yet be recharged on the surface, and Status was specifically responsible for all aspects of human safety.

None of this was conscious thought for Maria at the moment, just background knowledge. Status information, in fact.

Just north of one of the small, presumably alluvial tar "fans" was the entrance to the tunnel she was digging. It was about two meters high, with a five-centimeter sill of piled ice sand across the bottom, and about as wide, since equipment as well as suited people would have to get in. It was dug in the clear, nearly pure low-pressure ice—ice I—which formed the lower two-thirds of the cliff under the sediment layers. The latter was thinner than average here; one might use that to date the impact which had formed this crater— no, the sediment was gone from the cliff foot, and there seemed no way even to guess how much the stuff on top had been affected by the same erosion. Or why there was a difference—never mind that now, Collos.

Back to work. Research and fun could come later. She stepped across the clear ice and the rill of liquid methane running southward along the foot of the scarp—it had been raining ever since her arrival—picked up the chipper, and turned it on. It hummed obediently, so she descended the hundred and twenty meters of completed tunnel and pressed it against the end wall. Its iridium-armored teeth resumed shaving and swallowing ice, and blowing the resulting powder toward the tunnel mouth behind her. The group had learned; this machine had a double head and counterrotating blades. It did not try to spin her in either direction no matter how hard she pressed it against the wall.

She was getting more skillful in its use, too. It could only exhaust straight back, but she was now able to aim the heads most of the time so that "straight back" not only missed her suit but blew the dust much of the way to the tunnel mouth. She only had to pause every ten or fifteen minutes to clear her exit path. Her relief would bring a newly grown blower to handle that job, she had been told; most educated adults could still do improvisational programming on equipment seeds. The new factory now growing near the central lake nine hundred meters to the south even had locatable roots, a quality lacking in its predecessor. In two or three weeks it should also have produced a remotely controllable tunneler, and Maria and the others could get back to their proper, planned overseeing work.

That was if the iridium brought from Earth held out, of course. Cannibalizing labs for tools was a dubious idea at best, when one considered long-term planning.

She was angling the tunnel downward, and already had nearly twenty meters of ice and sediment overhead. Human beings under Titanian gravity, she had noticed, seemed not to feel much fear of cave-ins, a comforting if unrealistic attitude. This confidence had started to change for her recently, she had noticed, as ground tremors became more frequent, but she still did her best to enjoy it. Details of the planned base had not yet been completely worked out, since planning took so much more time than execution, but it would certainly have to be deep enough to be walled and ceiled by clear, seamless ice even if they decided to change to Titanian air pressure inside.

The fallen smog layer was about as strong as sand except where methane rains had caused it to crust. There it was more like sugar exposed to varying humidity—sturdier, but still not a reliable ceiling, even in local gravity and with balanced pressures.

The need for the downward slope had therefore been obvious. That for the sill at the tunnel mouth had not. The stream along the cliff face was intermittent, and had been dry when the digging started. Now there was methane sloshing around Maria's feet as she worked. Blowing this outside with the chipper had seemed an obvious solution when the liquid first trickled in, but the drops wouldn't fly as far as the ice chips in the heavy air. They also ran back downhill before she could reach the area where they had landed in order to blow them still farther. At least the ice dust waited for her.

She had taken care of some of the problem by digging a sump a few meters back, but this, unfortunately, had meant plastering some of the ceiling with an ice-methane mud which seemed always to choose the moment she was underneath to drop by handfuls onto her helmet. Water even on Titan did not bond closely with hydro-carbons, but the digger was an effective blender.

Maria, even in a philosophical mood, still spent some of her work time distracted by curiosity over which items of this rapidly growing crop of trivia might turn out to be lethal. She was not alone in this, though only she was in the tunnel.

She did what she could about the lack of company, reporting every action and its result to the station and to Status, though she put more faith in human imagination than in data-based calculations as a source of warning.

"More vibration!" she called suddenly. Belvew replied.

"Could it be your chipper getting out of balance, or biting deeper with one head than the other?" GO6 alternative hypotheses were a moral imperative, not just on Titan; being too sure too soon—the Aarn Munro syndrome, as some classicist had long ago named it— had proved a fruitful source of trouble throughout human history.

She turned off the machine as the most obvious way to test this one.

"Right, I guess, but—no, there it is again." She reactivated the digger and pressed it once more against the wall in front of her. The quivering stopped briefly, then resumed. "It's not that."

"Local quake? Titan still has plenty of tectonics, we know." This time it was Pete Martucci.

"Wouldn't the seismometers be telling us?"

"Not necessarily," Status's calm voice answered. "Seismic events have occurred often since the first can line began reporting, and seem to be regular Titan phenomena. However, the outer ice I layer does not carry waves as quickly as silicate rock. None of the can lines is close enough to Settlement Crater for an epicenter under that point to be recorded promptly. I advise you leave the tunnel until that idea can be checked, Commander Collos."

"But that'll delay—"

"Not as much as would the collapse of the tunnel, and it would be better for the overall project if you observed such an event from outside."

"Yes! For General's sake get out of there!" snapped Belvew. "And if you want to remind me that Arthur left you in charge, do it as you run!"

"Why didn't you mention the quakes before we started the tunnel, and if you knew about them why did you plan an underground station at all?" interjected Yakama. It was obvious to all, including the machine, whom he was addressing.

"Because no temblor has yet approached an intensity likely to damage the sort of structure we plan, and—"

"Then why did you order me outside?" snapped Maria, without slowing her pace back toward the open.

"Because theory must yield to observation, and this is our first chance to observe the actual effect of such an event on anything like the proposed structure." No one tried to argue this point; Maria changed the subject.

"I'm outside," she reported. "The rain seems to have stopped, if that matters to anyone."

"It may be relevant," Status commented, recognizing no irony. "Most of the quakes recorded in detail so far have originated at the ice I–ice II and ice II–ice III interfaces well below the surface, and redistribution of surface mass caused by rain, with resulting changes in deep pressure, could well be the basic cause. The correlation is statistically—"

"All right, keep track of it. When can I get back to work? I'm still using oxygen, you know."

"I know. It will take nearly twenty minutes for a wave front starting at your coordinates to pass enough network stations for reliable analysis. Are there any new local data which you could report? That might speed a possible decision."

Maria looked around thoughtfully. As she had said, the rain seemed to have ceased; none of the marble- to orange-sized drops could be seen drifting downward or blowing around. Not surprisingly, so had the rill trickling along the foot of the cliff. The crew had already dismissed this as just part of the drainage pattern which returned most of the crater's rainfall to the central lake and made Settlement Crater a nearly closed weather system.

Water ice is too polar to be soluble in liquid methane, and Maria had not been surprised that the temporary brook showed no signs of having cut into the foot of the cliff, even when she was thinking of possible ways to date the latter. Neither had Ginger Xalco, who had been first on the scene, done the testing at the quarry, and started the tunnel. Now something she didn't remember seeing earlier caught Maria's eye, and she looked at it thoughtfully for a moment.

"Ginger!"

"Yes?"

"When you started to dig, I know there was no stream along the cliff, so there was no reason to make a sill. Did you start the hole right at the bottom of the face, or a little bit up?"

"At the bottom, of course. That was planned, remember? We didn't want anything to interfere with rolling heavy stuff inside. It was just starting to rain when you took over, and you had water—I mean methane—inside in two or three minutes. That's why you had to make the sill."

"That's how I remember it. Now I see about three millimeters of edge outside and *below* the sill I made. Status, how fast could that stream eat its way down—remembering that it doesn't seem to undermine the cliff or cut the ground at all?"

"It couldn't." Two voices besides that of the computer answered simultaneously.

"Then what, besides a three-millimeter lift of the cliff itself since I built the sill, could have happened here?"

Neither Status nor anyone else answered that one. Maria thought furiously for some seconds—no more furiously than any of the others, but she spoke first.

"Status, what summary do we have on this crater? And how far back does the information go?"

"I assume you mean in time," the computer answered. "There is very little, actually. The area had not been covered by the regular mapping program when Colonel Goodall first centered his attention on it. His original data came from jet-based pictures taken from altitudes too high for good data, because of poor air transparency and steadiness and the jet camera resolution. When he became really interested in the site he secured more material from orbit without calling either your attention or mine to it; I now find that I have good pictures over a period of about two Titan orbits, ending about twenty hours before his landing. I cannot show you these where you are; you would have to come up here or at least board a jet. I can, of course, give verbal and numerical descriptions. If someone will make appropriate requests I can present current data very quickly."

Maria nodded, pointlessly.

"I want to find out how high this cliff was when Arthur did the area, and whether that height has changed measurably since then. I don't want you to tell me it's growing really fast, but I suppose I'd better know if it is. Pay no attention to my feelings."

12

SCOUT

I CAN ANSWER THAT now, since the cliff was observed during the ice testing. It was not there at all when Commander Goodall made his investigation."

"And you never noticed a difference when we started to dig?" asked Yakama.

"The matter was not specifically brought to my attention. Commander Goodall had not yet filed his information with the cross-indexed survey records, so I was not at first including the area in my ongoing comparisons. When he released the files, no one told me to back-check. When the scarp was first noticed and selected for the tunnel site I therefore had nothing to compare it with."

Maria cut in. "We understand that. Now, Status, do everything you can to make sense out of the fact that the cliff *is here now*. Especially, tie it in as closely as you can with all the seismic data we have; it looks as though Titan may be really alive in a very different sense from what we had hoped. And check over all the surface imaging we have, from the very beginning, to see whether anything of this sort has been happening anywhere we've mapped so far. Have quake waves from this area reached any of the cans yet?"

"None identifiable as such. There is frequent seismic activity at many points on the satellite. What you ask will take some time—

not much for record search, but possibly a great deal for comparison and analysis."

"Just a moment. Another question. There's more vibration now—Status, I'm at the foot of the cliff. I'm on the west side of the fault, which should be staying put or going down, since I'm at the bottom. It's the *cliff* which should be rising. Why was *I* just tossed into the air?"

The living listeners, the ones with imaginations, said nothing; each was furiously seeking a reasonable, or at least plausible, answer to this question. Status alone replied, posing another question which, however reasonable, could hardly have been more annoying to Maria if she had believed it guided by malice.

"How high were you thrown?"

She yielded briefly to the irritation and answered sarcastically, "Seventy-two point three one four millimeters."

"Center of gravity or boot soles? And how measured?"

"Disregard that datum." She had command of herself again. She was also back on the surface, still standing, and for a moment thought of using her time off the ground to calculate the height she had reached. Then she realized she had no accurate estimate of that, either. But even a guess would mean something, she reflected. "I was off the ground about three seconds. That's only an estimate."

"Were your legs straight, or equally bent before and after the event?"

"Straight. I was simply standing when it happened."

"Then you were lifted approximately one hundred fifty-one centimeters, with an uncertainty depending on the square root of your time-estimate error. With your suited mass of one hundred ten kilograms, the force against your feet must have been—"

"Status, I don't care about that. I'm on the *down* side of the cliff. Why was I thrown *up*?"

Belvew beat the computer to a response. "Has the three millimeters of cliff under the sill changed?" Maria had to pause to check before answering; being hurled into the air, even when one comes straight down again in practically the same place, is disconcerting.

"It's *about* the same. I only estimated it before."

Status cut in. "I advise setting up two more lines of seismometers at standard spacing, each one hundred kilometers long, at right
angles to each other, and intersecting as close to the center of Settlement Crater as may be practical. There are enough cans already manufactured to do this."

"Where?" asked Belvew.

"Aboard *Crius*."

"Which is headed up to you. Are there any on *Theia*?"

"Enough for about half of one of the lines I suggested."

Maria made an instant decision, and used her authority. Like
the others, she needed no explanation why Status wanted an on-
the-spot deep scan. "Get *Theia* here as fast as possible, and have it
make the two lines with four times normal can spacing. You can get
lots of information, even if resolution won't be as high—blast! I just
got tossed again. We *are* really having quakes. And this time the
three-millimeter sill went up to about five. The cliff did go up; I
should have had the ground drop from under me, if anything. What's
happening?"

"How high were you thrown this time?" and "Is there another
cliff somewhere behind you?" came the questions of Status and Belvew simultaneously.

"Maybe your ground was dragged up slightly with the cliff as it
slipped," came another voice, recognizable as that of Emil diSabato.
"If the area is being radar-scanned, that can be checked."

"How?" asked Seichi. "We already know the ground came up,
which is all the radar can tell us. The question is *why*?"

"If it rose more next to the fault than away from it, it will at
least suggest drag forces," pointed out the lieutenant after a moment.
Several people nodded approvingly but invisibly in their quarters;
Belvew alone spoke aloud.

"Good thought. Status?"

"The area is not being scanned by anything just now. It is below
horizon from the station, and none of the relays is working that area.
I advise committing relay units to cover it from now on."

"Make it so," answered Maria, "even if we come up with a possible answer right away. To answer Status's earlier question, I didn't notice this time, either. I have no way of guessing about the other; you're closer to the mapping gear than I am. Please get that jet over here! Who's driving it now?"

"I have it. On the way," came Ginger Xalco's voice. "I haven't seen another cliff either, but if I'm on the high side and it's any distance away I wouldn't expect to. Which is more important, Status? Going west to find another fault, which is probably there but probably not important, or starting the quake lines?"

"Sow the cans," ordered Maria before the processor could answer. "I'm going back to dig again."

"Stay out of there!" Ginger's and Belvew's cries were almost together.

"Check the tunnel as far as you can see without actually entering it, for evidence of new faults," was Status's more practical contribution.

Maria glanced toward the top of the scarp, and then to each side along its foot. Neither ice nor sediment seemed to have been shaken down by the recent shocks, and if anything was, she reflected, it wouldn't be falling far or fast. She could dodge, and even if she didn't dodge fast enough or far enough the stuff didn't seem likely to be dangerous.

They did need to know as soon as possible whether the whole idea of an underground station would have to be abandoned. Could they build *any* sort of surface structure? How? Test of compressive strength on ice blocks had not been encouraging; that was why they were digging instead of building. What materials could be used? No choice; there was essentially nothing but dirty ice available. It contained small quantities of silicate and sometimes carbonate dust, and often much larger ones of tar; but the process of separating these from the ice, packing it into building blocks, and binding it chemically in some fashion would take far more time than anyone would want to budget—even Status, with human safety in the equation.

She was distracted from the problem for a moment as the ground trembled again, not hard enough this time to throw her clear of it. Aftershock? Was the show nearly over? Would Status be able to decide about that even with the new lines in place?

The computer was not, of course, infallible; should she follow its rulings—no, suggestions—uncritically?

Of course not; but she couldn't act without them, either. She resisted the urge to call Ginger again to hurry; *Theia* was, she was sure, at full thrust already.

"Any faults in the tunnel?" Belvew's voice recalled her to the present.

She approached the opening and, after a moment's hesitation, took a single step inside. At least the sediment at the cliff top, which seemed more likely than the ice to be knocked free by any more temblors—it was a dirt-compared-to-rock situation, really—wouldn't hit her here. She examined the tunnel walls carefully with her hand light. Even Titanian outdoor light below the smog was ten stops or so darker than a sunlit Earth landscape.

"I can't see anything," she said at last. "The walls aren't perfectly smooth, but the only grooves I can see are along them. I must have made them myself with the digger."

"You should resume digging," said Status calmly.

"No you don't!" Belvew almost screamed. Maria frowned silently for a moment.

"Sorry, Gene," she said. "We need the new station."

"Not the way we need live brains!"

"I think it's safe enough."

"How safe is safe enough—oh." The man fell silent as a certain landing incident flashed into his conscious memory. The commander gave no answer, and no one else was rude enough to comment. She started back down the tunnel.

"You wouldn't have let me do it." Gene's voice was much quieter.

"You don't know that." Maria resumed work with the chipper.

"Nehemiah Scudder, if you've included Heinlein among your classic readings, didn't know the earth was made in six days."

Belvew omitted the "he just believed it" part of the rather trite re-mark; there was no point in either being grossly insulting or leaving himself open to a devastating retort about his own adolescence. Ma-ria probably wouldn't have made one, but still . . .

The rest of the group must be listening, after all.

"I'll be there in about ten minutes," Ginger interjected tactfully. "I'm letting down now. Status, does the absolute direction of the can lines matter? You said to make them at right angles to each other, but nothing more."

"No. Even the right angle needn't be exact," was the answer. "In any case, the absolute orientation will be found when we cali-brate them. You can drop the first line on your initial pass over the crater."

"Only if you tell me when I'm at the right distance. I know I'm heading right, but I can't see far enough ahead to spot the crater from fifty K's out."

"I can take care of that," came Martucci's voice. "I have your position and vector through one of the relays—the station is below your horizon. Tell me when you're down to drop height."

"Five more seconds," the pilot answered promptly.

"Then cut to sowing speed right now, or you'll overshoot."

"Right." Both speakers were physically in the station, of course; it would have been easier to let Pete take over the jet directly had he been competent to fly it. No one mentioned this.

"You start to drop in six minutes from—*now*. Remember the wide gap on these lines; is your intervalometer reset?"

"It is now. Thanks. Maria, any more jolts?"

"Yes, but nothing to send me off the floor."

"And nothing to shear the tunnel?" asked Belvew.

There was a brief pause while the digger looked back along the bore. "Nothing I can see inside. Ginger, can you see anything funny ahead? The sky looks paler than a couple of minutes ago, at least the little bit I can see through the entrance."

"Nothing shows from here. Not even the crater yet. The sky from here is the usual orange-tan, or whatever you like to call it, with the usual cumulus presumably about over the lake. Maybe you're seeing that."

"Maybe, though that shouldn't be the right direction. I can check that out later. I'll dig until I have to rest again, or until there's some other reason to go outside. Everything here seems solid enough, now that the mud I plastered on the ceiling has all fallen back down. The real shocks seem to have stopped, but there's a fairly steady continuing vibration."

"Keep an eye on the tunnel mouth," Gene suggested. "If the motion along that fault reverses, you could be in a tight spot."

"Why should it do that? Do they ever?"

"Ask me again when I know why it's there at all—I mean in detail; we already know Titan can build mountains."

"And why should I worry? I have the digger with me, and there's only a few meters of ice overhead."

"You can't go straight up. I doubt if you can slant up at twenty degrees. That reads *quite* a few meters of new tunnel if you have to dig out. Think time, not distance—Commander."

"Right. Thanks. I have about twenty-four hours to go in this suit before tapping emergency storage, and two after that."

"And that includes two or three to get up here, depending on when you start. At least take your rest breaks outside."

"We should have built recharging equipment into the jets," remarked Martucci.

"There are a lot of things we'd have done if we'd known enough." Anyone, including Peter himself, could have made remarks to that effect, and most of them did; Seichi beat the rest by a split second. There was silence for a few minutes while Maria continued to chip ice and Ginger's aircraft approached Settlement Crater.

"Twenty seconds to first drop. You're on heading, assuming no wind," Peter announced at last.

"A Titan hurricane wouldn't make that much difference. I've set start and interval—there goes the first!"

"Can you see the crater yet?"

"Not at thirty-plus kilometers. I'd guess visibility about ten or twelve, ordinary for this height. I'd rather not play with wavelengths while I fly a line; you're all getting the same picture, though. Some of you can try for more penetration."

Again Seichi was first; he had probably been scanning the spectrum before Ginger made her suggestion.

"I have the crater. You're headed all right, Major. There's something funny there, though."

"What?" Again several voices overlapped.

"A very low cloud, I'd say, nearly white in this wave band. It has a very sharp, straight edge on the west side, running almost north and south. It starts about a kilometer south and three west of the lake, less than a K from the near rim, and runs nearly straight north into the northwest wall. It's interrupted there, but resumes and continues for at least one crater diameter—seven kilos or so—outside. The cloud itself is about two or three kilos wide, though the east side is a lot less sharp. It fades out pretty well by the time it reaches the north-south diameter of the ring, so I can see the lake all right. That may be what's lightening your sky, Maria."

"Should I investigate, or lay out the cans first?"

"The cans." Status's voice of course showed no emotion, but the answer came quickly enough to *sound* emphatic. Maria had been about to say the same.

"That's three quarters of an hour at standard. Maria—Commander—maybe you should go outside and at least take a look," suggested Belvew. "The only low clouds I've ever seen here are cumulus, formed over lakes and raining back into them or near them, and those clouds weren't as low as the major described. This shows no connection with the lake."

"Status?" Maria uttered the one word.

"Sergeant Belvew is probably right. There is a good chance you can obtain useful data by going west."

"And a better chance of your living though the next big shock." Gene made no effort to keep the words to himself, but no one else commented on them. Not even the commander.

She kept the chipper with her as she leaned forward twenty

degrees to Titan walking attitude and started back up the tunnel. The visible area of sky increased as she approached the entrance, but to her surprise she could distinguish no ground even when she was within a few meters of the opening and her line of sight over the sill was clearly downward. Surely the cliff hadn't . . .

There was nothing but the vaguely orange-tinted gray, much lighter than the familiar color produced by the suspended smog—tar—particles constantly forming high above.

Only when she was outside and several meters from the scarp did the regular orange-tan become visible to the east, beyond the cliff edge. Overhead and to the west the color paled steadily until, looking toward where the horizon should be, there was only a featureless and impenetrable near-white.

"I can see it now. It's moving. It's blowing from west to east," came Ginger's voice. "There must be some wind. Can you tell, Maria?"

The commander took a gloveful of the ice dust which had been blown from the tunnel, raised it to helmet level, faced south, and let it spill from her palm.

"Yes. Not much, even for Titan, but the air's moving east. More to the point, the surface west of me has been covered with something; it's almost white, too. That's why I thought I couldn't see the ground from inside the tunnel. It's as near as no matter to the same color and brightness as the sky in that direction."

"Are you still feeling vibrations?" asked Status.

Maria paused before answering. "Yes. I'm getting used to them, I'm afraid; I may not be able to give an objective report about them before long."

"I suggest you walk slowly westward, looking for changes in visibility and thickness of the white ground covering as you go, Commander."

"All right."

"Hold it!" It was Gene, of course. "If visibility goes down too far, how do you keep track of direction?"

"You can be observed and guided from the jet, and if necessary from orbit," the computer pointed out. There could have been no insult intended in its use of "you" rather than "she," since Maria was the logical person for Status to address, but Belvew felt snubbed just the same.

"I've started," was the commander's only comment.

A human being fully equipped with environment gear can make a standing broad jump of four or five meters on Titan, if he doesn't care which way up he lands. A walker reasonably careful about keeping helmet upward and at least one foot toward the ground will take nearly a second to complete a one-meter stride.

This is about four kilometers an hour, considerably less than the speed of a healthy young adult on Earth. The difference is not in spite of the low gravity on the satellite, but because of it.

There were relatively few healthy young adults on Earth and still fewer on Titan, but Maria could make reasonable speed by her colleagues' standards. She started westward, wondering what walking for a few hours would do to her oxygen consumption and wishing the station would rise even though she wouldn't be able to see it. Not all its sensors could be used reliably through the relays, and some could not be thus employed at all. It would have been nice to have a towering, highly visible mountain like that near Factory One in sight.

It occurred to her that Factory Two, west of the lake but well south of her present course, should also be checked; the tremors might have affected it. Without asking for advice, she announced what she was doing and turned south-southwest. She was assured from the station that the factory was behaving normally for its age, but she went on anyway. A kilometer and a half could be spared, even if one measured it in terms of time and oxygen, and it would be a relief to be sure.

The structure was so far operating normally, but a new Collos patch about five meters across had appeared two hundred meters away, roughly halfway between factory and lake.

Maria reported it as calmly as she could, without making any comparison with the Factory One event, and turned west again.

13

SNOW

BY THE TIME GINGER had finished laying the seismic detectors, Maria was nearing what Seichi had described as the west edge of the cloud. By this time she felt sure, and had reported, that it consisted of solid particles far too small to see individually, but dense enough to settle quickly even here. The stuff now formed a layer two to three centimeters deep under her feet, hiding the smog sediment beneath. The latter might have extended for as much deeper, or a whole meter, or fifty meters, or not been there at all. Its thickness, they now knew, varied widely over Titan's surface. It had been moved—drifted?—extensively during the aeons, settling very slowly as near-molecular dust. Even Titan's feeble winds could move it easily until it finally caked in the methane rains—which did not fall everywhere. This, at least, was the general consensus, which had been through much GO6 processing.

The most reasonable guess at the white stuff's identity was water ice, but no one had suggested a plausible origin for it. This was only partly because of earlier experience with other observed white powders.

Ginger, her run finished, had made another low, slow pass to spot the new Collos patch the commander had reported and attempt to drop a lab on it. She had missed by nearly a hundred meters, but that was acceptable. The device had survived the fall even without a parachute, and diSabato was now steering it toward its target.

Status had been told to maintain a running comparison between its readings once it arrived and those of the one stationed where Goodall had performed his last experiment.

Ginger was now flying perhaps imprudently low along the west edge of the cloud, but she could make out no details. It was Maria who got the first good-enough look at the source to feed hungry imaginations.

Afterward, she could not deny that there had been some warning. A gradually increasing roar, which she had unthinkingly attributed to *Theia,* and a steady, faint quivering of the surface underfoot, which she soon tuned out, might have alerted her.

Quite abruptly, within the space of a few steps, she found herself seeing the familiar near-orange sky in all directions overhead. The dense white mist now reached only to her shoulders, swirling gently around her body in what passed for a high wind here; thinner, more transparent fluff still reached several meters above her, but she could see a horizon of sorts. A few meters ahead, beyond the drifting white, the ground showed in its usual patchy smog color, about the same tint as the sky but much darker except where bare patches of ice were exposed. A few such patches could be seen from where she stood.

Her eyes had just registered that the surface ahead was lower than the one she was walking on when her feet made the same discovery. She had stepped over the edge of another fault.

The fall would have been only about a meter if she had simply fallen. Instead, she was hurled upward by a blast of wind, not violently and not far before starting down; but she made an almost complete back somersault, landing mostly on her shoulders on a bare patch of ice. Her helmet took some of the impact, and for an instant she felt an intense, terrifying chill, which fortunately proved to be subjective.

She brought herself upright with a push of her left hand and looked around.

She had left the vision-hampering cloud. Westward, as she had seen before stepping over the edge, the bare ground extended to the crater wall half a kilometer away. To the east was the smooth vertical

step, a meter or so high, which she had failed to see in time. Its face
was almost totally hidden by roiling streams of white which spewed,
also vertically, from a narrow crack at its base. Maria started to approach it, remembered the upward kick, became conscious of the
roar, and stopped to report before getting any closer.

"I'm out of the cloud, Ginger. Can you see me? There's another
fault here, vertical, with something blowing up at its edge. It's the
source of the cloud, I'd say; there seems to be nothing more of it to
the west. My best guess is still ice dust, but we need labs here
pronto."

"I'm a couple of minutes north of the rim, too far to see you. I
still have labs aboard; I left only one at the new patch. How many
should I drop?"

"I'd say two—one just inside the cloud, one on my side of the
edge. There's a fair amount of snow, if that's what the white stuff
is, on the ground to the east; it shouldn't take long to get samples.
This side looks like ordinary titan, but we'd better make sure." The
commander stopped talking and listened.

"Coming around, five hundred up . . . I see you. I'll slow down
as much as I can. The labs don't have parachutes—should I land
and plant them properly?"

"Take another chance with them from where you are," Belvew
advised. "The one a few minutes ago made it, and they're more
replaceable than *Theia*."

The commander agreed, adding, "Don't get down too close to
stall—any kind of stall—and don't get below five hundred. There's
an updraft at the fault strong enough to pick me up. Drop toward
the west; that's into what wind there is and will take a little from
the impact's horizontal component, at least."

"All right." The commander watched the jet bank overhead and
thunder eastward over the whiteness. Its deeper sound, she now
realized, could easily be distinguished from the whistle of gas from
the crevice. After dwindling for a minute it swung back, heading not
exactly toward her but a little to her left.

"I don't suppose there's much chance of damaging you with

either of these," the pilot said conversationally, "but let's plan for a clear miss."

"I could dodge, or shelter near the cliff, but thanks for the thought. Are you dropping on this pass?"

"Yes." The craft swelled in the commander's field of vision and the thunder of its ramjets made parts of Maria's suit vibrate. Ginger was not risking a stall even of the pipes, much less the wings, and of course didn't want to waste mass by using rocket mode. The commander saw the two black dots separate from the hull scarcely a second apart; the pilot seemed to have confidence in her bombing skill.

It was justified. The first lab vanished into the cloud sixty or seventy meters east of the fault, and the second struck a little farther west of where Maria was standing. It rolled to a stop about fifty meters northwest of her. She moved quickly toward it and watched with relief as it extended its sampling appendages and got to work.

"Someone read those as fast as you can, especially the one in the snow," she ordered.

"I'm handling it," came the voice of Seichi Yakama, who was gradually, with the help of Status's memory, working his way into Goodall's former niche. "It'll be a few minutes."

"Right. If it's something weird like the vinyl in the pools let's find out the first time." The voice, to the surprise of some, was Ginger's rather than Gene's.

"Commander, can you provide more data on this cloud-emitting fault?" queried Status. "It is impossible so far to set up a coherent picture. Specifically, can you judge the width of the opening and flow rate of the escaping gas?"

"I'll try. It was fast enough to lift me, though not very far. If Ginger will make a wind run you may be able to figure out something from how high the stuff rises before it gets blown east."

"All right. That'll be a few minutes, too," replied the pilot. Maria stood still; she was presumably the most visible small surface object in the area, and Ginger might want to use her as a reference marker. Even if she didn't, moving was becoming hard work; another spell of fatigue was approaching, she judged. It didn't matter much; she could examine the fault from where she stood.

"The crack at the foot of the step is very narrow, not more than a millimeter or two," she reported. "Right where it opens, the cloud is too dense to let me see through it, except in glimpses. A few centimeters higher it thins out, and I can see turbulence in the gas currents."

"What's the face of the scarp show?" asked Seichi.

"Plain ice up to about seventy-five centimeters, then smog sediment, then a couple of centimeters of white—I suppose the same stuff that makes the cloud. Whoever is running it, when you get a chance walk the lab that's in the cloud westward—no, forget it. I'll pick up the other and put it on the top at the edge."

Not even Belvew remembered the updraft soon enough. Maria herself was not lifted this time, but felt the trivial weight of the spheroid she was carrying disappear as she was about to place it on the white rim. A moment later she gave a grunt of surprise, which naturally produced a response from Gene.

"What's happening?"

"More trivia," was the calm answer. "The lab was lifted out of my hand as I started to put it past the edge. Now it's bobbing around in the air about six or eight centimeters above the cliff and about a meter to the right of where I was reaching in. It's oscillating about ten centimeters each way north and south, about three east and west, and about the same up and down. I've seen that sort of thing before, of course; I just wasn't expecting it."

"What? Oh, Bernoulli effect." Belvew's pilot experience responded to the description. "Status, there's the information you need about the updraft speed. You know the mass, area, and shape of the lab."

"I will have to assume the gas density is the same as that of the general atmosphere," the robot pointed out. "It probably is, that far above the vent, if the commander is right about the turbulence. She has just over twenty hours to suit-emergency status; she has been using more oxygen than usual."

No one was particulary surprised at Status's sudden change of subject, considering its built-in priorities.

"Thank you," Maria acknowledged. "Should I put the lab in the snow, or leave it where it is while you run a gas analysis?"

"The gas, by all means." It was Seichi who answered. "That'll let us check Status's guess. I have some readings from the other lab now, but I don't understand them all."

"What's the trouble?" came several voices.

"The elements in the white stuff are hydrogen and oxyen and nothing else. It should be water, ice I at this pressure, but shows no crystal structure at all. There's just a diffraction blur corresponding to H-O bond length—"

"How about oxygen-oxygen?" Again several voices sounded almost at once.

"It is *not* hydrogen peroxide. No O-O bonds, single or double or hybrid. I said it showed *no* structure, just an average molecular spacing, like a liquid or a gas." The pro-tem chemist's tone, and even his voice, for a moment took on a surprising similarity to those of Arthur Goodall; once again Maria felt a chill not due to her surroundings.

"You have no ideas right now," she said, trying to keep any questioning intonation out of her voice.

"Not right now. I'm running the gas analysis. Do you need that, or shall I just tell Status?"

"File it." Maria made the latter choice promptly. "It's probably pure local atmosphere even if the white stuff is water, considering water's vapor pressure here.

"But I should be doing something besides listening. Status, will it be better for me to go back to digging, or should I explore along this new fault? My guess is that it would be better to let you build pictures from the new seismic lines before we run that tunnel any deeper."

"The fault can be mapped adequately from above," the processor answered promptly. "The cliff in which we started the tunnel is now partly obscured by the cloud, and it would be valuable to check any of its recent changes. There is reason to believe now that these may become quite rapid. I suggest you go back to the east but make no attempt to seek the tunnel itself. You still have the digger, I believe. Rather, bear to the south—"

"Why not the north? Wouldn't the region of the crater rim give us more information?"

"It probably would, but that would take you farther from any practical landing area, especially if the cloud continues to move eastward. I have just reminded you of the limitations of your suit."

"You don't think the information would be worth the risk?"

"No." The answer was in Status's calm voice; Belvew, to the surprise of the commander and several others, said nothing.

"All right. Ginger, have you had time to make the wind check? Is it all right for me to move?"

"I wasn't using you. There are places along the fault where there are fountains, if that's the word I want—anyway, the stuff isn't blowing up equally high everywhere, so I had plenty of reference points; and for one component I Dopplered on the cliff face. Your wind is seventy-one point one centimeters a second from azimuth two-eighty-four. Practically a hurricane by Titan standards; don't let yourself get blown away."

"All right. Status, you can fit that in. I'm jumping the face—I'm being careful, Gene—and heading east. Ginger, get whatever Status asks for that you can manage without risking the plane. Between its requests, just map. Pete, track me. There's no profit in my walking around in circles. There must be some radiation that can see through this stuff—after all, I was never out of voice contact while I was in it."

"Right, boss. Any reading will take a minute or two; I'll have to average half a dozen. If you want a direction it'll take even longer, but I don't think there's any chance of losing you."

"Neither does Status, apparently, or I'd have been sent south around the cloud. I won't need direction for a while; I can look back at my own tracks in the snow and tell whether I'm circling."

"Have you checked that, or is it extrapolation?" asked Belvew.

"The latter. Stand by a minute. I'm about to jump the cliff, and want to give it all my attention in case the updraft tips me. I'd rather land on my hands than my helmet." There were a few seconds of silence. "It was neither, and I'm back on my feet. I'm checking the footprint prediction now. . . . It seems valid."

"Your tracks aren't being blown out by the wind?"

"Not for as far back as I can see."

"Which is how far?"

"Twenty or thirty meters. That should improve as I get farther from the source and the cloud thins."

Gene said nothing to this, but Maria was not the only one who realized how the word "should," which she had carefully not emphasized, was affecting him. She suspected that Martucci was not the only operator tracking her, and hoped Belvew's regular work, or possibly his recreation, wouldn't suffer. She hadn't known that he, too, enjoyed reading classics. There was another GO against dividing attention when doing certain jobs, but she couldn't recall either its number or all the items on its list.

On Earth, being lost in a blizzard has been deadly to many explorers of the planet's mountains and pole caps. It has even killed blissfully ignorant and ordinarily competent people engaged in casual amusement within a few kilometers or even a few meters of safety.

Maria Collos was not ignorant and was well over a billion kilometers from anything like a really safe place, but she felt no actual terror. She didn't expect to see Earth again anyway; there had been nothing surprising in Barn Inger's death, nor in Arthur Goodall's except his own cooperation with it, or any of the earlier ones. There would be nothing surprising in hers when it came, though she hoped this would not be until she had done something else really useful— and learned a little more, of course.

In any case, although she was immersed in weather and could see little but blowing whiteness, she did not consider herself lost. Not just yet. Hiking a hundred meters, turning and looking back to see that her trail was straight, and repeating the process for several kilometers was more boring than immediately useful, but every investigator lives with this. Status's occasional personal report such as "You now have nineteen hours before emergency status" slightly relieved the boredom but was not otherwise helpful. This was also true of the occasional seismic shocks, two of which in the first hour were violent enough to throw her off her feet.

There had to be something odd going on. The area of the first factory had experienced nothing similar in the weeks since its planting, unless the new tar pool counted. Barn Inger's death had occurred there, but could not be blamed on quakes. Goodall's had occurred *here*, in Settlement Crater, but there was surely no connection—

No. Definitely none. None that Maria Collos could see, or that anyone else had suggested.

The white dust thinned as she drew farther from its source, and the sky started to show a trace of its natural color, though the wind seemed unchanged. The thickness of the white deposit underfoot, determined by scraping down to the substrate with a boot, had decreased to about a centimeter.

Her back, she suddenly noticed, felt warmer than her front. That was odd; the wind was mostly from behind her. If her suit's temperature-balancing gear wasn't on the job her back should be *colder*, and if it was there should be no difference. Another trivium— perhaps. There was little else to think about, so she considered the problem for a time.

"The new lines spot four more faults on the crater floor in the last hour," came diSabato's voice. "All of them run nearly north and south, all are vertical, and radar says the high side faces west. The tunnel scarp is now half a meter higher."

"How about the tunnel itself?" asked Maria.

"Can't tell. No sign of collapse of the region above it. Maybe you should slant north and see."

"Status? Relative value of such information?"

"Low. You should keep on your present track. Changes around the lake and Arthur's Pool will probably be comparably important, and you will remain closer to possible pickup sites."

"Have any changes been seen?"

"The lake's area has decreased slightly, a little less than one percent. Arthur's Pool is changing color; its long-wave reflectivity is increasing."

"How about the new patch? Has the lab told us anything? Has either its size or shape changed?"

"Its composition is not quite identical with that of the one near the factory or, as far as the limited data show, the one by Lake Carver where Sergeant Belvew landed. The differences among these are small. The ones between them and Arthur's Pool seem significant, but can probably be attributed to his own contribution. The differences became observable shortly after his death and have been increasing since."

Nobody asked just what the differences might be.

Maria did ask more about changes in the central lake.

"It is now shrinking slowly. It may be relevant that the cumulus cloud normally over it has drifted nearly to the east side of the ringwall. This is probably why the rain ceased while you were digging; it is now falling partly on the eastern slopes of the feature, and some of the liquid must be draining to the outside."

"Keep track of the lake's changes, and the flow in the various streams which empty into it, any way you can. Report any correlation you can detect between the flow and the lake area."

"*And* the depth of deposit of this snowstorm, if we can call it that, over different parts of the crater floor," cut in Belvew. "You can probably measure it by radar reflectivity."

"I'll try that in different wave bands and tell you," replied Martucci.

Maria scraped the white stuff to one side with a boot until the darker surface showed. "It's thicker now. There's just over five centimeters here, if you can use the figure for checking anything," she reported.

The processor acknowledged the information but didn't thank her. The commander kept on walking.

14

STRATA

ARTHUR'S SUIT HASN'T reappeared, or anything like that, has it?"

"No. It's a change in the general surface, not just a small spot affecting the average. Ginger could fly there in a few seconds and report what she can see from near at hand."

"All right." The pilot didn't wait for confirmation. "Maria, you're keeping direction well enough; you don't really need either me or Pete."

"Have *you* been watching me too? I thought you were mapping the crater."

"Between times. It wasn't just radar that spotted the new faults. Status, I can't see any difference in the lake, but your memory is better than mine. The cumulus cloud has moved, as you said earlier, and the rain is over to the east."

"Can you see Arthur's Pool?"

"Yes, but the color seems the same to me. Look, all of you use your screens. The whole floor of this crater is acting up. There's a scarp to the southwest that certainly wasn't there when I arrived, and one extending a little way from the south rim spitting white stuff like the one Maria just visited. No wonder you've been feeling jolts."

"Are all the faults running north and south?" asked Belvew.

"Pretty much, so far. Maybe I'd better land and get Maria off the ground while there's ground left."

"There's no hurry about that," insisted the commander. "You can't land in the fog where I am now; it'll have to be down by the lake as usual, and you're not to do that until I'm nearly there. Besides, I need to look at the pool—how about more samples from there right now, Seichi? Or have you been keeping track already?"

"There are lots of samples analyzed and filed," was the answer. "I don't know the details myself; I've been doing them, not thinking about them."

"Status?"

"There has been a steady increase of complex organics in the pool. Material presumably from Commander Goodall's body and armor seems to have been diffusing at a rate much higher than the temperature would render likely. Whether this can be the cause of the color change is uncertain; their two rates do not match at all closely."

Again, if any of the group felt discomfort at this calm report, none made it audible. Once a friend was gone, his body was a data source; one remembered *him*, not his flesh or his face. At least Goodall's experiment was providing data as he had hoped.

Maria thought a moment before speaking.

"We have a lab at the other pool here in the crater. Does it show anything happening there?"

"No. No significant change."

"How about the ones near the factory—the one here?"

"The small changes I mentioned earlier. So far of no apparent significance."

"Check all these change rates, and any which come up from now on, against probable effects of electron tunneling. Anything interesting from the seismic net?"

"Yes. There seems to be a body of liquid below the crater, its horizontal cross section about three times the crater area at one hundred twenty kilometers depth. Its top is at a depth of fifty-three kilometers, its bottom at least one hundred fifty. The resolution decreases with increasing depth, but should improve with time."

"Maria, get out of there! Get off the ground! That's got to be a magma plume!"

"More likely water, Gene. Are you asking Ginger to land beside me in this fog?"

"Well, no. But hurry down to the lake, and remember water *is* magma here!"

"The commander has eighteen point five hours before emergency status," the processor interjected.

"So who's worrying about your suit?" snapped Belvew. "That crater's trying to become a volcano. Eighteen hours could see its floor all cut up with faults or covered with fog or with supercooled water ready to freeze around you or a landing ship."

"Is any sort of prediction possible, Status?" Maria was not quite as calm as she tried to keep her voice.

"Not from present data. The liquid may be the source of the fog, but I have found no trace so far of a feed from the depths to either of the fog sources. The probability that both the fog and the liquid are water seems high, in spite of the lack of ice crystal structure in the former."

"I can make a guess at that," lePing cut in. "The gas coming out of that crack is mostly nitrogen, with a healthy trace of methane. Its temperature at the height where the lab is bobbing is about a hundred and ten. I suggest the white stuff is water, carried up from the magma chamber, showing no crystal structure either because it cooled so fast when it got outside that it's a glass, or because the drops are so small that surface tension keeps them liquid. Either would explain the lack of structure."

"Maybe it would explain something else," the commander put in, using a tone that bothered Belvew.

"What's that?"

"I've just been knocked down by another shock—"

"Why didn't you tell us, or at least Status?"

"Because it's becoming routine. I landed on my back as usual, and this time rolled over to push up with my hands instead of my elbows. The white stuff is sticking to the front of my armor, I see; and I think it must have been sticking to the back for quite a while. That part has been feeling surprisingly warm for the last half hour or more. I can't see or reach my back, but I bet the stuff's there, too. It could be not only acting as insulation but providing heat as it really freezes—crystallizes.''

"Why should it freeze?" asked Martucci.

"Loss of spherical shape would drop the surface tension and the pressure," said Carla. "Ask Gene why rime ice forms on wings—"

"Of course, but theory later," cut in the commander. "I'm pretty well covered by the stuff now. It sticks, whatever the cause. At least it's not interfering with my walking."

"It's interfering with something else."

"What's that, Pete?"

"I can't see you anymore—at least, I can't distinguish you from the rest of the white stuff, from the station. I hope you're still having no trouble with your trail."

Maria made no direct answer to this, but gave an order which Belvew naturally interpreted as one.

"Ginger, get down to one hundred meters and circle over the area where I should be. Look for me as carefully as you can without risking the jet with low speed, and if the white stuff is higher than a hundred don't go into it. Even if you didn't lose visual contact Carla might be right about the ice. Call out if and when you see me. I'll keep moving, which should help."

"Does that mean you *can't* see your back trail?" asked Belvew.

"I can see it, but not as far back as before."

"Is the fog getting thicker?"

"I can't tell. There's nothing *but* the trail that shows at all in this white fluff. It may be heavier fog or faster filling-in of my tracks by wind or some of both."

"Then travel! Get as far as you can as fast as you can! Try to get out of the fog before you lose orientation entirely."

"That's what I'm doing. But there's a limit to my speed, remember. If I try to run, I automatically jump, and if I jump there's a very good chance I don't land on my feet. That doesn't help either speed or orientation—I hear you, Ginger. You're almost overhead. I caught a glimpse of you; this stuff can't be as dense as it looks. You went not quite overhead. I was a little on your right."

"How long was that before you spoke?"

"Two or three seconds before I reported hearing you I caught the glimpse."

"Good. I'll be coming back over that point in sixty seconds from—*now*. I'll be heading straight toward the lake."

"You can still see that? The fog hasn't blown over it yet?"

"Not enough to hide it. I'm turning. Can you still hear me?"

"Yes. Lucky this isn't Earth; in a blizzard like this the wind would never let me hear anything else."

"On Earth we wouldn't be this worried about you," snapped Belvew.

"In a blizzard? You'd better read about Scott and Shackleton. Even Earth isn't always a really nice place. Ginger, you're coming—*now*! Right overhead!"

"Good. You're only about thirteen hundred meters from the lake, and should be able to see your way in half that. Can you hold your heading now? Should I go back to filling in geography-time derivatives for Status, or would it be best to keep near you and give you direction every minute or two?"

"Work on the data." Maria spoke firmly, but not loudly enough to drown out the start of an answer from Gene. He failed to finish the first word, but no one doubted its general flavor.

"All right." The roar of the ramjets faded, and Maria resumed her hike. Her suit was beginning to feel a little stiff, presumably because of the accumulation of whatever-it-was at the joints. She turned her mind firmly from that phenomenon, and asked Status to update her on seismic information as she walked.

"There has been no major change, though finer details are being added. The new can lines are providing much data in spite of their wider spacing. The magma or water reservoir is as I described it before. I can now trace the crack which is feeding gas to the vent

line you examined, but not to the new one the major reported. Six
more such faults exist, their lower ends starting at the liquid body.
They outline a vertical prism but have not yet reached the surface.
Practically all the activity is under the crater; it may be that the
impact itself has some connection with what is going on.''

"That would suggest that it's very recent," Maria commented.

"Quite possibly. However, there is little difference in the average
thickness of the smog sediment inside and out, so either the crater
is quite old or the general surface is being reworked much faster
than we have supposed.''

"Status," Gene cut in, "tell us more about those six feeder faults.
Where are they? Are they *changing*—getting any closer to the surface?''

"They are much shorter horizontally than any of the others.
Projected upward they intersect to frame the lake and immediately
surrounding area in a rough hexagon or, in three dimensions, to
place it at the top of a rough prism. I can give you precise edge and
depth coordinates if you wish. They are extending fairly rapidly, and
will reach the surface in approximately eight hours at their present
upward rate. I cannot tell which side of the resulting surface dis-
placements will be the higher, though pressure considerations suggest that the prism will rise; I have no reliable way to infer other
stresses from the behavior of the seismic waves.''

"But there's a good chance that the whole lake area will lift up
on a six-sided platform in the next few hours," the commander
mused.

"Or sink. A chance, certainly. It would not be a reliable prediction.''

"What would that do to available landing space?''

"That is already decreasing, assuming a two-hundred-meter
landing slide. If these faults extend straight to the surface it will be
necessary to land farther to the north or south than before, if we
continue to use east and west approaches. Any other run direction
would have to be farther from the lake.''

"And from the commander?''

"Yes."

"Hear that, Maria?"

"Of course I heard it. I'm hurrying. I still think it's important to get a good look at Arthur's Pool."

"Do it from the air! Get out of that crater as fast as you can—Commander!"

"As long as I'm heading near it anyway, let's not argue. I assume, Status, that the tunnel is no longer of primary importance. How about the general plan to move to the surface?"

"That will have to be dropped until a new settlement site is found. The crater is now unsuitable."

"And Arthur's—uh—experiment is wasted?" asked Ginger.

"Not necessarily. The area is supplied with labs, and we can keep track of what happens there unless it and they are all destroyed. Even that could be informative."

"Then I should land as close as possible to that spot."

"Not until I get there and tell you to!" snapped Maria. "The jet is less expendable than I am right now; you know it."

"I know it, but I don't believe it. Are you able to see any better yet?"

"A little. And you believe it, all right; you just don't like it. I'm having to move more slowly, though; the knees of this suit are getting stiff. I suppose no one can see me yet; I must be pretty well covered with this stuff, and there still aren't any bare spots I could stand on for contrast."

"I'll come back and make another pass. You should be getting out of that cloud by this time. There—I'm heading where you ought to be. Can you hear me?"

"Not yet. Where are you?"

"Just crossing the south rim, inbound," answered Ginger. "Half a minute should bring me about over you. I'm at standard."

The commander waited briefly. She heard the jet in a few seconds, looked up in the hope of seeing it, and just barely succeeded.

"You're a couple of hundred meters off. I'm to your right—*now!*"

"You haven't held course, Maria. How about using the wind? It's still from the west, and I can see the stuff blowing."

"Too turbulent to be useful this close to the ground. I'd thought of that. Getting knocked off my feet, and I suppose picking up more covering, every few minutes doesn't help."

"You know where she is. Pick her up now!" cried Belvew.

"Stop thinking of that!" Maria had never sounded so much like a commander. "Make another pass over me, or as nearly over me as you can, Ginger, heading as straight as you can for Arthur's Pool. You can still see it, can't you?"

"Sure. All right, coming back. Call when I'm closest, and tell me which side you're on and how far if you can. I'll be a minute or so with the turn. All right?"

Silence.

"All right?"

Silence.

"All right?"

Maria couldn't answer. She was off the ground again, totally disoriented. She snapped both hands above her helmet to protect it in case she landed head downward, and ignored Ginger's increasingly frantic calls until she struck the surface again.

Her heels touched first, with her body extending back and up at about forty-five degrees. On Earth she would have slammed down on the back of her helmet; on Titan the rest of the fall took well over a second and she had plenty of time to spin cat-style and land on her hands. A medium-hard one-handed push-up brought her back on her feet; she felt a fleeting glow of pride that she hadn't overdone it—much. One short backward step kept her from falling the other way.

"I'm all right. I got tossed around by another quake. I don't know whether you passed me then or not."

"I must have. I'm halfway to the rim—Maria! My screen shows a new cloud erupting all around the lake! Is it blocking your sight?"

"The eight-hour prediction was extremely inaccurate," Status interrupted, "but the qualitative extrapolation offered by Sergeant

Belvew was very good. The lake is now near the north rim of a hexagonal area well marked by fume-emitting faults. It will take a minute or more to determine the new height of the area. The lake itself has shown no significant change in shape or area. If Major Xalco will try once more to find the commander—"

"Is that area big enough for landing?" and "Is the pool inside the prism?" came Belvew's and Maria's interruptions simultaneously. Status untangled the sound patterns, though none of the human listeners could. The processor answered the commander first.

"The pool is inside the area described, though quite close to the northeast corner. It has not been visibly affected by shock. It may be possible with care to land the jet within the hexagon. I would advise landing slightly north of westward, touching down as near the southern east corner as the pilot's skill permits."

"Take it, Gene," Ginger called promptly.

"Not yet. Finish your run. We need to know whether Maria's inside the hexagon, too. If she isn't, and the boundary is hard to cross for any reason—remember how she got blown into the air at the other place—we *don't* want to land there."

"Right. Give me the call, Maria, if and when. Here I should be coming."

"I hear you but can't see you. The fog's a lot thicker, I'm afraid."

"Not even a glimpse?"

"No."

"Any guess at the direction of my sound?"

"Not in armor."

"Shall I make another pass?"

"No use, I'd say. If the new fog allows, you might go as low as seems safe over the hexagon and help Status find out if it's higher or lower than the rest of the floor. I'd guess it dropped, or rather that the outside rose—I was tossed upward again."

"You're assuming you're outside."

"Yes, Gene. Unless my earlier position was wildly off or I got tossed several hundred meters, which I'm sure I wasn't, I *have* to be north of it still."

"I suppose so. All right, just go on, I guess. You can see your track still, can't you?"

"As a matter of fact, no. The snow seems to have been tossed around too, I'm afraid."

Not even Status had an immediate answer for this. After some seconds, Belvew asked, "Can you see the tracks you make right now—after the shock?"

Maria experimented—the answer seemed obvious, but she was taking no chances of being surprised by another trivium—and answered affirmatively.

"All right, just start walking, and keep a straight line as you did before, I'd say. If you're lucky and get into clear air, fine. Sooner or later you'll have moved far enough so Ginger can get some idea of distance and direction from when you can hear her pass over, even if that doesn't give much resolving power. Can anyone think of anything quicker? Staying put certainly won't accomplish anything."

Maria admitted this, and decided not to mention that the joints of her armor were getting stiffer. There would be time enough for the others to face that worry if and when she was actually immobilized. It would have been nice, she reflected as she started to walk, if she had had a rope, or a few meters of wire, or something like that to drag behind her. Even if that were tossed off the ground, it would have to fall back somewhere near its original position.

Theia boomed overhead, and the commander reported the sound as soon as it started to fade. Two minutes later she heard it again, this time with a fainter maximum, and she passed on this information as well. The third time was fainter still.

"All right, I think I have you fairly well boxed," came Belvew's voice—he had evidently taken over the jet. "Just keep traveling, and report any sort of change you catch. You're about where we thought, only a few hundred meters from the nearest of the new faults."

"You said they were putting out fog too. I can't see any difference in the vision range yet—of course, I don't really have much idea of how far I'm seeing. I *think* I hear something besides the jet, though."

"What?"

"It's like the deep whistle of the stuff coming from that other fault, but that may not be objective. Keep your fingers crossed, those of your who aren't flying. I'm still walking." The last statement was not a complete truth: her armor was continuing to get stiffer, and the walk was becoming a totter.

But she did manage to keep moving. Twice in the next few minutes she was thrown off her feet. Three times in the same interval the jet thundered past near enough to let her give Belvew some sort of direction report. The last time he was able to be encouraging.

"Stay with it, boss! You're only a hundred meters or so from the north face of the prism. If it rose, you should see it. If it went down, r-e-a-lly watch your step!"

"It went up. I see it. It's not plain ice, Status. It's alternate white and dark layers of different thicknesses. Half a meter of smog at the top, a few centimeters of white—ice I, I suppose—it looks like the face at the quarry, a little—more tar, more ice—four layers with a total thickness of ten or a dozen meters, mostly dark stuff. Y'know, with fifty or sixty drill cores inside and outside it, I bet we could *date* this crater!"

"Someone get pictures!" Mastro's voice sounded frantic; lePing, younger and much junior in rank, managed to control herself and only asked quietly, "Have you time to use your suit camera, Commander?"

"It's on, but I can't be sure its view field is clear. Is anything coming through?"

"Just the fact that you've been tossed into the air again and aren't down yet," Martucci answered dryly. "I grant the importance of dating, but—"

"I'm getting up on that thing," Maria cut in. "Plan your landing, Sergeant."

15

SHAVE

ALL RIGHT, COMMANDER. Where do I land?"

"No wonder I was tossed around, even if the prism went up more than I did. Your hexagon is over two meters above the rest of the floor, at least on this side." Maria had shifted back to reporting as though she hadn't heard Belvew. "I wonder whether this is something common here, or whether Arthur just picked a very bad spot."

"It will take the detailed review you ordered of the worldwide mapping records to tell," Status replied. "This is not yet complete. Nothing of this sort came to anyone's attention earlier, but I was initially instructed to compare albedo changes, not heights."

"You can get up on the new level and check Arthur's Pool in a few minutes," Belvew said, giving up for a moment. "I can't be sure where you hit the edge, but it almost has to be the north face. The pool could be about in front of you, or anywhere up to three or four hundred meters to your right. You'd know it, I suppose, if you were right at a corner."

"I might, but not if the corner was more than a dozen or two meters away. About getting up . . ." The commander's voice trailed off.

"You can jump two meters—or are you worn-out again?" Belvew made no specific reference to Maria's ailment, of course.

"I'm afraid that's not it. This white coating has been stiffening up my joints, including the ones I'd need for brushing some of it off, for quite a while now, enough to make walking difficult. I'll try, but I'm not sure I can jump at all." There was silence from the station while she tried, reported failure, and tried again.

"How about the digger?" asked Pete. "You still have it, don't you?"

"I do, but I'm not using it on my own suit. I can't get up half a meter. Check the pix you have so far. Is there *any* place which looks as though it *might* be anything but a vertical cliff? Surely you can't just push a prism of ice up like this, especially if the ice is effectively rock, without some irregular cracking somewhere."

Again Status took unintended parts of the remark literally. "Not enough is known about the mechanical properties of ice, either crystalline or glass, at these temperatures. Remember how Sergeant Inger was taken unawares by its expansion coefficient, and how much time it took to make sure we could safely hollow out rooms in the surface layers. Our only pictures of this new feature cover the minutes since it formed. There are several irregularities around its perimeter, on all six faces including the north one where you presumably are. If you can still walk, I advise you do so in either direction along the scarp."

"If—" Belvew choked off the exclamation. Then, "I'm setting down. Go left, Maria. It's clearest to the east. You *can* walk, I hope."

"Oh, yes. But we need to check the pool, and should do the lake too, and they're up top."

The jet's roar suddenly became audible over the sound of escaping vapor, then faded again. Belvew continued as though the commander hadn't spoken.

"I *can't* land up there."

"Why not?" came the usual multiple voices.

"The area is just barely wide enough for a landing at all, approaching just above wing stall. At that speed the turbulence from the fog blast—I felt it with the gauges a hundred meters up—as I cross the edge would wreck the plane unless, by pure luck, updrafts under both wings were exactly equal. I know I'm safe up here, but one wing dip is more than enough to kill you. Also, the surface is white stuff, not smog; if it's loose powder, as Maria has been finding, the landing slide may be longer than usual; and going off the edge of that raised area—well, if anyone else wants to risk it, take over and apologize in advance to Maria. *I* don't.''

"I can get down again after I get up," Maria replied calmly. "But don't try to land anywhere until I'm through here and ready to do it. That's an order."

"How do you mean that word 'through'?" Belvew let the question out, and immediately regretted it. Maria had tact as well as firmness, however.

"I think I see at least two ways of getting up," she said, still calmly. "At the other fault, the updraft tossed me off the ground; this one seems a lot stronger. With luck, Bernoulli effect will keep me inside the stream until I get to the top."

"And maybe longer. What will you do hanging a couple of meters out of reach of the ground?" A little to her surprise, the voice was Seichi's, not Gene's. She had to hesitate only a moment before answering.

"I'm a lot bigger and denser than the labs, and can do more about my overall shape. I won't be out of control."

"What's your other idea?" asked Belvew predictably.

"Build a ramp. The snow is three to four centimeters deep."

"How much snow will she have to move, Status?"

"It depends on the angle of repose of the particles, another unknown quantity. Its behavior under Earth conditions is irrelevant; it is sand or dust here, even if it actually is ice chemically. Assuming a twenty-degree repose angle, the volume would be approximately thirty-two cubic meters. If the commander's estimate of snow depth is correct and general, it would require all the snow within a distance of some sixteen meters of the climbing point, assuming no loss of volume to packing or gain to freezing when she builds her ramp. Enough material is apparently available, but the time required to move it without tools may be excessive. This ignores the problem of building against the updraft at the inner side of the ramp. The commander has about eighteen point two hours, extrapolating from the last two hours' consumption, to reach suit-emergency status."

Long before this sentence was finished, Maria had approached the whistling crevice at the base of the scarp. By the time Martucci had pointed out that she could accumulate a large volume quite rapidly by the snowball-rolling technique, and Seichi had reminded him that snow did not self-weld New England style at ninety kelvins, and Martucci had pointed out that water drops kept liquid by pressure most certainly would, she had leaned for the first time as close as she could against the smooth ice face and been hurled backward with satisfying violence.

By the time she had tried again, backing against the wall and pushing as hard as she could with her legs, which was not very hard under Titanian traction conditions, someone else had pointed out that the stuff had at least stuck to the commander's armor, so maybe Martucci was right after all.

Before the argument got any further, Maria interrupted. "What I can see of my armor is now nearly clear of its white coating. I can move quite freely. Something in the vapor stream got rid of it, I guess," she concluded.

"It was hot enough to remelt it and blow the liquid away," Belvew proposed at once.

"The dust particles sandblasted you clear," Seishi came back at once with the GO6 counterhypothesis.

"If they stuck in the first place because of altered surface tension, they'd have just added to the coating this time. It has to be temperature."

"That couldn't have been why they stuck. Surface tension won't hold any size water-drop liquid down at ninety K. And pressure would work the other way on most other things."

Maria again ended the debate without suggesting this was not the time for it; she was interested in the reason herself, but had not needed any of the recent reminders about her suit's depletion or what work had to be done.

"I'm jumping—now!" There was a silence of two or three seconds.

"Make it?" asked Belvew.

"Not quite. High enough, but I bounced off the fan of vapor—it's all right, I was able to land on my feet. It must have been a matter of armor shape; I should have been pulled into the stream."

"Pushed." This was Martucci.

"Don't be a purist. Here I go again . . . I'm in this time. Bouncing around, as someone suggested, a meter or so above the top of the scarp. I can regulate my height with arms and legs—there. Now—blast, up again. I'm oscillating. I can vary the rate and amplitude by reaching—there. Resonance. I'm out, and on the right side. Oops—there's a breeze trying to push me back into the current—"

"I told you so," said Martucci, violating Rule X, which was not military but dated in its original form from sometime before Archimedes. Maria ignored him.

"No traction to speak of—wait, I'm all right—I'm away from it now. The wind is noticeable only within a couple of meters of the edge. You were right, Gene; don't try to land here. The visibility isn't very good, either. I'm heading right to look for the pool."

"It's only about seventy meters," Martucci informed her.

"You can see me?"

"Sure. There's contrast again, now that your whitewash is off. Head along the edge to your right till I tell you to stop, then turn straight away from it and hike about thirty meters. Not too close to the edge; remember that Bernoulli wind."

"Is the seeing worse than outside?" asked Belvew. "That west wind is covering the hexagon with fog, or dust, or whatever's blowing up on that side. Is the stuff blowing along the surface, or overhead?"

"Surface or both, I'm afraid. I can see the rim, but not the pool yet."

"It's time to turn," called Martucci. "Right angle, left turn, away

from the edge. Tell us when you see the pool, so we can give Gene
a real measure of the visibility."

There was a brief silence.

"I think it's there . . . yes, I can see its near edge."

"Sixteen meters," muttered one of the watchers.

"The color *is* funny, a lot redder than any I've seen. Certainly
redder than the one you got stuck in, Ginger. I can see a lab now; I
hope it's working. I'm right beside it now. The color isn't the same
all over; some of it, away from the rim, is almost black, and there
are a few spots where the snow seems to be sticking. They're all
several meters from the edge, and no lab is anywhere near one; shall
I get a sample to bring up?"

"No!" cried Ginger and Gene together. "All we need is to get
you stuck the way I was," added the former.

"This is just another tar pool, and you got loose."

"From stuff that looked different and could behave differently.
Don't take any chances. Pick up a lab and toss it onto the white, but
keep your feet out of trouble."

Maria followed this suggestion, and scored a center hit the first
time. She was getting used to the gravity. The lab sank at once;
Seichi said promptly that it was still transmitting.

"I won't step on it, but I'm going to get a sample from the lake
to take up. It's only a few meters, and I know which way. We can
do more with it in the station than the labs can manage down here."

"Be careful!"

"Relax, Sergeant. I didn't step in the pool, did I?" There was
silence for over a minute, a tense one for the watchers in the station;
real-time instrument resolution wasn't good enough to show what
parts of Maria's suit were above the liquid, especially when another
shock tossed her upward.

She landed feet down half a meter past its edge. It turned out to
be only a few centimeters deep where she arrived, and she waded
ashore with neither trouble nor delay.

"Now," Maria said firmly enough to prevent even Belvew from

arguing, "I also get a sample or two from Arthur's Pool. Then I'll meet you, Gene."

There was silence for several minutes.

"I have a chunk," she called at last. "It's gooey, like the stuff that caught you, Ginger. I don't have anything to put it in, but I can carry it in one hand—the piece is about fist size. I'll leave the digger. I don't know why I carried it this far. We can—"

"Better not," countered Seichi. "It has nearly a tenth of our available iridium in its teeth."

"Right. I should have thought. Now, Gene, I'm willing to make you happy. Where *can* you land?"

"Closer than I thought. If I go into the wind, though that isn't really fast enough to matter, I can touch down half a kilometer from the corner at the east end of your edge—you're near the west end, about the same distance from it. Go back to the edge, turn right, start hiking, and please don't let any new cliffs form in the next few minutes. I'll skid to about three hundred meters of the corner, and drive closer on rockets. Jump through the updraft when you hear I'm down. Don't do it any sooner; if I have to abort and land somewhere else, it'll be quicker for you to cross the hexagon than go around it. I'm lining up now . . . slowing down near pipe stall . . . letting down slowly . . . I don't want to get too low until I cross the crater rim." There was half a minute of silence while the commander walked lakeward. "Over the rim. Rocket mode. Height one fifty . . . one hundred . . ." The pilot ceased reporting for several endless seconds. "Touched down, sliding as usual. I'm coming into the fog and can't see very far ahead, but I made the approach a little north of your edge so there'll be no trouble if I slide too far. There—stopped. Pete, how far am I from Maria? Should I push a bit closer?"

"You can go another hundred meters. Maria, you know about where you are."

"Yes. Be patient, Gene."

"All right. You'll get to the edge *pretty* soon."

"Wait a minute, please. This tar sample—"

"As sticky as mine?" asked Ginger.

"I'm afraid so. Wait a minute—I'd better not put my hands together. I'll be jumping in a few seconds."

"All right," replied Martucci. "Just concentrate on getting down on your feet. Good. Don't hurry. Watch the edge. Getting picked up again by the updraft would waste time."

"Your suit has seventeen point six hours."

At least walking was now easy, between tremors.

"Recalculation based on recent usage. Your suit has seventeen point four hours."

Martucci's voice again: "You're there, Commander. Go ahead and jump. Try to land so you don't pick up another coat of paint."

"The updraft will have more to say about that than I, but here goes. I'm backing off . . . picking up speed as fast as I can—thank goodness ice isn't slippery here—*there!* I'm through, but I'm somersaulting—don't know how I'll land—got a fair kick upward—coming down now—feet first but leaning forward—good; I caught myself with one hand. Pete, I can't see the jet. How far and which way?"

"One hundred thirty meters, the way you were traveling when you jumped—about forty degrees north of east. Just keep going as fast as you can."

"That's not very fast. The ground's shaking again."

"So the accelerometers say," Belvew agreed. "Status, record their readings. They should help make sense of the can reports." Maria silently gave thanks that he could work as well as worry.

"I see *Theia,*" she called as the dark bulk loomed in front of her. "Good guiding, Pete. Twenty meters . . . the fog's thinner now . . . ten . . . I'm there. Climbing aboard . . . hatch open . . . inside, sealed up."

"You want to fly out yourself?" asked Gene.

"No. You keep it." The commander let it be assumed that she was acknowledging Belvew's piloting skill; she was not going to mention any other troubles yet. Worry might interfere with his piloting, and he was almost as good at worrying as at flying.

"Fine. I can't see ahead well enough to risk a westward takeoff. It'll have to be downwind. No matter, with that wind speed." The left engine roared, and *Theia* slid slowly forward, turning gradually to the right until her nose pointed back along the landing approach.

"Ready, boss?"

"When you want."

Both pipes thundered, and Maria gratefully felt the acceleration which Gene could only read from his instruments far above. Her coffin screen showed little detail, though it was set in a wave band which gave several hundred meters of fog penetration, and she tensely watched the center of the Mollweide ellipse.

The ground was fairly smooth, but with enough bumps to let her tell by their cessation when *Theia* was airborne. Her tension remained; the crater rim couldn't be very far ahead, she knew. How far had the run up to flying speed taken?

She remembered the flight instruments, and glanced at them. Less than two kilometers even now, and it had been a little over three to the rim—good—altitude fifty meters . . . a hundred . . . a hundred twenty as the wall flashed into view below the center of her screen. At the same moment she felt, just barely, the slight jolt as Belvew let ramjet take over.

"Want to fly now, Maria?" he asked.

"No, you'd better keep it. I'm not sure I can."

"Why not? Fatigue again?"

"A little, but that's not the problem. I can't get this sample of the pool off my right glove and for some reason I can't feel the hand. Do you think it would be smart to let this compartment warm up?"

"Commander!" Martucci cut in excitedly. "We wondered why you were tossed upward from the low side of those faults. It's just friction! The rising side dragged the other with it for a moment! It probably snapped down again while you were still in the air. Ice isn't slippery there, as we've all been telling each other!"

Belvew, speechless for once, gave his attention to *Theia*. It was left to Maria to point out as tactfully as possible that this suggestion had been made earlier. Martucci didn't seem bothered.

"I know. I couldn't think of any other idea though, so I tested that one. I had radar covering the top of the prism and a dozen points around it. The prism went up nearly a meter again just after you left the ground, and the surrounding area followed it—I had enough spots covered so I could tell that the surface actually *bent* up for a couple of hundred meters out and then snapped back."

"Good work. I shouldn't have put you down so fast. So ice is rock even under those pressures and motions. Note it, Status. Is the lake still there, Pete? I got samples, but maybe we'll want to get more."

"It's there, but doesn't look the same anymore. It's a *lot* smaller."

"It is spilling off the north edge of the plateau," reported Status. "Correlation with stream flows will no longer be possible."

"And Arthur's Pool?"

"Still there, unchanged in shape, color change continuing."

"Are the labs there still reporting?"

"Yes."

"Good. Then we come back to the question of what we do about the tar in my hand, or the tar my hand's in. I remember now there's no choice about its heating up here in the coffin. I'll try to get *some* of it into a specimen locker, but there isn't much room to move here. And the hand's still numb for some reason."

Actually, the main difficulty was not getting some of the stuff into the locker, but getting her arm out afterward. This specimen was far stickier than Ginger's had been.

No one suggested that Arthur's remains were in any way responsible, at least not aloud or directly. Radiocarbon dating was mentioned briefly, but Belvew pointed out stiffly yet again that no one had any idea of the rate at which the isotope formed in Titan's atmosphere, so only relative comparisons between Collos patches could be made; absolute dating was not yet possible. This was common knowledge which had been covered in earlier discussions, and the discussion ended; diSabato, who had made the suggestion, lacked whatever nerve or insensitivity was needed to point out that relative measures might tell all they needed to know this time.

Martucci changed the subject. He called attention to the pictures he had obtained of the stratified side of the lifted prism with *Theia*'s camera, using carefully chosen wavelengths during the rescue of the commander. This definitely ended the radiocarbon discussion; Mastro and lePing were still dominating the debate when *Crius* and Maria reached the station.

PART FOUR

SOLUTIONS?

16

SURGERY

NO ONE, NOT EVEN Major Xalco herself, thought of her as being in her own quarantine section within meters of everyone else, though they all knew she was. For all practical matters except vulnerability she was driving *Theia*, seven hundred kilometers below and a third of the way around Titan's globe from the station's present orbital position, trying to hold the jet at the official, standard observation true airspeed of one hundred meters per second.

Even after weeks the illusion of actually being in the aircraft tended to take over at dangerous moments, with resulting panic. The fact that occasionally the pilot was really on board probably made matters worse. The optimists who had believed at first that random reality reminders from Status would eventually cease to be needed had by now given up the hope.

Ginger Xalco had never been an optimist. She was commonly one of the first to comment whenever things seemed to be getting worse, and her voice now was practically a snarl.

"I don't—know what would—constitute a K-T catastrophe on this—silly moon." She got the words out in spasms, when some of her attention could wander briefly from piloting. *Theia* at the moment was not so much flying as being blown around, four kilometers above the smog-stained ice and ice-patched smog of the surface.

Turbulence was not new; it had been met by all the pilots in reasonable places, mostly within and under the thunderheads which commonly grew over Titan's numerous lakes. Horizontal winds of more than a meter or two a second, however, had originally been rare. Recently they had become routine. So was the seismic—actually now volcanic—activity which had ended the first attempt to set up a surface base and was now racking at least four new areas on Titan's surface.

One of these was centered less than a dozen kilometers from the first factory. This might, of course, be coincidence; no one but a pessimist could feel sure either way.

While Gene Belvew's noncommissioned rank made him formally a mere observer rather than a theoretician, he seldom let that fact keep him from talking, much less from thinking. He answered Ginger's rhetorical remark with a more literal question: "Why should we assume this is something catastrophic? We've been here only a tiny fraction of a Saturn year, and we're near the equinox. That's a stormy period on Earth."

Ginger's attention was not too occupied to permit a retort.

"You mean on some *parts*—of Earth, where—the sun—makes a lot of—difference. And since when—were volcanoes seasonal—whoops!"

"Trouble?" Maria, still group commander in spite of her recent hand loss, cut in instantly.

"Downdraft. I overcorrected—and had a pipe—stall. No danger—plenty of altitude—there. Fired up again. Status, that'll put a—kink in my line. Allow for it."

"Checked," came the data handler's deliberately unmistakable voice. "It may be relevant that the increasing turbulence of your last few dozen kilometers shows a rough correlation with increasing methane content of the air."

"Probably is." Belvew's voice sounded thoughtful. "Most of the thermals I've ever run into are over lakes, where the evaporation would drop the air density—"

"And drop the—temperature too. I thought we'd—agreed not to call them 'thermals.' Or are—you just reminding us gently—that you were a pilot long—before this affair started and can't—bury old professional knowledge?"

Maria, nearly certain that this charge was justified, changed the subject again. "Are there lakes below you, Ginger? I don't see anything special on my mapping stuff, and haven't been watching your Mollweide. What part of the spectrum are you using?"

"Long-enough waves to see the ground—I'm below most of the smog anyway. There are four—lakes I can see from here, but none right—under me and none specially big. There's no obvious reason—for extra methane—wow!"

"Another stall?"

"Just a bump. If I'd really been riding this machine—I'd—you show 'em the accelerometer records, Status."

Exclamations like her own sounded in other human voices. Nearly all of the group were experienced enough, and identified well enough with their craft while flying, to "feel" the jerks shown by the instruments just as Ginger did. The input from the waldoes could be felt even more literally. The gaps in the pilot's sentences were now really understandable.

"That's close to red line," Belvew worried aloud. "No one expected real turbulence here."

"If you'd hit that at four or five times standard speed we'd be looking back at your wings," Peter Martucci remarked uneasily. "Shouldn't you slow down?"

"And risk having—all the lift go out—from under me?"

"You have plenty of altitude."

"And that's the—way I want it. How much longer—should I hold this—run, Status? I don't—suppose the original timing means—much anymore. Is—there any trouble compensating for this—bucking? I'll slow down if—the readings really need it."

"There is no problem calculating from the readings. Aircraft safety is still paramount."

Silence, except for an occasional annoyed mutter from the acting pilot, ensued for several more minutes. Maria had been tempted briefly to offer a suggestion, which might have been taken as a command, that Belvew take over the piloting; but the jet seemed in no real danger, and morale was important even, or perhaps especially, among a dying crew. She couldn't compromise by taking the controls herself, for two reasons.

She was no better a flier than Xalco at the best of times and everyone knew it, and this was not the best of times.

The waldo suits, which could direct the aircraft from thousands of kilometers, were complex devices. They used input from many parts of the wearer's body including toes, chins, and noses, not just fingers. Some potential group members on Earth at the time the project was being planned had been rejected for poor control of their facial expressions. The possibility that someone might need to fly with a missing right hand had not been foreseen, and in the fortnight since Maria's loss no one in the station had been able to think of a way to compensate for it. Total redesign and rebuilding of the jet control systems was impractical, and nothing less seemed workable.

The commander looked across her quarters—actually a rather luxurious and extremely well equipped living space and laboratory—at the two tanks where most of her specimen from Arthur's Pool reposed. It had seemed harmless enough to scoop up, in a glove designed to keep her hand from turning to glass at a surrounding temperature of ninety kelvins and in a fairly conductive atmosphere, a sample of the viscous matter in which Goodall had died. Xalco's worrisome sticking in a similar pool had proven merely frightening, with no resulting damage.

Maria's inability to clear her glove of the stuff during free fall up to the station had been merely a nuisance; outside contamination meant nothing to the waldo controls, and Belvew had done the piloting anyway.

Back in her quarters, however, the stubbornness of the sample had graduated from an annoyance to a problem; and when she discovered—visually: she hadn't *felt* anything—before even shedding the suit that part of her glove had been dissolved and the stuff was starting to work on her hand, she had to declare an emergency. Of course all the individual quarters were equipped with remotely controlled surgical equipment, and a laser amputation had been a minor job well within Status's competence, fortunately. The alternatives would have been quarantine violation or letting nature take its course.

Even while the operation was in progress Maria had been almost more interested in another matter; she had joined with gusto, and seemingly full attention, the discussion over why the sample had failed to be inactivated by a temperature rise of over two hundred kelvins. An egg starting at a normal three hundred ten would be much more than hard-boiled at, say, the melting point of aluminum—a comparable *ratio* in temperature increase.

Seichi Yakama was still talking as though the stuff were alive, but no one else went that far. Alien suit-penetrating and flesh-eating monsters had seemed at least as unlikely to the sober and rather conservative project planners as the alien kidnappers of UFO mythology. Besides, no one could believe that a major goal of their mission—establishing that either life or prebiotic chemistry was present on Titan—could have been achieved in such a short time and with so many of the original group still alive.

Maybe they didn't *want* to believe it. What would they have left to live for if it had? What could they do if their problem was *solved*?

No need to worry about that, most of them knew deep inside. Nothing has ever been that simple since the invention of agriculture.

But Maria Collos could no longer fly. And the stuff in the tanks across the room—one containing mostly the sheared-off forearm and gauntlet of her suit plus adhesions, the other the more personal material which had been extracted from them—was probably relevant to the problem even if it was not an answer. It was certainly interesting to others besides the victim. An obvious first experiment was under way; a scrap from the second tank's contents was taped to the hand of one of the mausoleum's occupants, under remote observation, to find what the stuff would do to human tissue at the Titanian temperatures maintained in that chamber. The strapping had been accompanied by another memorial to the hand's owner, now once more contributing to the project.

Maria had of course made the proper gesture, offering to resign the command so recently inherited from Goodall, but no one else wanted the job. It was too often a distraction from more interesting work, and the crew unanimously, promptly, and firmly agreed that neither a theoretician nor a commander needed two hands. Maria wished fleetingly that she had had as good a chance to argue with her own late predecessor, but she accepted the situation. At least the bunch of argumentative daydreamers had now committed *themselves* to following her *recommendations*.

And the daydreams, more formally called speculations and hypotheses, were still being produced, luckily. She wouldn't have to stimulate any imaginations. Martucci's voice was relieving her of any such worry right now.

"Y'know, Ginger, that point of Gene's about equinox may have something. Remember it's eclipse season, for the first time in fifteen years. I know the sun's a long way off, but a quick change of heat input over a whole hemisphere as Titan ducks into Saturn's shadow might do *something*."

Not even Belvew really spoke for some seconds, though many voices muttered at Status's calculating units.

"It's worth checking," Maria agreed slowly. "Intuitively, I'd say the input was very small, as you suggest, and if there is any effect it'd be lost in chaos. Still, one and a quarter percent of Earth's solar intake over the sunward half of the satellite adds up to a lot of gigawatts, I'd guess—no, don't anyone bother to tell me the right number. It takes Titan about half an hour to move its own diameter along its orbit, and except at the middle of the eclipse season it would take even longer to get completely covered or uncovered by Saturn's shadow. Longest possible eclipse at midseason, which we haven't reached yet, is only about ten and a half hours. Could be a respectable amount of heat involved at that. Pete, you and Seichi think of some ways to word useful questions to Status on that one, bearing the chaotic possibility in mind." She knew that everyone else would try to beat the assigned pair to the idea draw, but that would do no harm.

"The air's quieting down, I think," Xalco finally reported. "It's been over an—hour. That's quite a storm cell for Titan, if it was a storm cell."

"It was not." Status's tone showed no change, but its firmness was taken for granted by everyone. "There was nothing cyclonic about its wind patterns, and there seems to have been more descending than ascending current area, though that cannot be certain; you traced only a single, rather irregular line across the region. The cause is not clear. I am making the obvious correlations which have been suggested as routine, but any others you want will have to be added by living imaginations. Nothing significant has appeared so far, and with the volume of data now involved it will take at least ten more minutes to make the remaining routine comparisons."

"Please include eclipse data in them," Maria replied.

"I interpreted Corporal Martucci's words as an order to that effect. Only the fact that eclipse season and large-area turbulence started within a Titan orbit of each other, and in that order, is so far obvious. Both starting times are too recent for a causal relationship either way to be reliably inferred."

"What next?" asked Ginger. "There are a few more seismic lines to lay out, aren't there? I mean the originally planned ones, not the stuff we've had to improvise around the new volcanoes."

"You'll need to restock on cans first." Belvew spoke before the robot managed to do so. "The extra patterns dug into the reserves pretty deeply."

"I know. There should be plenty at Factory One—Status, you didn't stop manufacture when the stocks we originally planned were finished, did you?"

"Yes, but I resumed after the change in operations was implemented. There will be a full load waiting when you reach the factory. Iridium is running low at the factory, however. When restocking is needed, gold and platinum should also be taken down to save a trip."

"I still don't see why they didn't use just one of those metals," growled Pete. "I'd say iridium would be the best; it's hardest. Then we'd have a lot less trouble over which and how much to use for labs, cans, and maybe new jets.''

"I don't know either,'' answered Ginger. "Then I'd better start back there now. Heading, Maria or somebody?''

"Do you still have labs aboard?'' cut in Yakama.

"Sure. Why?''

"I'd like very much to make some comparisons between Arthur's Pool, the one by the factory, and the one at Lake Carver where Gene set down a while ago. We dropped a lab there at the time, but it got blown away when he found he was sinking and took off in such a hurry. There are units still working in Settlement Crater and lots at the factory site where the—where you're going anyway, but I'd give a lot to be able to cross-check all the places where any of our stuff has touched Titan's surface physically. D'you suppose you could drop another lab there by Lake Carver before you settle down at the factory, Ginger?''

"I don't see why not. Wait a minute, though—we know we'd better not drop it in the lake, since we couldn't hear the first one after it went in, and we know the ground there is pretty hard. Wouldn't I have to land to get a lab down intact?''

"Gene landed, but you dropped labs from flight during Maria's hike, and they stood it all right—''

"They landed in snow!''

"About four centimeters deep, as I recall. And there were other drops—''

"Four centimeters can make a big difference, especially under Titan gravity. But aren't there any snow patches reasonably close to Carver? The labs can travel, after all.''

"I take it you'd rather not make an extra landing.''

"Is that criticism?''

"I'll do it if you like,'' Belvew cut in. Maria played this one safe, too.

"Ginger can do it if it needs to be done. I agree with the importance of having labs there, if only to get an analysis of that lake; we never found out why we couldn't read from the unit we lost there.

It could have been depth or composition of the lake or blast damage to the lab itself. Nothing in the analysis of the lake at Settlement offered a clue. Go ahead down, Ginger—but do check the area for snow patches first."

"There were none nearby at that time, or at any of the routine checks of the area since then," Status informed them. "All the ice we have seen has been massive, except possibly the dust being produced from the volcanic vents."

"And maybe the lighter layers in the strata!" interjected Carla lePing, beating her coworker to the suggestion. "At least they're the right color!" Status made no comment.

"I'll look anyway. Heading, please?" Ginger relaxed; at least this should be a more comfortable ride. It was, though no one would have been paralyzed by shock if it hadn't been.

There was still no snow, and relatively little surface ice showed in the dirt; Lake Carver was on Titan's darker trailing hemisphere. Ginger was not, as she had tacitly admitted, eager to land, but she had no intention of handing Belvew the responsibility. She made all reasonable delays, looking unsuccessfully for nearby snow patches, doing a careful wind run, and even topping off her mass tanks at a nearby thunderhead—she had used rocket mode once or twice in the turbulence—but it seemed clear that dropping a lab even at minimum speed and altitude was likely to wreck the equipment. Even if the device were still able to heal itself afterward, that would take much longer than a landing.

The pilot still hoped that Maria would decide to risk a drop in spite of all this, but the commander concluded that the balance favored touching down. Ginger sought and found Belvew's Pool with Carver in the background, lined up *Theia* toward it, and began her approach. She had found no wind and observed neither rain nor turbulence along her flight path, so there was plenty of time to adjust letdown rate. She wanted to touch just at the bottom of the near side of the gentle slope—she wondered suddenly why neither of the other named pools had shown either such a large bulge or a dimple like the one originally spotted here by Inger, but put the question firmly

aside. This was no time for theoretical work. She was a little above
pipe-stall speed—closer than Belvew had gone before shifting to
rocket, she recalled; but he'd been enjoying a small head wind. Not
that that made any difference with *air*speed. Fifty meters above
ground, six hundred from touchdown—

She closed the intakes and began to draw from *Theia*'s mass
tanks. She could feel her bare scalp—her nickname dated from her
teens, years before she had qualified for Titan, and even before her
infection—trickling with perspiration, and she was fleetingly glad of
her isolation. Belvew, his screen and other instruments copying hers,
hoped his relief at the near-perfect mode shift was inaudible. Someone else gave a grunt which might have been approval; the change
to rocket mode had barely shown on the accelerometers.

Thirty meters up and three hundred to go. Now she had to watch
for imminent wing stall. She was overshooting a little. Nose and
power both down just a trifle, but watch that airspeed. The bulge of
the pool now hid the lake. She should still touch down on this side,
but might not stop sliding before the top. Still overshooting—was a
tailwind picking up? If another updraft was starting to grow over the
lake, that would be its effect.

She couldn't touch now less than halfway up the near slope.
The air *must* be moving. No matter. She could still—but yes, it *did*
matter; beyond the top the slope was downward, and that was when
even Belvew—cancel that "even," blast you, Xalco—had expected
trouble. Not much, but some.

Her keels touched before *Theia* reached the top, but not very
much before. There was a swelling black cloud at either side of her
screen just as Gene had had, and she cut thrust the instant her accelerometers showed the ground drag.

Not soon enough. The jet ballooned, probably only a few millimeters, but failed to touch again until it was halfway down the
lakeward side. She had had to nose down, of course, which raised
airspeed slightly. It wasn't much of a slope and the aircraft didn't
have much wing area, but Titan doesn't have much gravity.

Then she was firmly down and slowing rapidly.

Not as rapidly as the now very visible lake was approaching, however. There *was* a thunderhead growing over it, she noted in surprisingly detached fashion as the jet crossed the shoreline and the splash blanked her Mollweide for a few seconds. That should explain the unexpected tailwind, she thought; but she didn't voice the speculation. There were more important things to consider.

17

SEGMENT?

WELL, WE HAD TO find out sometime." At least the remark hadn't come from Belvew, and there was no way for anyone to tell how frantically the commander had striven to beat the sergeant to it. "What's the lake density, Status? You have *Theia*'s mass and volume parameters and can read how deep she's floating." Maria seemed completely calm.

"A little higher than expected for a ninety-ten methane-ethane mixture at that temperature, but not outside reasonable variations in such a mixture. If the major will eject a laboratory we can—"

"Not till you're ashore!" Belvew did get that exclamation in first. "We know the lab won't float, and we can't hear its output from under the surface."

"Strictly speaking, we don't know it won't float," the commander pointed out. "The density of lab and lake certainly aren't very different. We never really looked for the other on the surface, and it might have been damaged enough by the exhaust that blew it away so it failed to broadcast. However, I agree it would be best to get ashore first. I'd suggest very, very gentle thrust in rocket mode, Ginger."

"And expect it to be pretty bumpy even then," pointed out Belvew. "The liquid will boil around the arcs and the bubbles will drive huge masses of liquid out the pipes. That'll stop as the arc clears itself, and repeat when juice sloshes into the fire again. It'll be like pouring from a narrow-necked bottle, I'll bet, and the sloshes may not stay in step between the engines."

The "I'll bet" was encouraging. Not even Belvew, it seemed, was certain what would happen with the pipes submerged and flooded. The point, as someone had realized early on the Earth-Saturn orbit, was another factor overlooked during planning of the aircraft, but no one had seen any way of rectifying the design without risking further complications. The ramjet is simple in principle, but the simplicity does not extend to machines using it. Not one of the original fifty crew members had had confidence in his or her skill in aerodynamic engineering. Getting the needed information from Status would certainly take a worrisome amount of time, and with terrible luck no one would ever ask the right questions.

Xalco wasn't sure whether Gene's uncertainty was a relief or an added worry. She lit the arcs with even more caution than she had used in the landing.

The jerking wasn't bad—*Theia* was massive and the lake offered its share of inertia—but the sergeant had been essentially right. Also, the process was *loud*.

As she bumped away from the shore, Ginger experimented with cambering the vertical stabilizer in ordinary steering fashion and found it ineffective. The obvious alternative was to lower the fire in one engine until *Theia*'s nose pointed back toward shore and hill. This worked, complicated by the predicted lack of synchronization in the jolts. Then, even more slowly and carefully, the major began to retrace her path.

"Hadn't you better tank up?" asked Martucci. "You used juice to land, and will use more getting ashore." Ginger didn't answer directly, but followed the sensible suggestion.

"Status, check how much mass I take aboard, how far it sinks me, and cross-check the lake's density," she said. It took her a moment to remember the appropriate controls; all previous refills had been made in flight from air scoops, and opening an inappropriate valve just now seemed unlikely to be habit-forming. Again she fought off the temptation to abdicate responsibility and let Belvew take over.

The mass percentage change was small and the rise in fluid line perceptible only to instruments. Status reported a small difference in the newly computed lake density and claimed it exceeded reasonable measurement error, but the collective human judgment dismissed the difference as unimportant. It was certainly minute. *Theia* resumed the bumpy drive shoreward.

She was close in when the keels touched; the slope of the lake bottom appeared steeper than that of Belvew's Pool, now called by some Belvew's Hill. Without consulting anyone, Xalco gently eased more energy into the arcs.

Theia bumped further inshore as though being tapped from behind by a giant putter on a very wet green, and her bow began slowly to rise. Then forward motion and hammering stopped for fully a second. Before the pilot could decide what to do, even before Belvew could offer advice, there was an even louder thud and a stronger forward jerk. Both repeated themselves in a fraction of a second, but less violently. Motion and sound ceased again; then Belvew gave a cry of warning.

It was unneeded; the pilot had also felt the arc warning which the sergeant had seen on a different instrument and reacted properly, feeding liquid to both chambers. Another blast from the pipes, much more violent in terms of acceleration but much less noisy than the others, sent the jet completely ashore.

"When the arc section got above the liquid—," Belvew began.

"I can see what happened," snapped Ginger. "The pipes are drained now, I expect. I'm dropping a lab right here, Seichi; you can try getting a lake sample without having it lost in the drink. I'll hold off on thrust until you can walk it to one side far enough. Then I'll push a little closer to the pool, or hill, or tar pot, or whatever we're going to call it and drop another—or do you want even more?"

"Two should be enough, but if you can spare more a backup would be nice."

"All right. Just a moment." The rockets thundered briefly as

Theia bumped a little farther from the lake. "Here go two labs. Get them off to the sides, or to one side, or whatever is handiest as fast as you can, please."

"I have control of them both. They seem to be responding normally. I have them moving aft . . . now they're clear of the keels. Another couple of minutes." Even Belvew was silent during the wait. "All right. They're both about fifty meters to your left, almost at the shoreline, and should be clear of your wash. You're getting closer to the stuff?"

"Yes." Again everyone heard rocket thunder, and watched instruments and screens as *Theia* slid closer to the rise. "All right, here go two more for you to use on the tar or whatever it is. Move them aft and a little to the right—my left, that is. I'm going to use the right engine to turn parallel to the foot of the slope before I try take-off; that should use less mass than trying to accelerate up the slope, especially if it's going to pull the sticky trick. The first two are enough closer to the lake so I won't be risking them. Nothing else needed on the ground?"

No one answered, and the aircraft swiveled clumsily to its left until it was parallel to the shore a few dozen meters away. Then it accelerated northward, a dark cloud again appearing behind as hot gas swept the lowest fringe of the hill/pool. Ginger had not recited the checklist aloud, but she had followed it. The wings were cambered for maximum lift, and *Theia* was airborne in less than three hundred meters. The moment it was safe—perhaps a fraction of a second before Belvew would have done it—the pilot shifted to ramjet mode, smoothly enough so that the sergeant nodded approvingly if pointlessly in the solitude of his quarters far above.

Without a word Ginger headed for the now well-developed cumulus cloud above the lake, climbed to four kilometers, and drove into it to refill. She didn't expect any remarks from Belvew, and there seemed no point in asking for them.

She got one anyway.

"Look at your chamber temperatures and exhaust speeds, Major. There's something there that shouldn't be in both pipes, clogging

them maybe two percent. It's lucky you didn't open the intakes any
sooner; you'd have been pretty low for a pipe stall and a lot worse
for a front fire."

"Right." Ginger was thoughtful. She wasted no worry on what
hadn't occurred; pessimism is a tendency to brood over what might
be, not what might have been. The fact that she wasn't actually
riding the jet was irrelevant; losing the craft would have been emotionally worse, she felt, than losing herself with it. She strongly
doubted any afterlife, and even more strongly doubted the chance of
being able to correct mistakes once there. Her usual irritation with
Belvew suddenly sank, though not too deeply, in a ripple of sympathy.

But there was a piloting problem to be faced, and she gave it all
the attention she could spare from steering the jet through the nearby
cloud and operating the collection equipment. She even asked for
help.

"Status, watch those engine readings and let us know if you
detect any change in any direction. You needn't recite the readings
themselves, but let me know whether the obstruction they indicate
is increasing or decreasing."

"It is decreasing," was the instant response.

"Something sticky got into the pipes while they were submerged
and is burning out now," Belvew concluded promptly.

"Or into the tanks," Mastro and Wei snapped out almost simultaneously. Belvew kept his annoyance to himself; he should have
thought of that before opening, or at least before closing, his mouth.

"Let's hope it's just the obstruction that burns," Ginger said,
acknowledging obliquely the higher probability of the first idea—the
other would obviously have called for increasing pipe blockage—by
failing to comment on the alternative.

"A reasonable *speculation*," the commander put in, out of a
sense of duty. Belvew did tend to become positive in his ideas rather
earlier than regs or rationality advised. "Seichi," she went on before
the sergeant could react defensively, "have you any analysis of the

lake yet? Is there anything which might explain this?"

"The lake is mostly methane, ethane, and small amounts of higher but still simple hydrocarbons," the analyst replied promptly. "The key word, though, does seem to be *mostly*. Maybe half a percent of the stuff is extremely complicated, and it'll be a long time before I can get even a rough composition. It's certainly a mixture, not one or two nice, clean compounds with readable structures and writable formulas."

"Tars, in other words?" the commander queried.

"I couldn't say yet. Using the word even more loosely than we have so far, not just for the stuff in the smog, I suppose so. That's about as meaningful, though, as the word 'protoplasm' was back when it referred to the few powers of ten between the smallest thing you could see with a microscope and the biggest you could recognize in a test tube."

"Are you trying to say 'life' again?"

"It won't—wouldn't—surprise me."

"And jellyfish swam into the pipes?"

Seichi ignored Belvew's sarcasm. "That *would* surprise me," he responded, keeping straight what was left of his face even though no one could see it.

"How about a heading for the factory?" It was Ginger this time who changed the subject.

"Sorry. Wasn't thinking," replied Maria. "Status?"

"Wait, please." It was Yakama again. "One of the labs you dropped beside the slope has stopped reporting. Major, could you look it over before leaving?"

"Sure. Where was it?"

"I moved it to the edge of the hill, if that's what we're calling it now, as soon as you were away. It should be at the edge of the tar—pardon the word; we *will* have to find some more specific labels—within half a dozen meters of the other, which is sampling the ground between lake and whatever. It should not be more than half a meter into the whatever."

"All right. I'll concentrate on flying. The rest of you do anything you can think of with your screens, and look for that egg. Any better ideas?"

None was offered, and the jet glided back toward its recent landing site, easily enough identified from above. The smoke had drifted out over the lake, but the hill itself still contrasted in color with the ground. Ginger flew over the area at three hundred meters and standard observing airspeed.

The two labs by the lakeside could be seen easily enough, and after a few seconds Martucci spotted what was presumably the still active member of the second pair. He indicated it on his own screen, and Status emphasized the image for the others. No one, however, could see the fourth lab, and Ginger banked out over the lake to make another pass. Scalp once more sweating, she dropped to a hundred meters altitude and two per second above pipe-stall speed and straightened out, tensely ready to close air scoops and turn on reaction mass at reflex notice.

Several screens showed the errant lab almost at the same moment. Maria and even Belvew waited for Seichi to report; he should, after all, have the most to say. Peter, however, was less restrained.

"It's sunk in! It's nearly half—"

"Look closer," Maria interrupted softly.

"What?"

"It hasn't sunk. There's a little hill around it."

"I told you!" exclaimed the chemist.

Belvew cut in, to no one's surprise. "The lab is pseudolife. It was grown from molecular patterns. Its shell is organic—close enough to chitin. All sorts of things would react with it—"

"And climb up around it like ants around a jar of—"

"Or like the other one around my boots?" Xalco cut in.

"General Order Six, Sergeant." This was not Maria's voice.

"No! No! I mean *dissolve* it—*absorb* it—and swell up as the lab's molecules took up room! I'll bet you'll find molecules from the lab spreading out in that stuff like . . ."

Maria refrained from interfering this time. Science might have become more military under need, and it had always needed discipline as much as combat ever did, but Lieutenant Colonel Maria Collos believed strongly that a scientific debate was better not stopped until it grew acrimonious enough to involve personalities. Belvew *was* suggesting a way of testing, after all.

"How do I find out?" asked Seichi more specifically. "The lab's not working, or at least not reporting." Belvew paused for a moment's thought as this question was raised, but no one expected him to be silent for long.

"If this thing really eats carbon polymers," he finally suggested thoughtfully, "it shouldn't be too hard to grow a lab with—oh, silica armor, or maybe a heavy-metal plating, if we can spare enough metal. That should at least last long enough to make some analyses."

"Cheru, please check the practicality of that, and if it can be done at all, estimate cost in time and material." Maria displayed her usual prompt decisiveness. "Gene, you seem to be speculating that the hill by Carver represents something which was absorbed—recently—by the patch. What would it be? Just speculate, for now. Forget Six."

"Meteorite would be my first thought."

"What kind?"

"Ice would be most likely out here."

"Then why aren't there a whole flock of these tar pools near the factory? A lot of ice fell there when Barn knocked the mountain down, and the mountain itself is ice!"

"There's one forming among the fragments already, Pete; and they weren't shed very long ago. Also, the pieces of cliff couldn't have hit the ground at anything like meteorite speeds. And there's carbon—carbonate dust, anyway—in those ice chunks. Arthur reported it, didn't he, Status?"

"He did."

"But you don't suppose a stone or iron body got this far out in the system, do you?"

"I don't know. We've found only one pool like this so far, anything can happen once, and don't tell me what a coincidence it would be for us to find it this early."

"We're getting a bit abstract for real planning, Gene," Maria said, closing the discussion. "If it proves practical to make a lab such as you suggest, I'm willing to try it. After all, if Belvew's Hill really is unique, we should learn that as quickly as possible. We should also find out what made it. In the meantime, back to routine."

"Commander."

"Yes, Seichi."

"We maybe don't need to wait for Cheru's feasibility study. The regular labs have two collectors each with inert-metal plating, gold for the fluid samplers and iridium for the scrapers. I can reach those maybe thirty or forty centimeters in without getting the rest of a lab in contact with the stuff. Maybe that'll let us find out enough to tell whether Cheru should go on."

"Go to it!" Gene's and Maria's voices were too nearly simultaneous to be distinguished; perhaps the commander didn't realize that the sergeant had also spoken. At any rate, she said nothing about his issuing orders to a captain.

Yakama spoke again a moment later, sounding crestfallen. "I can't judge distances well except where I have items in sight to provide scale. The lab has only one eye, and that doesn't have much resolving power; it's mainly for travel guidance. Getting close to the pool may be riskier than I thought."

"The eye's on a stalk," Martucci pointed out promptly. "Wave it around to provide parallax and have Status build you a 3-D image. You can keep the lab out of danger easily enough, and if you do slip up there are always more. It's not as though they were jets."

"Not exactly, but you pointed it out just now. Parts of the labs need inert metals like gold and iridium for sampling tips and electrical and chemical equipment. We brought reserves of those along, since it didn't seem very likely we'd find them here, given Titan's density. Unless we manage to salvage and recycle used labs, though, we'll run out of those metals sooner or later."

"What's the difference? Isn't that true of the jets, too? And the jets need a lot more—"

"No, they don't. Believe it or not. Not very much more. And we've been pretty casual with labs. Ginger's going back to the factory now for cans, and she can get more labs while she's at it, but we'd better be less free with them from now on."

"The 3-D trick should work," Maria interjected firmly. "Ginger, your heading is two-zero-two. Seichi, get to it—no, first make sure the labs at the factory site are all working."

"They are," was the report after a brief pause.

"All right, you get back to your lake and Belvew's Hill work. Status, keep track of *all* the labs and tell us if any of them, anywhere, either stops reporting or sends readings inconsistent with its own earlier ones. Use one-sigma consistency criteria. Cheru, use at least one eye as you're doing the study to cover my mapping program along with Status; I want to keep on top of the tar-pool count and sizes. Gene—"

"It's almost time for me to relieve Ginger with *Theia*," the sergeant interrupted.

"Take *Crius* instead and make a really tight air-current grid through the turbulence region she just left. Modify it to fit any new information Status may supply; use your own judgment on aircraft limitations. Keep repeating it at decreasing altitudes until either you get too tired to fly, or Titan has been out of Saturn's shadow for two hours. That time's arbitrary; stay with it longer if things are still happening. Carla, plan your R and R to be ready to relieve Gene when he needs it. Ginger should last long enough at what she's doing, but Louis can be ready to relieve her if necessary. Don't either of you even think about wanting more strata pictures until I clear you; you should be happy enough checking over what's on hand already. If anything surprising turns up, of course, let me know and I may reconsider.

"Ginger, get to Factory One and start earning your pay."

No one laughed at the p-word; there was serious work to be done. Even those not receiving specific orders had routine to continue—routine which included rest and recreation, but might have to be interrupted at any time by a medical alert from Status or a sudden meaningful fact from Titan. By the time *Theia* reached the factory site, Yakama had learned, with some mild but natural irritation, that his analyses seemed to support the Belvew diffusion hypothesis. The lost lab had now disappeared completely into the tar, the bulge which had formed around it was now slowly flattening out to match the surrounding slope, and the confusion of molecules in the now-presumed-to-be-monovinyl gel definitely included many which almost had to be fragments of the lab's pseudolife outer shell and inner machinery. They contained trace elements not so far detected on Titan, even copper and startling amounts of iron and nickel; their polymer makeup was consistent with bits of ordinary industrial pseudolife, and nothing very like them in structure had been found anywhere else on the satellite.

There were even a few atoms of really heavy metals. The lost lab had apparently been well digested. Seichi was able to report all this without revealing too much annoyance, and Belvew refrained from any triumphant remarks. He was far too busy by this time, in any case; he had taker over *Crius*, and flying a planned grid pattern through and around a heavy-turbulence zone was straining even his skill. He found it comforting to remember that he had made no tactless remarks about Ginger's handling of the same task. She would never have missed a chance to return them.

"The ice cliff's in sight," reported Xalco. "I'll make a wind check before I set her down." No one argued or even commented; not even Maria felt this time that the pilot had or should have any qualms about the landing. Yakama made a request, but not of the pilot.

"Status, check the camera records as she goes over and give me any changes in albedo or topography at and near *Oceanus*."

"And record any details you can about the strata at the top of that mountain as you pass, too, please." This time Mastro got in ahead of Lieutenant lePing. The commander decided not to comment; the request was technically insubordination, but it involved no change in flight plan or loss of time.

"Topography changes seem minor," came Status's prompt answer. "Less can be seen of the craft. I will need a moment for stereo interpretation to tell whether *Oceanus* has sunk or the pool has risen. Strata at the top of the block have been recorded again; do you want the records themselves or comparison with earlier ones, Major?"

"Both, please," replied Mastro.

"It wasn't even—in the pool last time I—knew!" Belvew's attention was diverted even from his present flying task. "Why didn't—you tell us? Did the pool—or the ship move?"

"Your statement disagrees with my memory. The pool had spread to include *Oceanus* at the time of Sergeant Inger's death. Have I been shut down without proper warning for any significant time?"

"No, Status," Marie replied at once. "Sergeant Belvew's attention was distracted at the time, and his memory of the pool is unreliable. Don't attempt record-conflict resolution."

"You were told to—report changes—"

"The command was much more specific than that, Gene," Maria pointed out. "You know it would have to be, or Status would have been swamping us with unusable and probably meaningless data. Ginger has passed the site now, Status; do you have a stereo comparison?"

"Yes. The pool is now a hill, if our naming is to be consistent. Its slope is even greater than the one by Lake Carver, everywhere within about twenty meters of *Oceanus*."

"Has the expansion gotten as far as any of the ice boulders, and if so what has happened where they met the tar? Were they absorbed, or what?"

"Yes. Four of them. They are resting motionless on the slopes of the hill, and show no signs of sinking or being absorbed or engulfed."

"So the stuff isn't interested in ice," commented Yakama.

18

STRESS

I CAN SEE THE ice being rejected," Seichi put in, "but the hulls and especially the keels of the aircraft are also chemically very different from the lab shells. How could the same solution process be occurring here?"

"What do your labs say?" returned the commander. "All the ones near Factory One are still working, aren't they? Or have we lost some here too?"

"All are reporting, including those on the pool itself. I have kept the latter moving, and none so far have been caught."

"Better stop one of them, Captain. Just don't let *Theia* get—uh—into it, Ginger." Belvew seemed back to normal after a few minutes of silent thought in a background of turbulent flight; he couldn't hold back the superfluous advice.

"I'm landing to the north. There's a five-meter wind from there." Ginger might have been replying indirectly, or merely reporting to Maria. The wind direction was not surprising, but the speed was, and for just a moment Maria wondered whether she should have Belvew handle the landing. There could be a lot of ground turbulence.

She decided against it, but was not sorry to note that practically everyone's screen was copying *Theia*'s. It seemed unlikely that the pilot would be allowed to overlook anything serious.

The wind, a gale for Titan, was indeed producing strong ground turbulence in the heavy atmosphere. Ginger stored for possible future Rule X use the fact that Belvew had not predicted this.

The accelerometers showed the jolts as Ginger rode down the approach, and she felt grateful for her recent practice. Wings stayed almost perfectly level once she had set up her heading; pitch angle remained unchanged; she was able to handle descent rate with thrust alone. She intended to touch down heel first, with the keel toes only a centimeter higher at that instant if the ground was really level. The attitude change would be barely perceptible, but lift would fall sharply below weight and keel drag would start almost instantly. She would be west of the factory and the remains of *Oceanus;* she had paid no particular attention to the latter as she passed over it on the wind check.

Neither, for some reason, had anyone else. Status had no relevant orders.

She had picked the approach line to keep away from the ice cliff and the larger scattered fragments at its foot. The small ones should be harmless.

To her own surprise, everything went exactly as planned; she was disappointed to find that Belvew had been far too busy to watch. *Theia* slid to a halt half a kilometer west and slightly north of the factory, with a record low of reaction mass used during the rocket-driven part of the approach.

"Nice job, Major," Maria remarked, seeing the tank readings.

"Just as well. I'll need to use a lot of juice taxiing. Is the factory ready to deliver, Status?"

"It indicates so. You will want the full complement of cans. There are fifty new labs also ready, and even if you take them all you will still have room in the jet for a dozen more from those already operating in the factory area. These would of course be harder to load."

"Think we'll need 'em, Seichi?" asked the pilot.

"I can hope not," was the dry answer. "I've picked up nearly fifty samples from the base of this hill of Gene's without losing any more yet. Of course, if dope is needed from nearer the top, I can't promise anything.''

"It will be," assured Gene.

"The lost one, assuming material diffused about equally in all directions and the tar layer itself is thick enough for vertical motion to—''

"Tar layer? Didn't it go into the lake?'' Ludmilla, usually quiet, cut in this time. No one asked whether recreation or duty had kept her out of touch. Maria, who had been trying to persuade the corporal that reading was greatly preferable to visual shows, felt slightly guilty.

"Not according to present data . . . for vertical motion to count, seems to be accounted for,'' the acting nanochemist went on without seeming bothered by the interruption. "It appears to have dissolved completely, even the metal in the sampling heads and reaction stomachs. I find quite a bit of gold and iridium, far more than the occasional random atoms that are of course always there even on Titan. Unfortunately, there's a lot of background material—polypeptides, carbohydrate polymers, and probably stuff similar to but not identical with either—so a lot of time will be needed to specify the mixture details.''

"Maybe we *should* call it protoplasm," suggested Martucci. "Just for the historical implication," he added hastily. "Something sitting between the high side of low resolution and the low side of high.''

Maria gently ruled against this without trying to find out how seriously the suggestion had been meant. Any such word would be far too likely to influence what should *not* be wishful thinking, and thus help feed the Aarn Munro instant-certainty syndrome. "But it wasn't a bad idea, at that, Peter," she finished tactfully. "We do seem to be in a sort of in-between situation calling for some such improvisation.''

"Whatever it is, let's keep the jet out of it." This was Belvew rather than Maria, and Ginger allowed her irritation to show once more.

"Don't worry. She's—I'm—down and stopped, and there's plenty of juice for taxiing. Tend to your own driving, Sergeant." Belvew detected her feelings both in her tone and her use of the formal title, and said no more for a while; but his attention did not go back entirely to his own jet.

He committed a gross piloting error. He set his Mollweide to copy Ginger's, flying *Crius* with complete confidence by the waldo instruments. This should have been a court-martial offense, and he *must* have known better.

He didn't stop to think, this time, that attending to a visual display from one aircraft and tactile readings from another at the same time might strongly resemble trying to fly simultaneously by instrument and contact, a mistake which had killed far too many people through flying history.

Worse, Status had never been given instructions about appropriate reality breaks for anyone driving, in effect, two aircraft at once. The processor also lacked human common sense; the fact that one of the jets was on the ground would have affected human judgment, but Status made no attempt to reorganize the independently random breaks. It was pure chance that Belvew's own error rather than Status's inadequate procedure caused the first trouble. It had been inevitable anyway.

The sergeant fell into the trap he had set for himself. As Xalco started to swivel her charge, his reflexes for a moment responded to *Theia*'s attitude change rather than *Cruis*'s.

Theia was nearly motionless. *Crius* was at standard observing airspeed, which was already close to pipe stall for the present turbulence. Belvew's jet nosed up slightly as he entered an updraft, his reflexes tried to handle conflicting yaw and pitch inputs, his airspeed dropped further, and both his fires went out as *Cruis*'s sensors responded to inadequate ram pressure and her electronic reflexes sought to forestall a front fire.

Mentally, Belvew recovered instantly. Reflexively, he overcontrolled. This did not endanger the aircraft, which had plenty of altitude, or even deceive the waldo suit, which had built-in safety cutouts to cover shivering, startle reflexes, and even convulsions. The suits had been designed, after all, for terminally ill wearers. The overcontrol was strictly in Belvew's own body, the results purely biological. Everyone in the station, including Xalco, heard him yelp.

"What's wrong, Gene?" the commander cried. The answer came from Status, not the sergeant, who was already doffing his waldo and emphatically did not want to talk.

"His right ulna is broken some four centimeters above the elbow. He seems to have forgotten momentarily his bone condition."

"Gene! Can you fly?"

" 'Fraid not."

"Carla, take *Crius*!" snapped the commander. "Don't worry about the pattern if you can't follow it without practice—the aircraft itself is more important. Status, provide Lieutenant lePing with full-detail guidance for that observing grid after she recovers from the present stall until she tells you it's not needed. Gene, are you out of your suit yet?"

"Yes."

"Good. Get onto your cot and let Status do what's needed."

"Does he know? I haven't actually broken anything until now. Only been expecting it."

"We'll soon find out. Ginger, what's your status?"

"Still taxiing, a couple of hundred meters south of the pool, nearly three hundred from the factory. I assume I carry on." There was no question in her tone at first; then a thought struck her. "Or do you want Mastro to take over here and me to handle *Crius*? I've been in the turbulence already."

The commander hesitated only a moment. "No," she decided. "Carla has plenty of altitude if she needs it, and you've been down at the factory before. Louis hasn't. Pick up the cans, and at least a dozen labs. You said there were more than that, Status?"

"Yes. Everything previously suggested is ready to load when the jet reaches position. I assume the standing order to look for detail changes around *Oceanus* should be supplemented from any relevant *Theia* camera data as she taxis."

"Right. What are you doing about Gene's arm?"

"The bone ends are set and the elbow and shoulder immobilized. There are few data on what to expect in the knitting process with CPRS, but it will be several days before he can use a suit for either flying or environmental protection. I will maintain continuous watch over his blood calcium and phosphorus as well as bone analysis. Do you have further suggestions?"

"Not right now." She did not bother to ask for other ideas which seemed promising, reasonable, or even slightly relevant; that was common sense even Status would take for granted. She went back to the basic problem.

"Status, how do the chemistries of the pools we've actually touched with ships, labs, or armor compare so far with each other and with any others you have on file?"

"All are alike in being essentially gels with apparently monovinyl alcohol as the dispersing agent. I have no basic data which would have let us predict that this compound would be so stable even at Titan's temperature. The most up-to-date bonding information I have suggests that the activation energy for its conversion to water and acetylene should be low enough to make the reaction explosively rapid even here. We are of course in a temperature range where tunneling strongly affects reaction-rate calculations, but so far no combination of Arrhenius formulas and tunneling theory seems to match any observations. Commander Goodall was investigating this point."

"I suppose," Yakama interjected, "that this will all be very useful if humanity survives and we have nothing to do but unravel the mysteries of the universe. It complicates the human survival problem, though, if this project of ours is really part of it."

Even Belvew chuckled at the complaint, and Maria briefly but uselessly pitied the computer, which presumably could not *enjoy* learning. Status went on as though there had been no interruption. "Subject to conflicting orders, I strongly advise moving the sample now under study in the mausoleum outside for safety, though the condition and behavior of those still in the commander's quarters at normal life temperature suggest that trouble is not likely. I advise also that the same precaution be taken with these, Commander. They are at a far higher temperature than the mausoleum.''

That brought silence. Status was not supposed to have an imagination; any foresight it showed should be a very straightforward extrapolation indeed. Therefore it should suggest only very probable events. Everyone who had ever heard of nitrogen triiodide monoammate suddenly remembered about it.

The work, however, went on, even among the knowledgeable. They belonged, after all, to a species whose members are highly skilled in convincing themselves that if something they don't want hasn't happened yet, it probably won't. Even Maria rejected the hint.

Ginger looked a little uneasily at the remains of *Oceanus* as she slid past, but didn't allow the memory of Belvew's landing misfortune to distract her seriously. Loading from the factory was straightforward but needed care. She had to get close enough for the dispensers to reach the jet, but not too close. Also, wings could not be allowed to damage themselves against ground objects; and getting into a position which could not be escaped without exposing the factory to rocket exhaust would be highly embarrassing.

The factory could of course be replanted, probably even with an improved model, but if the wasted time meant that the staff would all be dead before its job was done, this would still be a net loss. Ginger did not take seriously any of the half-lives for the group which had been calculated en route to Saturn—or even the later ones.

She nudged the aircraft slowly into position, wincing slightly as the tank gauges forced themselves on her consciousness, and signaled the factory to start loading. A tube promptly reached out from the main structure, passed over and along *Theia*'s right wing, and approached the fuselage. She relaxed slightly as the proper hatch opened to accept it, and her instruments showed that cans were settling into the proper magazines. She felt even better as these filled and labs began to come aboard.

She was almost completely happy when the tube withdrew and

left her free to fire up once more. Almost, not totally, because the
fuel gauges were still looking at her—the nice economical landing
had been followed by much taxiing. Also, it had crossed her mind
during the recent conversation that no one had thought to replenish
from the orbiting station the heavy-metal stocks which had been
yolk to the factory's original egg, and which must be getting low by
now. Since nothing could be done about it this trip, she filed a reminder with Status and resumed maneuvering.

There were a few boulders of fallen ice from the eastern cliff to
be avoided during departure. She felt quite proud of managing this
without sending exhaust anywhere near the factory, but by then the
tank gauges wore an even more reproachful expression.

She considered the wind, and decided that a slightly downwind
takeoff would use less extra mass than meters of extra taxiing. She
swung around to the northwest, lined up carefully with no visible
ice fragments directly ahead within some hundreds of meters, and
pumped liquid into the arcs. She noticed on her Mollweide an ice
boulder behind *Theia* caught in the exhaust and shattered into flying
fragments, wished briefly that this could have happened in time to
warn Barn Inger, and relaxed slightly as her keels left Titan's surface.

Looking for a thunderhead once into ramjet mode was routine.
Tanks full, she relaxed even further.

The monovinyl alcohol explosion warning had little effect on
the general personnel of the station, and apparently none whatever on Seichi Yakama. He seemed to have gone through the it-
hasn't-happened-yet-so-there-must-be-some-reason-it-won't stage so
quickly that he was never conscious of it.

His next words followed Status's explosion warning so quickly
that they should have formed a response to it, but there was no
instantly obvious relevance in what he said.

"When a situation is chemically unstable but long-lasting, as
when a planet loaded with reducing agents has an oxygen-rich atmosphere, there's always one reasonable explanation," he remarked.

"I'm glad you didn't say *only* one," the commander responded.
"Have you ever seen a diamond decay to graphite, which is more

stable? The loose word 'life,' which you seem to have in mind, is not, without mention of specific items like 'photosynthesis' or 'dynamic equilibriums' or 'activation energy,' much better than 'protoplasm' or even 'the supernatural' as an explanation.'' Once again she managed to keep the reproof from sounding personal. Belvew wondered less about how she did it than why. She went on, ''Do you have any such specifics?''

''Not yet, but I think something's cooking. I need some more comparisons.''

''Status is listening.''

''I think this may be a bit abstract for mere statistics, but give me anything unexpected you spot, Status.''

''Unlimited?''

''Relevant to any equipment on the ground or in the aircraft.''

''Starting now, earlier, or later?'' Maria couldn't see Seichi's face and didn't want to—she knew his ailment, of course—but she could imagine its expression.

''Now!'' The exclamation point leaked slightly into his tone.

''There is a discrepancy heavily masked by turbulence effects, small as they now are, between *Theia*'s power setting, attitude, and airspeed. Move slowly, Sergeant Belvew, if you must move at all. You have other bones at risk, there is no obvious immediate danger to the aircraft, and you are not now either flying it or even in a suit.''

The sergeant may have stopped moving, but not talking.

''The pipes picked up something in the lake, remember? Something that we thought burned out later. You can see all the fields of all the cameras; show us *Theia*'s skin—wings, stabilizers, what you can of the fuselage.''

The Mollweide in the sergeant's quarters did not change, but smaller screens suddenly displayed sections of the jet's surface. Maria quietly requested the same data, and both scrutinized the images carefully. Neither felt certain of what was being shown, and the commander spoke thoughtfully: ''Status, you have enough viewpoints to build 3-D images of these fields.''

"Most of them. I have such images already, but doubt that you could perceive anything significant without my adding exaggerations along one or more axes which would destroy the image meaning for you."

"If you can't show us, abstract verbally. Describe them to us."

"Irregular areas carry a coating, never more than a fifth of a millimeter thick and usually much less, of a varnishlike material colorless to human eyes but absorbing strongly in some infrared bands. These spectra, plus recent events, suggest the material is probably organic."

Yakama smiled broadly with what was left of his face, happy for more than the usual reason that no one could see him. His expression would have made his lack of objectivity—downright wishful thinking, in fact—far more obvious than carefully chosen words should.

"This is on wings and fuselage, but not on stabilizers?"

"Correct."

"And on the bottom of the fuselage, and part of the sides, but not on the top." This time the words were not a question.

"Correct."

"And stabilizers were not immersed in the lake, but underbody and parts of the wings were." This was declarative also, and Belvew certainly did not argue. He was not silent, of course.

"Commander, I suggest we slow that jet down enough to make it safe, and play with wing camber. It would be really nice to know whether this stuff is frozen and will crack off if we change the curvature under it."

Maria, silently thankful that the suggestion had not been given as an order, asked the actual pilot, "Major, did you hear that?"

"Yes, Commander."

"How about it? Practical? You're high enough?"

"Not yet. Give me a few minutes to climb, and maybe half an hour for the tests."

"All right, do it. If it still seems safe, go on and make the drops at Belvew's Hill."

"And Status!" added Belvew. "Keep close track of the thickness of that stuff, especially on the wings, starting right now. Don't wait until Ginger starts trying to stretch or crack it."

"I am recording and will call general attention at once to any change."

Gene Belvew was feeling sleepy by this time, but his arm hurt. The only way to keep the pain out of his mind seemed to be concentration, with study about the only form of this now available. Reading fiction was not, to him, fun, in spite of Maria's missionary work. He enjoyed more passive forms of entertainment such as vision shows, but was sure from conversation with the late Arthur Goodall that this was probably too passive to take attention from serious pain. He had Status raise the detail level of the chemical abstracts the sergeant had been skimming from the huge knowledge bank, in order to keep himself busier and less aware of his discomfort. This worked fairly well, but he also found himself less certain that he was understanding the material. He even found his mind wandering—wishing for the mechanical educators of the classical literature he *had* been persuaded to try, for example. Too bad the human nervous system didn't work that way. Information came in through the senses, and then analogy took over. The puzzle had to be assembled, and there was only guessing which piece should be examined next. One could hope it would be in the Titan box, and even in the biochemistry color, but this was only hope. Life, and not just human life, was coming apart on Earth; but was it really coming *together* on Titan? And if it was, would the knowledge really help humanity?

Was the reason for the human catastrophe really chemical, as seemed so likely? Life, after all, is basically a chemical phenomenon; this concept had inspired the whole Titan project, which represented a major commitment of resources even with pseudolife and casual fusion energy absorbing nearly all the former costs of manufacture. Planning and design now took most of the heavy thinking and time.

If it really was chemical, how well could the details of one life-producing process steer anyone to the right details of another? It had never occurred to anyone that life on Titan, if any, would be identical with life at the same stage on Earth.

He watched words and diagrams flow across his screen, sometimes ordering a rerun when he could tell he was missing something, sometimes letting it pass when his mind wandered further than usual.

Proteins. Carbohydrates. Condensation polymers. Activation energy and reaction rates—no, that meant less on Titan. Fragmentation. Random reassembly. Autocatalysis. Chemical evolution—were preconceived ideas steering him, and the rest of the group, aside here? Chains and folds. *Dev*olution. Viruses, prions—at least the diagrams were getting simpler again. Too simple? Similes instead of analogies?

Status stopped the input when the sergeant fell asleep. It seems unlikely that processing also stopped in the man's head, but he failed to hear the report that *Theia*'s wing varnish was rubbery; it bent and stretched even at Titan temperature.

Ginger Xalco dropped the additional labs close enough to target to be useful, though Seichi had to take a little time from pure chemistry to direct them to the spots he wanted. The area of Arthur's Pool was still foggy and shaky. She got from Status the heading toward the start of her next seismic layout and started for Titan's anti-Saturn pole.

19

STRAIN

MARIA DID NOT LET the next few minutes go to waste.

"Seichi, how are your analyses going? Or did this new item distract you?"

"The analyses are going well, but the event *has* distracted me. There is more information than before coming in from Arthur's Pool, which will take much longer to digest; but I want a chance to analyze that wing varnish. Can that be done without landing Ginger near a lab or bringing her up here? I mean the plane, of course, not the major."

"I don't see how," the commander replied slowly and thoughtfully. "Any suggestions, anyone?" Silence ensued. "All right. Ginger, head back for the factory when your grid is done. Status'll give you a heading when you need it. You don't mind landing again so soon?"

"I don't think so, unless it turns out this stuff on the wings causes problems I can't foresee now. If it's just going to affect wing stall, I can handle that—just land a little hot. Gene?"

"Probably not even that. At transsonic and near-stall speeds even tiny changes in airfoil shape can be tricky, but not this time. My change wasn't tiny. You'll be doing a lot more to the shape yourself as you make the landing."

"That's what I thought. Thanks."

No more was said about *Oceanus*'s last landing. Status would now advise without special request about accumulations on the wings, but neither it nor anyone else knew what other warnings might also be appropriate. Ginger began to plan in detail just what flight tests she would make, but didn't bother to discuss them with Belvew; her own piloting experience might not be quite as great as the sergeant's, but she trusted it. Belvew's lower rank had nothing to do with this decision. Like nearly everyone in the group she was more scientist than either pilot or soldier. This in spite of being a scientist only by attitude, not training.

The question of what was coating *Theia*'s wings was officially up to Seichi and Status, Belvew realized. Even "mere" observers were expected to think, however. Belvew smiled as he remembered that consciously; he had of course been doing his share of this— more than his share, he often felt—all along.

After another two minutes' brooding, he told Status to abstract at a level halfway between "business interest" and "engineering specialist" and to resume feeding him biochemistry.

Random encyclopedia scanning is not a very good road to organized knowledge, but it is an excellent way to find ideas, at least when the ideas needn't at first be right. Once inspiration comes, of course, the scanning needs to become more ordered.

Actually, the sergeant started with a trace of order, perhaps inspired by the nature of his own ailment. He concentrated on the biochemistry of calcium, decided that that was too narrow, and spread the search to include other metal ions. It was a lucky choice, he thought later.

Or might have been.

Hence, Ginger had barely started her stall tests when he got an idea. Being Belvew, he decided at once that only the latter part of GO6 really applied, that the questions he wanted to ask were actually tests of a hypothesis and needn't be accompanied by an alternative one. He could have been right.

"Captain Yakama, have you been looking just for organics in

the tar, or have you given some machine time to heavies—to metals?"

"Structures mainly. They take more time, and are more in line with what we are hoping to find. We have a reading for metals from one or two sources, but they aren't in general surprising; nothing much was expected out here."

Belvew shook his head negatively and uselessly. "I'm not sure of that. Think about magnesium in chlorophyll and iron in blood. There was some iron in—"

"We're looking for prelife. We did look for metals occasionally; you're right there. There was iron in your hill and gold in Arthur's Pool. But you're talking pretty highly evolved life."

"Are you sure? Some very early life forms on Earth got their energy by oxidizing iron."

"I didn't know that, but—"

"Look, even I know the structure analyzers are independent of the pore units. You could look for metal ions without delaying anything. What metals could you detect on the atom-count scale, anyway?"

"I don't know offhand. Status?"

"In principle, anything from lithium to cernium. Some would require several stages of selection to narrow down to one possibility," answered data handler.

"Then why not—?" started Belvew.

"No reason, I suppose. Do you want everything, or will the mag and iron make you happy?"

"Well—those plus calcium to start with. Okay?"

Seichi might have sighed, but Belvew wasn't sure and didn't care. "All right. If it's atoms per mm-cubed amounts, you may have to wait awhile. I know a little silicate and carbonate dust is scattered through most of the surface ice, but don't count on too much heavy stuff getting up from the core even if this silly moon does have tectonics. The dust isn't all that soluble in ice, whatever it may do in liquid water. Loose ions could still be few and far between."

"I suppose so. Thanks for trying. If you *want* to add any others while you're at it—"

"We'll see." The sigh was definite this time. Belvew returned to his studies for fully ten minutes before Yakama called back.

"Gene."

"Yes?"

"I was thinking about conceivable causes for Belvew's Hill, since none of the other tar pools had any hump that big, and I did add another metal or two to the list."

"And?"

"The goo in your pool is filthy with iron, remember? Whole nanograms per liter. There is also nickel—and phosphorus, remember?"

Even Belvew was silent long enough for Maria to react.

"Status! How long did it take for the lost lab there to cease reporting after it touched the tar?"

"Three minutes twenty-one seconds."

"And how long would any lab take between picking up a sample and giving any sort of metal report?"

"Fourteen to twenty-five seconds, depending on program settings and the metal."

"Maria! I have lots of labs," snapped Ginger. "I might as well go back to the lake as to the factory, and—"

"Not until we find out what's on your wings. I don't want you near the ground before then, except for that one landing. Carry on with your present program. Carla!"

"Yes, Commander."

"Finish the grid at your present altitude, then head for Carver. Ask Status for a heading when you need it. When you get there, make passes over Belvew's Hill as low and slow as seems safe, dropping labs on it and near it until you've used up half your stock. We'll save the rest for any repeats that seem needed, and we still have enough inert metals to make more. Status, determine the landing spot and operational status of each lab as it stops moving, and have it test for iron, nickel, sodium, potassium—every metal through period four. Seichi, start up through the periodic table with at least some of the labs you're using at both Arthur's Pool and *Oceanus,* and tell Status of anything surprising which should be looked for by the other labs when Carla drops them. Understood?"

She was understood.

Lieutenant lePing was not particularly tense as Lake Carver came into sight ahead. Low flying was of course risky, but she had followed through on many such maneuvers and performed enough on her own.

She was coming in from the south because that was most convenient. She assumed incorrectly that Belvew would be watching, and felt relieved when no remarks followed her first pass. She could see the three working labs, and knew that the other was now completely submerged or dissolved in the whatever-it-was. LePing was developing some sympathy for Seichi's wishful thinking.

She found she could drop four labs on each pass. Even though two of the first four missed the hill, one of the others made up for it by rolling to the center of the dimple. LePing waited before making another drop until she heard Status report that all four were still in working condition, at least for now.

She did better on the next drops, averaging only about one miss per seven tries. By the time she finished the allotted number of labs, the early ones had all gone out of service. The hill seemed still to be hungry.

"Should I slow down even more and see if they're disappearing, too, Commander? I'm a bit uneasy; I've used quite a bit of juice."

"Go up and refill. It'll take us a while to digest this material," Maria responded, unconscious of any pun. "Seichi, I suppose you're thinking meteorite."

"Of course."

"I'm startled to find an iron or even a stony iron this far out from the Sun, but I can't argue with the labs. Go ahead, Carla."

There was at the moment no thunderhead immediately above Lake Carver, a fact which Maria noted as also needing explanation sooner or later, but the pilot circled slowly as she climbed, spotted a likely mass source a score of kilometers away, and headed toward it. General attention shifted from aircraft to analytical instruments.

"You said phosphorus?" asked Maria, recalling Goodall's readings of weeks before.

"More likely C-N-O." Belvew's return to the conversation was less surprising than his choice of subject.

"Why on Earth?" Maria started, and stopped. The sergeant ignored the tempting lead.

"Right now I'm betting on low-weight polypeptides. The iron adds possibilities. Nice, thin glue for Ginger's wings, too," he added. No one could see his face—few could imagine or even remember much of it but ferociously black eyebrows after the months of isolation—but no one missed the smugness in his voice. No one missed the implications of phosphorus, either.

"It will take a while to find what part if any the iron takes in the structures, even the ones we have so far," Yakama reminded them, "but your inspiration seems to have some merit. Should I do an optical macro search for coarse structure, such as cell walls, before I report? The lab's not really designed for it, but I think I could do something with the crystallography gear."

"I'm not *that* optimistic," Belvew replied more quietly. "Let's check my chances of being right about the rest first, unless you can't wait yourself."

"I find no phosphorus in this batch," Seichi reported.

"There was before!" Belvew insisted.

"I know."

"So it's near the edges. Just where it's growing—"

"Sergeant, aren't you getting a little ahead of the data?" Maria cut in as smoothly as she could.

"Well, I suppose so. But I'll be really surprised if we don't find amino acids and maybe nucleic acids there. I've said it and I'm not apologizing," he added.

"You needn't," the commander responded soothingly.

"You needn't," Seichi came in almost simultaneously. "There

are carbon-nitrogen single bonds and carbon-oxygen doubles, but no oxygen-nitrogen either single or double. Your chances of being right have just gone up several thousand percent, I'd say."

"That's all I want to know for now," Belvew replied happily. "Unless you need me, Commander, I have some more studying to do."

"Are you looking for something specific?"

"No, just pieces." The jigsaw-puzzle analogy needed no further explanation.

"Shape, or color?" the commander persisted.

"My stall tests are done," Ginger came in before Gene could answer, if he had intended to. "I'm heading for Factory One."

Minutes later lePing reported full tanks, and was sent back to Belvew's Hill to drop more labs.

Peter Martucci was spending as much time as he could spare in his waldo suit working simulated flying problems with Status, trying to foresee as many situations as possible in which his intrinsically slow reaction time would really put a jet in danger. He had known, in a remote way, that he might someday have to fly in spite of his disability, but he had never grasped the need as a likely reality until now. Reality was forcing itself on *all* of the dwindling crew.

Seichi Yakama was considering the accumulating analysis results from the areas named for Arthur Goodall, Gene Belvew, and *Oceanus*. He had originally reported them as being generally similar; now he was wondering almost seriously whether all were on the same planet. In near desperation and after some careful lab maneuvering, he got more samples from Lake Carver itself. The results seemed not useful except possibly in the Sherlock Holmes sense: eliminate the impossible . . .

If you can recognize it, of course, Doyle should have added. Seichi was another minor respondent to Maria's reading evangelism.

Maria Collos got some sleep. Lieutenant Carla lePing got good practice flying low passes over Belvew's Hill, and Yakama recorded what he could from each lab while it lasted. He took it on himself to have lePing cease dropping until he could catch up with the data; he was very aware of the heavy-metal stocks.

Status announced that the recent atmospheric oddities were statistically almost certainly due to eclipses and that specific mechanisms could be investigated if anyone with an imagination would suggest any.

Ginger heard this announcement and began to think; she was still far from the factory, the air was calm, and flying this high took little attention.

Belvew, still asleep, did not hear the announcement and in any case was not currently interested in planetary air circulation. He slept until Ginger was halfway to the factory.

He woke with no new idea in mind, wondered briefly how much chemistry he had missed, realized what Status would have done about that, ate without appetite—the station's foods were genuine meats, fruits, and vegetables grown from cloned tissues and perfectly palatable, but he just wasn't interested in food at the moment—and addressed a question to Seichi.

"Have you checked what's going on in the mausoleum?"

"No. I've been too busy with the other comparisons. Status must have its progress, if you need to know."

"I don't want anyone to tell me yet. I woke up with the web of an idea, and I want to add some threads. Just a test prediction: Status, I'm guessing that nothing measurable has happened to Jerry—the fellow infected from Maria's hand. Right?"

"Correct, Sergeant." The word "test" had probably influenced the computer's use of title, but did not move it to ask questions. Those would have to come from the living minds.

"Why not?" Maria, also recently awake and alert, pounced on the prediction.

She had no chance to get an answer. A dozen warning bells and lights clamored and flashed for attention. Ginger gave a startled exclamation as her accelerometers, both linear and angular, visual and tactile, gave weird combinations of signals.

"Turbulence! You said it was safe in this hemisphere!"

"You read too much into my report. I tried to warn of its limitations. Your present disorder is at least partly due to change in aerodynamic configuration—look."

The Mollweide screens, ordinarily showing no part of a jet's own image, changed for everyone. Part of the new field was hard to see, as the background scenery was spinning madly. The visible sections of *Theia*, howver, were stationary with respect to her cameras, and caught all eyes at once.

The left wing, from a few meters outboard of the engine, was gone, and no trace of it could be seen by anyone in the whirling background of Titan. The break was ragged but uninformative.

"Did I hit something? I was awake, and you weren't slipping a reality break on me, Status."

"You were, and I was not. You did not strike anything in the air. My images showed and still show no obstacles in your neighborhood. The wing simply broke, without anything I could interpret as a warning. There does not seem to have been any turbulence, or to be any now, since I have analyzed the current motion pattern."

"Have you any control? Can you possibly land without any more damage?" asked Maria.

"I can't stop the spin, even with the other pipe completely cut out," was the answer. Belvew gave a yelp of pain.

"What happened, Sergeant?" asked the commander.

"Don't mind me. I just broke another bone. Ginger—no, Status—were any tar pools in sight fron *Theia* just before this happened?"

"Yes. Two."

"Good. Ginger, if you can control at all, try to head for the nearest. We might as well get another test out of this. Crash in it if you can."

"You—"

"Do your best, Major. We'll understand if you miss," Maria cut in.

Xalco cut both engines completely and nosed down, but there

seemed to be no combination of thrust and airspeed which would let her override the vast difference in lift now existing between the two wings. The spin continued, but the ground was clearly approaching on all the screens.

"I could imagine its happening to me, after what Gene's been saying," remarked Carla thoughtfully as she remembered her turbulence grids, "but Ginger's contamination wasn't on just that wing, was it?"

No one answered. Even Martucci was trying to follow, or better to anticipate mentally, Ginger Xalco's efforts with *Theia*'s controls. There were faint cheers each time the dark patch which was clearly her target moved a little closer to the screen center, slight gasps and groans when it circled farther away.

"Ginger! Rocket mode! Full thrust on both pipes!" Belvew suddenly cried. Whether the pilot saw his intent or was merely in a mood to take any suggestion no one ever asked. "Flatten the right wing. Eight points camber on the left—and I thought the designer was an idiot to have those wings cambered separately! There!"

The spin stopped with startling abruptness. "Nose up carefully! Left engine half thrust, right at minimum needed to hold your heading! Get out of atmosphere! Status, give her a heading for station intercept while she can still steer!"

"I have it. Thanks, Gene."

"Not worried, were you? Remember you're not on board."

"I did forget. You would have too. I didn't really worry, though. And don't try look at my face, please." In the privacy of her quarters, Major Xalco wiped her bare scalp once more.

"Sergeant, has Status taken care of your new fracture?" The late Arthur Goodall had properly judged his chosen successor's grasp of values.

"Oh, sure. It's lucky he can take verbal commands."

"Why? What's happened this time?"

"My other arm, of course."

The last two words were echoed by Ginger, who then had the grace to add, "It's just as well you can still talk, though. I don't suppose I'd have been able to come up with that maneuver on my own.''

Belvew grinned in privacy. "Well, I have to admit I was talking without thinking.''

"I can believe that—sorry. Can you talk me into intercept orbit from this plane, or had we better use Status?''

"It's not mental arithmetic this time, especially with unsymmetrical thrust. Vacuum will help, but—Status, give her the dope.''

The processor obeyed, but Belvew's help was still needed, to his unashamed glee. The velocity changes were simple mathematical items, but actually achieving the velocities themselves was not. The lost wing segment meant a change in *Crius*'s centers of mass, pressure, and angular inertia, and complicated the actual maneuvers greatly even beyond atmosphere. By the time the acceleration integrators reported a set of velocities, they were slightly out of date and new ones were needed. By the time true orbit injection had been managed, the tank gauges were embarrassingly, but fortunately not critically, low.

The velocity match at apoapsis, involving both speed and orbit-plane change, took even more mass; but enough remained when docking was completed to permit another departure if one were ever needed. This was not the primary consideration for everyone; after all, there was still some spare water in the station.

"Ginger, turn loose a lab while you're still in there!" Yakama called firmly as his instruments reported docking complete. "I want the word on that wing varnish!"

"I'm not sure I want to know how close I came to dropping half the fuselage instead of half a wing, or the other wing, but all right. But what do you mean, while I'm still in there?''

"Sorry. I wasn't thinking. Get to your bed 'n' bath. I'll do the lab work.''

Seichi didn't find the lab work quite that easy. They did have appendages usable as legs, but no designer had considered a possible need for the labs in free fall. Even if they had had solenoids to hold them against a surface for traction, there were essentially no magnetic surfaces in either jets or the station. Yakama went to the dock in person, found the lab which Ginger had released and which was now floating uncooperatively around the jet, and held it in place while its scraper worked.

The results were neither surprising nor, at first, very helpful. There were none of the simple hydrocarbons which had been found in the lake; these would presumably have evaporated during orbit. None of the bonding pattern now being interpreted as monovinyl alcohol showed up. This relieved many; Seichi had forgotten, if he had ever noticed, Status's warning on possible explosion and had brought the samples to his own quarters. Status had not repeated its earlier extrapolation; all concerned had presumably heard it, and deciding whether to heed it or not was a human duty. The processor could evaluate risks by straightforward extrapolation, but could not weigh them against possible returns without highly specific instructions.

Belvew had paused to digest his latest biochemical-information meal when Seichi's preliminary report was announced. The sergeant reacted predictably.

"What it *isn't* may be a relief, but what *is* the stuff? Prions? Protein fragments? Not bits of lab, I hope."

"If I'd expected prions it wouldn't be in here—," Seichi started.

"There could have been. Why *is* it there? I thought you'd sent it outside for the work." Maria's voice was less sympathetic than usual. "Are you trying to pull a Goodall?"

"No, Commander. I just wasn't thinking of that. I—"

"Maybe that's what's happening to humanity. We've added so many things to the original saber-toothed cats in our environment that we can't remember all the ones we should be careful about. Consider yourself reprimanded."

"Sorry, Commander."

"*Are* there prions, or anything like them?"

"Well, there are what seem to be protein fragments. Whether they can replicate I don't know, and I don't see offhand how we find out."

"There's always the hard way. Better get them outside before we do." This was Belvew.

"I was careful to keep them sealed. If I didn't succeed, whatever can happen probably already has."

Maria was firm again. "Nevertheless, get them out to the vacuum lab. That won't compromise any data; zero-P must have done all it could to the stuff before it got up here. We don't want to find out what putting it back into atmosphere might do, just yet."

Belvew didn't actually contradict, but couldn't hold back.

"You mean we'd love to find out, but not by personal experience. Will it speed things up if I help you, Seichi?"

"I doubt it, with both your arms broken."

"They're splinted. I can use 'em to move low-mass stuff in free fall."

"Don't try, Sergeant. You're an experimental subject until we find out how long it takes those bones to knit, if they ever do. Until then, no unplanned variables."

"All right, Commander. But shouldn't *someone* help Seichi? The faster that stuff is outside, the better, it seems to me."

"You may be right, but the fewer the people who have a chance for cross-infection, the better, too. Get at it, Captain."

"I'm topping off my suit. I'll be bringing the main box out in about ten minutes. Check your doors. Status, monitor me and the suit as completely as you can."

"I am doing so. Your own physical parameters are within normal range, and your suit shows no clear sign of chemical attack or surface contamination not attributable to oxygen and water. Straight up to the axis and then to the antidock pole remains the safest route. Captain, I would advise not touching any of the material until your suit is ready and you are back inside it."

"Right. Sorry. I won't do it again. I was thinking of saving time by fastening the sample cases together so I could take them along all at once."

"Sensible enough, Seichi," Maria approved. "Just wait till

you're back in armor before you do it. That may cost a little time, but I'm willing to spend it."

"All right. The suit checks out now, and I'm getting back into it. Status, monitor my checklist."

"Watching, Captain. I suggest you be sure the waldo function is deactivated before getting into it."

This obvious recommendation would have been insulting from a human being but was within the range of Status's programmed concerns. Seichi merely nodded; the processor, after all, was watching him. He sealed and checked the suit, and began to assemble into a single bundle the specimen container and the half dozen specialized labs.

20

SATISFACTION

THE PACKING PROVED much more awkward than expected. The station labs were much larger than those grown and used down below, and were not intended to be portable even in free fall. The problem settled down to deciding whether to take out the specimen container first and come back for the labs, or reverse the procedure. Seichi opted for the former.

"I'm unsealing," he reported. "I'll have to make two trips; I can't carry all the labs with the big box. I could bring one or maybe two, but they can't readily be fastened to anything but tabletops and each other, and I'd hate to lose any of them once outside, so it's two trips either way."

Even with the smaller load, travel was not easy. Floating along free-fall handholds while carrying a half-meter cube—too large to be tucked conveniently under one arm—was another item no one had foreseen during station design, though the passageways were big enough and the effective gravity was much less than one percent. Yakama rested briefly, releasing his load and floating freely himself, when he reached the axis. He had the foresight to make sure he and his burden were a little off the line on the same side, so any drift would be in the same direction for both.

Status had not been told to stop the personal check of the armor, and now reported again.

"Captain, there is a film growing on both gloves and forearms of your suit." Seichi was too startled to react at once, and Belvew had returned to his chemical studies; but Maria responded fast enough.

"Get your load out to the air lock, and stand by there until we can get an extrapolation. Don't evacuate the lock until we have some idea of your chances of reaching the vacuum lab and getting back in before you leak—or pop."

"Right. On the way."

"Status, do what you can to correlate thickness of film with that wing failure while he's in range of your eyes. When he goes into the air lock give an estimate of how long that suit will be space-worthy, and how much you trust the estimate."

"Measuring. My sensing equipment can follow him through the lock and out to the vacuum lab."

"Good, but report while he's still in the lock. He won't open until you do. That's an order, Seichi. Sorry if it's unnecessary; no insult intended. Ginger, you're suited up." It was not really a question.

"Sure," the major lied, almost certain that Status wouldn't comment. She was not going to miss any fun.

"As soon as Seichi is in the lock, go up and wait there until he comes back. If he doesn't manage it under his own power, be ready for a rescue."

"And contaminate my own suit and the rest of the station?"

Maria may not have thought of that aspect, but answered promptly but vaguely, "First things first." Xalco may have had doubts about which were the first things, but she said nothing. If the commander wondered why a full two minutes passed before Ginger reported that she was unsealing her quarters, this too remained unvoiced.

"Don't come out until Seichi is into the lock. That'll be a minute or two yet. Is the film either spreading or going deeper, Status?"

"Yes. Both. It is growing much faster than it did on the aircraft skin, but it should be several minutes yet before the suit will be unsafe.''

"High temperature or different chemical environment," muttered Martucci, obeying GO6 in about as few words as possible.

"Open the inner door as he nears it, so he won't be trying to do two things at once," Maria said, maintaining her close supervision of the procedure.

Status responded by opening the door at once; Yakama and his load were now within a hundred meters of the lock, floating at a higher speed along the ice-walled axis than Maria herself would have cared to risk, and using each brief contact with the hand-holds and even the sides of the axial tunnel to increase his pace. As he approached the door, he worked himself around so that he was floating in front of the case. The commander tensed, imagining the man being flattened between the outer door of the lock and the massive block of extremely hard plastic he was carrying, but Seichi had recovered from whatever brief panic Status's warning had given him and was planning sensibly.

He went though the inner door feetfirst, with his arms holding the case as far above his head as he could while maintaining a firm grip on it. Status closed the door the instant it was clear, and a moment later Yakama's feet hit the outer seal. Even after years of zero-G he had no trouble controlling a deep-knee bend, bringing the load to a halt with over a meter to spare for his own crouching body. He took the block's relatively mild impact on the back of his suit at shoulder-blade level. Maria, whose screen had been shifted to an appropriate viewpoint by Status without orders, resumed breathing.

"You have four minutes on worst-case assumption before the handling extremities of your suit are likely to yield to internal pressure."

"What's the other extreme?" asked Yakama.

"You don't want that," cut in Maria. "Can you get out and back in four?"

"Probably not. I'll go slowly, just the same. I'd hate to lose this thing now. Status, open this door and the lab one."

Seichi's goal was a ten-meter cube made from interior partitions of the original ship, attached by a set of cables to a dozen points of the rotating station, "orbiting" under their restraint a hundred meters from the "north" pole, the one opposite the jet dock. It appeared from the pole to remain at a particular spot on the horizon, projected against the disk of Titan.

More cables held a comparable mass of ice equally far on the other side of the pole, minimizing precession forces, which, with the station's rotation period of two hundred twenty minutes, were small enough anyway. The unit looked like a very small target in a very large field, but the man made no comments as he hooked a leg about one of the cables without actually touching it.

He took a firm grip with both arms around his burden, pushed away from the station with the other leg, and promptly cocked that one around the cable too.

It had been a good push-off; he traveled the hundred meters in less than two minutes, with only an occasional contact between the cable and either leg.

For just a moment he floated unrestrained as he transferred from the cable to the doorway, keeping his mind firmly away from the hopelessness of even an attempt at rescue by the damaged and nearly fuelless ship only a kilometer away. Then he was inside and Status had closed the portal. Without too much haste, since carelessness could waste the risks taken already, Seichi attached the case to a worktable before asking anything about his personal safety.

"How's my suit?"

"The estimate is indefinite. The film seems to have stopped growing since you reached vacuum. Your suit material is, however, dangerously thin in several spots. You should be most careful of the affected hands and forearms. I strongly suggest that Major Xalco bring the other load from your quarters, rather than have you exposed to decompression before your suit heals."

Belvew rejoined the conversation. "Is that risk greater than having her suit infected?" he asked.

"Since the infection is stopped by vacuum—"

"Stopped permanently?"

Status admitted ignorance.

"We'll have to find out anyway." Maria took control again. "Seichi, get in as fast as possible without overstressing your gauntlets. You'll have to do your own guessing at what stress they can take right now. Status, watch for any resumption of film growth on his suit. Ginger, stay where you are until he's in the lock."

Ginger reacted typically at once. She was, after all, of theoretician grade. "Shouldn't I go to Seichi's place and get that other stuff? The sooner it's out of the station, the better."

Maria hesitated just a moment; even with Xalco suited up, the mental taboo against entering anyone else's quarters except in a medical emergency was stronger than mere regulations. The major was not wrong; GO6 had been applied before, in slightly strained fashion perhaps, to orders as well as ideas.

"All right," she finally said. "It's nice to know vacuum will take care of it at least temporarily, though I hope we don't have to use that on the whole station. Go on, Major."

Ginger didn't get far. She heard directly only the outer lock opening, since Yakama was outside; but the thud of its closing was covered by another announcement from Status.

"The captain's right gauntlet has ruptured. He is inside the lock. There seems no time for gradual pressurization. Major, I am performing inner-door emergency opening; get a handhold." Ginger failed to manage this, since no handhold was in reach, and was kicked toward the barrier by the gust as air filled the chamber. The sight of the drifting form in the lock left her undecided for a moment, until Yakama's voice uttered in very firm, though rather hoarse, tones, "I don't *like* vacuum."

"Did you get much of it?" asked Maria.

"Enough. I was inside the lock when it happened, but the outer door hadn't closed yet, and even with it closed the lock has a lot more volume than my suit. I didn't pass out, though."

"Good. Get back to your quarters and have Status give you a complete checkout. Ginger, go with him and get the other package.

Have Status check your armor for infection before you go out, and keep repeating it; if possible, get your load to the outside lab too. If your armor *is* infected by then, tell me and wait for orders. There's worthwhile work to do on the stuff out there, but I still have to think about the whole station. Now we have something which can infect aircraft material in the Titan environment, which is not a vacuum. That something, after several hours, can still attack suit tissue. This second infection, however, is *stopped* by vacuum."

"Maybe not the same something," interjected the doctor.

"True. And I'm not saying this affects our main project, but there are only nineteen of us left, and anything which seems likely to threaten all of us needs to be understood."

"Commander, there are only eighteen left," came the voice of Status. "Captain Yakama is dead." There was no pause for dramatic effect for this announcement, which helped reverse the slowly growing attitude among some of the staff that Status was a personality.

Ginger lost control of her load for a moment; Maria and several others repeated the last word in various tones of disbelief.

"But he seemed all right at the lock, and on the way back. He talked and moved well enough."

"He said only a few words, right after recompression. He was indeed conscious and coordinated then. He died forty-five seconds ago from suffocation. His lungs are nearly full of blood. There is no procedure available to me to repair the injury."

"He probably had nearly full lungs, and tried to hold his breath when the glove went!" exclaimed Belvew. "He'd have known better—we all do—but it's hard to get ahead of reflexes."

"His final statement before losing consciousness may have referred to that, though I am unable to relate the words to what actually happened to him. Imagination will presumably be needed. 'I should have thought. Heavy-metal coenzymes' were his last words."

There were some seconds of silence, which Gene spent wondering whether it would be wise to point out the processor's own neglect of GO6. He had just decided that admitting ignorance could hardly be called a speculation when the commander spoke again.

"Status, has the infection of Seichi's suit resumed?"

"No. So far, the stoppage presumably due to vacuum has lasted."

"Vacuum or particle radiation? We're outside Saturn's orbit and well inside its belt just now." Martucci was pleased with himself for obeying regs so promptly, but few heard his suggestion over Belvew's voice.

"Status! Is there any heavy metal from the lab pickups—iridium or gold—in the stuff from Seichi's suit? Or from *Crius*'s surface film?"

"Neither has yet been analyzed completely. Captain Yakama was at work on the latter when the decision to move the material was made. No one has even sampled his suit material."

"My job," Maria said instantly. "Someone has to move Seichi, and I can bring in another lab when I go for him. I can let it take scrapings from his suit, and use cordage to move him without contact."

"There are already several labs in his quarters, Commander. Also, I suggest you use the strapping now holding him to the treatment table; this can be freed from the table without touching the armor."

"Good. All hands: I'm unsealing and going to Seichi's quarters. I'll report en route to the mausoleum and again when I get back to my own room. Everyone stand by for memorial to another friend. Lieutenant Skokie, you seem the right one to collect and judge for relevance personal data for the eulogy.

"Status, keep checking my armor for infection, starting *now* to furnish control data, not waiting until I get to the captain. Cheru, complete the analyses on the wing sample he started, initiate the same kind when a suit sample is obtained, and answer Sergeant Belvew's question about heavy metals as quickly as precise work will permit. Everyone else, carry on."

The first answer came from Akagawa even before the commander's arrival at Seichi's door.

"The *Crius* samples average between forty and forty-one thousand atoms of gold per cubic millimeter, just a little less than a tenth as many of iridium, and about three thousand of platinum. This is roughly a tenth of a percent of what is found in Earth's oceans. More precision will require much more time, and ideally should have many more samples. Does this help your inspiration, Gene?"

"I don't see how."

"Maybe the rest of us can. Forget GO6 for the moment and tell us your idea." Maria did not quite make this sound like an order, but the sergeant needed little encouragement. He spoke less rapidly than usual, however; he seemed to be choosing his words with more than ordinary care.

"I've picked up quite a bit of biochem in the last few days. A lot of it has to do with the effects of metals on organics. For example, the iron in our blood and cells is framed in a porphyrin group"—he didn't pause to explain what a porphyrin group was; people who cared but didn't know already could consult Status for themselves— "and the magnesium in chlorophyll and the cobalt in vitamin B_{12} are similarly framed. All do very different jobs in our bodies, though. I still think—" He broke off suddenly. Then, "Cheru, how do those figures jibe with uncontaminated lake samples?" Belvew suddenly sounded even more excited again.

Ginger practically sneered. "If you mean uncontaminated by the collectors and lab reactors, how do we find out? Analyze uncollected samples?" She didn't sound exactly delighted, but she was not the only one glad to catch Gene asking a silly question. None of the others betrayed themselves, however: the sergeant riposted too promptly.

"Check something that was collected by scraper for gold, and something collected by tube for iridium, of course. The platinum is all inside the labs; test for it at different points along the procedure chain for different samples. Status will have records of every step if we don't wait too long. It'll be on the running log.

"Now we know why they used different metals in the labs, I guess. Remember we were wondering why just iridium wasn't enough? I'll bet *somebody* showed some foresight after all in planning this. We certainly can cross-check, Major. We used up lots of labs on my little hill, some on our late commander's, and I'm sure the collection routines must have varied here and there between solid and liquid sampling."

Status probably caught and even interpreted annoyed sounds in that part of its attention centered on crew welfare, but rightly judged them irrelevant. "All such information is on record. It will take some minutes to check and cross-check. You are right about the varying routines."

Most of the survivors spent the minutes ignoring current duties and trying to imagine what Belvew had in mind; but even the answer, which came well within the promised time, failed to help them.

"About ninety-one percent of all three metals appear to come from contamination from collectors and Colonel Goodall's remains. As was pointed out, many more sources should be sampled to make these figures really reliable."

"Don't waste the time here," replied the sergeant. "Commander, I suggest we report this to Earth, and advise they start checking for really heavy metal coenzymes *everywhere*. Remember, we've been using such metals in increasing quantities for two or three centuries now at home.

"Do it in tissue samples dating from now as far back as possible—before the general collapse if the data are still around. I suggest that increasing heavy-metal distribution has made new enzymes possible."

"You think—"

"I think Seichi's last words about heavy-metal coenzymes meant more than we thought—and possibly more than he thought. The trouble is, the quantities just reported, at even one metal atom per molecule, couldn't possibly be enough for what I'm thinking, unless I've missed something really important in my lessons from Status. The four metal atoms instead of one in each molecule, as hemoglobin has, would make it a lot worse. I'll check my arithmetic and the numbers Status gave me, too."

"But how could something like the population implosion, with the increase in metal and presumably in any new enzymes being slow and fairly steady, appear so suddenly?" asked Ginger.

"That's common sense. For any pandemic, the cause, either microbe or chemical, needs to reproduce, or at least increase, faster in the environment than it's decreased or immobilized by the deaths of its hosts or victims. It could *exist* for thousands or millions of years at an unnoticeable concentration, forming by random reactions or mutations or human hacking, and causing too few problems to be noticed. Most of its victims would probably die of an ordinary cancer or traffic accident before the new symptoms were taken seriously or even noticed. Lack of raw material would limit its expansion rate."

"You really have been reading," remarked Xalco. "It couldn't have been random. What was steering you?"

"I don't know. I haven't read any psychology. It wasn't conscious thinking, though. But let me finish your question. For the coenzymes, once we started high-energy living, the supply of heavy metals being *widely spread* over Earth began to increase more or less exponentially, both with rising population and improving technology if nothing else. More coenzymes could form randomly. I don't know whether the word *mutation* applies, but it sounds right. With a wider variety of metals available to bring their concentration up, new enzymes could suddenly reach a formation rate as fast or faster than the removal one. They'd reach—well, not a critical mass, but a critical concentration. And remember, the deaths of their hosts wouldn't remove them permanently, unless you toss everyone's body into space.

"I'm all for remembering good things about people, but until now I haven't been completely happy with keeping them around afterward. Yes, I know it's for data purposes, Major, but I never felt very sure we'd have use for that data. Now I see it.

"I haven't been all the way through Status's banks yet, and not even Pete could expect ever to have time to, but I've picked up quite a lot."

Maria thought she could see where this was heading, and took a chance.

"You're going along with Seichi—that this stuff is alive?"

"No. Not quite. I'd like to think it was in the chemical evolution stage still. Half alive, we could say. Different tar pools show different characteristics, which ought to be mostly chance; the only selection factor so far is the ability to replicate."

"You suggest that the search be for coenzymes containing metals which have become widespread in Earth's environment in the last few decades, then? Or that we should have done that if only Cheru's atom count had been more encouraging?" Maria sounded impressed but not quite convinced. "We can certainly run analyses on our friends—and on ourselves, for that matter.

"A more serious objection seems to me that most of the iridium and hafnium and similar rare metals now around have been circulated extensively only *since* the medical problems began."

"No." Two voices, Ginger's and Belvew's, sounded together. The sergeant might have been deferring to senior rank, welcoming support, or being polite. "Go ahead, Major."

"There's one heavy metal that's been around since long before high tech. We've been spreading it for thousands of years, in pretty close proportion to the number of people around. We wear it, and *wear* it—two different meanings. That's the one I'd concentrate on first. Jewelry! Think of it. Rings, bracelets, collars, pendants, coins, all sorts of items circulating around among human beings and rubbing off atoms all over the planet ever since human beings liked pretty things. Never mind high tech."

"You mean—," started Maria.

Ginger became polite, too, and waited. Some did not.

One word was overlapped among the voices of Corporal Pete Martucci, Corporal Cheru Akagawa, Lieutenant Carla lePing, Corporal Ludmilla Anden, and one other. It was a short word, and clear to all the hearers in spite of the overlap, but the last was the clearest. Since the Xalco speech had involved more behavioral than physical science, Status came in a poor last, and unmixed with other voices.

"Gold!" Excitedly and confusedly.

"Gold." Prosaically and clearly.

Silence. Thoughtful and critical.

Maria couldn't see how GO6 might apply. Certainly testing for gold in protein molecules could hardly qualify as an alternative to testing for iridium or other metals; only one basic hypothesis was involved. Furthermore, there was still the quantity problem, even with gold if Akagawa's figures were right. Still, the major *had* offered a reason for preferring it . . .

Even Maria Collos had never been one to follow the wording of a rule blindly, but she did know why there *were* rules. The general excitement which had followed the word—not for the first time in human history—gave her enough time to compose the wording of her next order very carefully. It must not imply that the speculation was probably correct and the end of their mission was in sight.

"Sergeant Belvew, you will write up a report of your suggestion for transmission home. You will no doubt prefer to offer a detailed procedure for testing it, but you are free to provide an alternative if one should occur to you—or do you have one already?"

"No, Commander."

Maria just barely refrained from thanking General aloud.

"You will take, or be given if you prefer to think of it that way, full responsibility for the speculation, which is far beyond presently established information. It will be interesting to see whether you are reduced to private, or commissioned. I will recommend the second if asked.

"Major Mastro, you will take four tissue samples from each of our friends in the mausoleum, recording in detail the source of each, sterilizing the outside of your collecting equipment both chemically and by radiation before and after each sampling, and bring them to the valve of Cheru's quarters.

"Each of us will also provide personal tissue samples, with Status's assistance, and place them outside our quarters for Louis to pick up. Each tell Louis when yours is ready.

"In the meantime, all mapping, meteorological, and other work will continue as nearly as possible as though the sergeant's suggestion had never been made. There's still a lot to answer about Titan, and no doubt many of the answers will inspire more speculations, as usual. Major Xalco, have you any idea what took the thunderhead so far from the center of Goodall Crater a short time ago? Cheru, why did the film on the jet wings, which had been well exposed to vacuum when it orbited up here, then produce something able to affect suits, but which was *stopped* by vacuum? Lieutenant diSabato—"

"Did it have to be only one stuff?" Akagawa was no more conscientious about GO6 than the rest, but had thought of this point already and was not sorry for a chance to let the rest know it.

"No, of course not. Look for variation among the wing and fuselage samples, and get more if you need them. Lieutenant diSabato—"

"Excuse me again, please, Commander. Sergeant, have you any idea how much gold, or anything else, should be in the samples in order to confirm your hypothesis?"

"Not yet. All the better for whoever's analyzing; he won't *want* to find some particular answer. But it would be nice to compare the gold, platinum, and iridium figures from the surface and wing samples with those from us and our friends, I'd say."

"Make it so, Cheru. Lieutenant diSabato—"

The commander finally got the rest of her assignments out.

The project would never really end, of course, no matter how solidly human survival was assured. If discovery ended, Maria felt strongly, there would be little point to survival. No fun.

And even if Belvew's suggestion—or speculation, or guess, or wish—were to prove right, it was a long way from cause to cure. Could you really strain all the gold atoms out of the Earth environment?

She brightened. Maybe Titan could tell them the results of *that* . . .

NOT, OF COURSE, THE END

POST

BEFORE BELVEW HAD a usable report ready, a problem developed. The tissue analyses showed no more, and very little less, gold than samples from friends on Earth dating from two centuries earlier. They did show far smaller in other metals, platinum, iridium, and even barium; it looked just possibly as though Belvew could still be right in his basic idea, but that Ginger and the others must be wrong about which metal was involved. This caused several invocations, aloud and otherwise, of Rule X during the ensuing weeks.

It was Peter Martucci who finally suggested a testable two-stage process in which the heavy metal could catalyze the formation of new and different enzymes, so that even one metal atom could be responsible for an indefinitely large number of product molecules. This, of course, favored metals other than gold, which should have started eliminating humanity a lot earlier if it were the real cause . . .

Ginger had trouble forgiving him until a report from Earth, weeks later, told of a strong statistical probability that gold was probably guilty after all. Of course, testing was being continued . . .

So the work went happily on. No one on the staff was ever bothered by the fear that there might sometime be nothing left to do.

They were still being useful.

Maria was having all the fun she could manage, finding things out.

There were lots of questions still to answer. GO6 was established habit, and Rule X cropped up about as often as it ever had in friendly arguments.

The last *possible* question of course is "Why?" It is never, equally of course, the last *question* because it can always be asked again of any answer.

Maria, rationally and responsibly, had assumed that while Belvew's idea was extremely plausible, it was also probably wrong and certainly incomplete.

But she was satisfied. The Titan crew would have plenty to keep them from boredom and morale loss, even if Belvew was right. Living on, and finding and assembling more pieces of the puzzle, would be much more fun than dying in Deep Sleep on the way back to Earth. After the several years they had spent in free fall, it would also be more fun than reaching the place.

Since some of the possible ailments which might claim members of the group were variations of Alzheimer's syndrome, Status had plenty of reading and recitation material for the mentally young in its fiction banks; loss of competence was not a reason for a friend to become a specimen.

So far, not even Maria had read or listened to them; Baum and Lofting were the closest she usually came to juvenile literature.

Status was of course aware of the material and could start reciting from it without notice; but it was not conscious of it. He—It couldn't even speculate about the likelihood that some time, with half or more of the group reduced to children, a particular phrase in his fiction memory might become a trite saying.

It could never, without careful explanation from a human being, recognize how the phrase would apply to the beings in its care. Presumably.

But the phrase did apply.

They lived happily ever after while they lived.